The Last Climb

A NOVEL OF SUSPENSE

Thomas H. Cosgrove

Simon & Schuster

SIMON & SCHUSTER
Rockefeller Center
1230 Avenue of the Americas
New York, NY 10020

Simon and Schuster and colophon are registered trademarks
of Simon & Schuster, Inc.

Designed by Leslie Phillips
Manufactured in the United States of America

10 9 8 7 6 5 4 3 2 1

Library of Congress Cataloging-in-Publication Data
Cosgrove, Thomas H.
   The last climb : a novel of suspense / Thomas H. Cosgrove.
   p.   cm.
   I. Title.
PS3553.07474L37   1999
813'.54—dc21   98-53467 CIP
ISBN 0-684-83414-6

For Frank Philip Hiner III,
Philosopher, Scientist and Mountaineer—
in gratitude for the time we had

Acknowledgments

Very little of artistic merit is accomplished in a vacuum; to be successful, an artist must be informed, nourished, and given opportunity. This requires people who are willing to lend their expertise and encouragement. In these respects, I have been uniquely fortunate. Michael Hamilburg, you are the best agent and friend possible, even if you did throw 20,000 of my finest words into the trash can. Michael Korda had no business inviting an untried neophyte to New York, but with shaking knees, I came and received a tutorial in novel structure that will remain. I thank you also for lunch, for the opportunity to try Simon & Schuster's patience, and for the kindest gesture of all, an introduction to Robert Mecoy, editor extraordinaire. In that same breath, I honor Peter Fornatale, who kept Mecoy in line and saw this manuscript to the copy desk.

Perhaps none of this would have transpired without the faith and support of my wife, Susan, who patiently read revision after revision and made her comments. My thanks also to Carol McInnis, canny reviewer and dear friend, who has encouraged me for more years than either of us will admit. Thanks also to Marta Stock, native Argentinean, whose contributions in language and Latin culture were invaluable. But before any of it, came Peru, its people, and those mystic mountains that work their way, inexorably, into one's soul. As I reflect on those sojourns into the sky, I marvel at what I owe and can never repay.

Foreword

Peru is a primal place, more linked to the past than present, the energy of its creation still resonating amid ice-clad mountains and across the vast puna. In the highlands, the ancestral gods keep their eternal vigil and the builders of its lost cities still wend their way on ancient footpaths. Long before the Supreme *Apu* took his seat upon the most lofty of all mountains, presences unseen and unknowable worked the primordial elements into the wonder of the Andes. Never was a land so carefully crafted, so embellished with the colors of earth and sky.

Into this realm came a people whose lives mirrored the land and there was great harmony in living. They wove cloth in brilliant colors and terraced the precipitous hillsides. They built cities to honor their creators and ease the burdens of daily life. Today's descendants do not know their names, but they remember, in that abyss of mind and soul where the voices of their ancestors yet echo.

Prologue
Father Bartolomé D'Annunzio

Where are you, Mariano Raimondi? Your spirit has been absent of late and I feel an unaccustomed chill descending on my shoulders. Do not leave me now. I have become so dependent on your counsel, the comforting whisper of your voice in my mind. I fear that Time has begun to stalk me at last. Twilight fades upon my window and the soft ring of yellow light beneath the kerosene lamp wavers as if in the presence of something heretofore unknown. Is it Death? What else could be left to an aging and corpulent priest?

All of these years, I have remained in Peru, a shepherd to your legacy. Now, time presents us with a new urgency. The Church Fathers, in their concern for my health, have written that a new priest will soon come to walk the cobblestones of the plaza and treat with the people. They will receive him kindly, it is the Quechuan way. But their eyes will turn to me. Lest our victory be lost, he must be prepared.

I sit here, the stub of a pencil in my ungainly fingers, and ponder the history of which we were a living part, you preaching the gospel of insurrection and I your stalwart Sancho. So clear are the images, I can almost smell the fresh stony soil dug for your grave, hear your people chanting the mass in their native Quechua. By the thousands they descend from the hillsides to see your face for the last time. As the service ends there is a vast silence.

On the opposite side of the grave stands the tall, rugged *norteamericano* who made our dreams a reality. His eyes are fixed on mine. What were you thinking that day, Jaime Bridgman? Were you angry at the conspiracy that made you a legend? Or, had you come to grips with Father Raimondi's vision and accepted the hand of fate? Not a day passes, but I think of you, your courageous leadership, your ascent into the dark Andean sky.

The chronicle of the indigene war for freedom and land is your story, Jaime. I struggle valiantly; but the foolscap is blank. I am no man of letters and the urgency of the task increases. Unless my successor is filled with knowledge and conviction, all that you won could be lost, for the forces of evil never rest. Speak to me, Mariano! Give me the words that will explain all these years of struggle and war. Let me make the saga of Jaime live. A new priest approaches, bearing the chalice of our faith. Of all that has gone before, what will I tell him . . . and how?

PART ONE

A Mountain's Wrath

Nevado Viracocha   *June 1965*

Jim Bridgman trailed behind the others as he ascended through the early darkness. After a short break for dinner it had been agreed to continue the march until they reached base camp. The *arrieros* had assured them that with the advent of a full moon, route-finding would not be a problem. The jingle of harnesses and low, muted voices from above made him smile. The thin-clad indigenes were tough; to survive in the Peruvian Andes they had to be.

Jim's companions, anxious to catch a glimpse of the mountain, were just reaching the pass. Twenty years ago, he would have been two hours ahead of them. Still could be, he thought, but at forty years of age, perspective changed. He knew that Nevado Viracocha would be there waiting for him. He would approach the mountain with a dignity befitting the creator god of the Incas.

Soon the sky above was bright from the rising moon and

he could see the narrow passage ahead take on an almost supernatural glow, as if it were a portal to another world. They were here at last. An immense burden seemed to lift from his shoulders in the knowledge that their precious cargo of film equipment and climbing hardware had reached its destination after three hard years of promotion and planning. Now, it only remained to lead his team to the summit.

Nevado Viracocha, never climbed, was the mountaineer's Holy Grail. Of those who tried, most gave up the struggle after a few pitches; those who did not had encountered disaster. Jim shrugged his doubts away. The granite around him sparkled in the moonlight as he reached the crest. Below was the valley in which they would set up base camp. Beyond it an immense glacier gleamed in the distance, beautiful yet sinister. Looming above him, the immense bulk of Viracocha shimmered in the light, dominating the landscape, a sullen, brooding, remorseless giant. Although Jim did not notice it, a peculiar hush had descended. The distant roar of glacial meltwater and cracking ice had ceased, almost like an intake of breath in anticipation.

~~~~~

Jim was the first to awaken, followed shortly by Hal Rich. As Jim tended to their big Primus stove, Hal quietly observed their leader, noting the many patches on his down parka, the faded stocking cap and old pair of running shoes he wore around camp. Jim's hair was long, almost down to his shoulders, and usually kept in place with a bandanna tied over his forehead. His eyes, a striking light blue, never seemed to rest, constantly playing over the landscape.

Hal felt a sense of awe when around Jim. The big man was more than just a legendary climber; there was an aura of substance about him that other men did not possess. Hal could not reconcile Jim's many qualities and accomplishments with the fact that he was an aging, insolvent guide with no apparent future. Perhaps the film would work for him. "Get us the climbing footage," he had been told, "and we'll take care of the rest." Jim needed the feature documentary that they had been promised.

The sun was still behind the mountain. Squinting into the glare edging over the ridgeline, Jim began to point out various features on the expansive west face. "We'll do the west ridge, starting over there," he said, pointing with his coffee cup. "It'll take us a day to make a route across the glacier; then we'll start hauling. Gotta take our time though. We're still not acclimatized."

Hal looked at the lined, but still boyish face. He could sense the excitement begin to emanate from Jim and the quiet confidence that comes of a man deep in experience and ability. Behind them, the voices of the other climbers stumbling out of their tents broke the morning calm. "I guess I'd better put our bags out to dry," he said, rising to his feet.

Across the meadow, the *arrieros* tended to their horses, removing the hobbles and carefully examining each hoof. Jim hollered to them that the morning tea was ready and set about making a large pot of oatmeal. He looked up as Hal returned, and threw his climbing partner a packet of powdered milk. "Make yourself useful," he chided.

Hal looked at the dull green label. *"Leche Pura,"* he said, *"hecha en los Estados Unidos."*

"Yeah," Jim said, "my ex used to stockpile this shit."

"You were married? I didn't know that."

Jim shook his head and turned toward the mountain. "Someday when I'm in a good mood, I'll tell you about it."

~~~~~

From the vantage of Camp II on the southwest ridge, Jim and Hal watched the sun brighten behind the mountain. It had taken ten days to work the five thousand difficult feet above base camp and they longed for a rest. Tucked into a declivity thirty feet farther along the ridge, the orange dome tent that housed Walt Wheeler, Chuck Dawes and Ralph Breckinridge showed signs of movement within.

"They're late," Hal remarked.

"They're tired," Jim responded. "They're probably waiting for us to yell over that there's hot water."

Hal nodded as he scooped another cup of snow into the pot and zipped the tent flap up, leaving just enough opening for ventilation. It was approaching nine o'clock; the sun was slow to reach the west side of the mountain.

"Do you think we can reach the step today?" he asked.

"Maybe," Jim answered. "It depends on how we handle that double-corniced section. The ice is . . ."

He stopped in mid-sentence as a sudden tremor rattled the tent poles.

"Jesus Christ!" Hal exclaimed as a gust of wind blew in through the vent, causing the walls to balloon outward.

"Get your boots on!" Jim snapped as he jerked the door zipper down and dove through the opening. Hal followed immediately, struggling into his down jacket. Only ten feet away,

snow dust blew skyward through an enormous gap which revealed the tortured twisting of a glacier two thousand feet below. At its furthest extreme, the orange tent with its three
occupants was snagged on a nubbin of rock twenty feet below.

Jim turned to Hal. "Belay me." He spoke in a hoarse voice,
though even as he began to maneuver along the edge he knew
that there wouldn't be enough time. Beneath him the tent
swayed over the vast, almost palpable volume of space.
"Don't move!" he shouted.

The three men lay in a jumble at the bottom of the tent, the
weight bob of a sinister pendulum that was ticking off the last
few seconds of their lives. Jim could see a shiny black patch
on the rock finger showing where the tent had already slipped.
Quickly setting an ice screw, he tied off his second rope and
let it drop. Down-climbing the ice to the tent, he attached
three carabiners to a knot and managed to work it through a
tear in the nylon, letting the rope run to the bottom. There was
a momentary tug on the line as if someone had grasped the
carabiners when the tent began to slip again.

Reacting instantly he lurched from his stance to try to arrest the movement, but it was too late. He heard a voice cry
out "Jim!" as his line pulled free through the opening, followed by a single forlorn woolen glove. As if in a trance, he
watched the tent plummet downward. A low, concussive
boom sounded through the glacial amphitheater, then the distant rustling of ice. Jim stared numbly at the expanding ring
of snow and ice particles which marked the point of impact.

Of those who had shared his dream of Nevado Viracocha,
three had become one with the mountain, never again to exult in the beauty of an alpine morning.

Jim turned his face into the ice and felt the deep cold against his skin. There was no time to grieve. One slip would send him careening across the steep, exposed remnant of the cornice. His hands slowly tightened on his tools and he began to climb. Taking in the rope, Hal watched intently as his partner struggled over the edge and made his way across the ridge. Jim scarcely heard Hal's "Off belay!" as he slumped into the shallow depression.

They sat staring into space. Neither man spoke for several minutes. "They're gone," Jim finally groaned, his breath coming in slow, convulsive gasps. "Damn it, Hal! I should have tied that tent off on the other side of the ridge. I thought about it; I just didn't do it!"

Hal noted the wet, swollen eyes as Jim pulled his goggles down and clasped his face in his hands. He knew that Jim had been something of a big brother to the three younger climbers, maybe the only real family he had. Placing his arm over Jim's shoulders, he tried to console him.

Jim made no response, his eyes blank and unseeing. Hal's concern escalated. "Shouldn't we move out, Jim?" he suggested. "The rest of this ridge could go any minute."

As Jim gathered himself to respond, a sudden shadow flickered across the bright sheen of snow and ice surrounding them, followed by a loud, piercing cry. In amazement, the two climbers looked upward, where, no more than one hundred feet above, a giant condor hovered in the wind shear across the ridge. Jim could almost feel the bird's intense gaze as the flaming crimson eyes looked directly into his own. Then, as abruptly as it had appeared, the great bird slanted off and dived into the vast space beneath the western face of the mountain.

Jim could feel his heart pounding as he stared at the almost invisible speck in the distance. "We'll take what we can and cache the rest," he murmured, his voice nearly inaudible.

~~~~~

Oblivious to the press of people, the two men made their way through the busy lobby of the Cuzco airport, the din of excited voices and the crackling blare of the public address system making speech difficult. "Shouldn't we have told the American consulate?" Hal insisted.

Jim switched hands with the heavy pack he was carrying to prevent an imminent collision with a porter pushing a large cart. "No," he answered halfheartedly.

They took a position in line. "If people could see you," Hal persisted, "it would be better. Without you, they'll be suspicious."

"I can't help what people think," he answered. "I've got enough problems with what I think."

"Are you at least going to talk with Chuck Dawes' wife?"

"Yes."

The line inched forward and Hal wrestled with his frustration. Jim had become almost uncommunicative.

"There's nothing to be gained here. It would be better if we were both available for the families."

Jim shook his head. "No," he said. "I don't want to talk about it any more." The voice was flat, without affectation.

"I still don't like the idea of leaving you here," Hal insisted.

Jim made no reply as he lifted the pack onto the scale. He didn't feel like making the effort to explain, even if he understood the strange feelings that possessed him.

"*¿Pasaporte? ¿Billete?*" the clerk asked.

Hal reluctantly handed them over and signed the customs slip. When he turned to continue the conversation, he was dismayed to see that Jim had left. Hastily looking about, he caught a glimpse of a tall man who paused at the building exit to look back and then disappeared into the blinding noontime glare.

PART TWO

Entrapment

Cuzco   *July 1965*

A waiter eyed the big *norteamericano* warily as he stopped in
the entrance to survey the room. The worn, soiled Levi's and
oversized pullover suggested another of the climbing bums
who frequented the Cuzco environs. With a casual finger, he
indicated a table discreetly removed from hotel patrons arriving for lunch and yet offering a view across the city to the distant mountains.

The big man nodded, moving past the waiter, who noted
the lined face and scraggly beard, the reddened eyes. He is
older than most, he thought, yet he moves well, like a big cat.

"Cerveza." Jim Bridgman spoke in a hoarse voice, leaning
back in the chair and looking up at the waiter. *"Grande."*

He could see the sudden start of recognition in the little
man's eyes. The waiter swallowed as he wiped the table,
dropping the bar towel in his haste to depart. A few moments
later he returned, bearing a tall bottle of dark Peruvian beer

and a chilled glass. Setting the items on the table, he stepped back. "No charge, señor," he said. "Courtesy of the management."

Jim watched the man retreat and felt the glances directed from the bar. A few tourists stared from their tables and then looked away. He gazed out the window and cradled his glass. "Let it go," he whispered to himself. The cool liquid placated the dryness etched in his throat from prolonged exposure to altitude. The sun was high in the sky, the red and orange tiles of the city awash in its glow. He felt his mind tug at its tether; his eyes moistened and closed.

"Mr. Bridgman?" The low, resonant voice connoted power, carefully restrained. A priest, shod in thick-soled leather sandals and wearing the black habit of the Benedictine order, stood by his table. His face was large and round beneath a close-cropped beard. "I hope I'm not late."

Jim looked up blankly at the source of the intrusion and tried to will the images away, but the grief-stricken face of Chuck Dawes' wife would not leave. The tearstained cheeks, the quivering lips that pleaded with him to give her some hope. Even though he'd put her on a plane back to the States a month ago, she still haunted him.

"Not at all," he finally managed, shrugging off a flush of irritation and rising to take the priest's hand.

Father Bartolomé d'Annunzio's grip was strong and his dark brown eyes on a level with Jim's. Although his girth was considerable, he settled into the narrow table space easily. The usual amenities were exchanged and the two men silently appraised each other before ordering from the daily menu of *Merienda Especialidades*.

Jim read the sense of urgency in the priest's face. He had been unsure about this meeting and had felt put-upon by Bartolomé's insistence over the telephone. Going anywhere near that damn mountain again would be almost unbearable, but he had to do something and going home seemed the worst sort of betrayal of his dead friends. Furthermore, taking a three-hundred-pound man into the *cordillera* would be a questionable task at best, although the money he offered wouldn't hurt. Even with the charity extended by the hotel and some minor guiding activity, he would be lucky to get plane fare home.

"How certain are you that this man is still alive?" he asked.

"For reasons that are too complicated to justify explanation at this time, let me just say that a conviction is growing in my soul."

Jim's face was expressionless. There was both a naivete and a certainty of purpose about this man that he could not reconcile. The priest could not fully appreciate what he was asking. Even if the locale was correct, it could take several weeks to locate this mysterious hamlet, *ayllu,* where the man was to be found. In addition, the indigenes could be a problem. One never knew exactly what to expect out on the puna and there were always *bandidos*.

It did not sound good. "Do you walk much?" Jim asked, the skepticism showing on his face.

The sudden tilt of Bartolomé's chin told him that he had taken the priest aback. "I can assure you that I would only be a minimal burden. Despite what you see, I am very ambulant."

Right, thought Jim. He could see the priest gasping for air on the altiplano like a beached whale. There was an awkward pause in the conversation as the waiter returned with their food. Jim's mind was racing. He felt himself being propelled toward something very unwise. Had he been sought out because of his notoriety? His circumstance? He was desperate, wasn't he? Why not face up to it? Do what you have to do.

Something began to crawl through his insides and he felt the energy drain from his body. Everything seemed so fucking hopeless. He had to establish control over his life, but until he did, he just couldn't leave Peru. No matter how much he wanted to flee.

"This isn't like the northern *cordilleras*. Down here the ranges pancake out. If you don't have a specific location, you could spend a lifetime searching for a tiny hamlet, wandering from one canyon to another."

"God will guide my way," Bartolomé answered.

An interval of silence followed in which Jim contemplated the priest's remark. To date, the manner in which God decided to pick and choose his beneficiaries left him unimpressed. The eyes that looked into Bartolomé's were cold. "I hope He does a better job for you than He did for me," he said.

Bartolomé had been watching him closely. He could see the anguish lurking behind the mask. He noted the big, callused hands, scarred and abraded from contact with rock and ice, as they fumbled unconsciously with the soiled baseball cap. A cheap battered watch was tied to his wrist with a shoelace, its face advertising some cartoon character. An emotion began to rise in the priest's chest that he could not quite divine. "Those of my calling share a long history of such endeavors," he said. "It is an adage among us that the pursuit of truth always incurs risk."

A fleeting thought of his cabin above Telluride, Colorado, turned Jim's mind aside. He had left the woodpile stacked high for the next winter, but the roof needed work and the glazing was probably cracked on the western-facing windows. He needed to be there. A strong sense of longing overcame him.

"Jim?" Bartolomé spoke inquiringly to create some distraction.

The priest's face was a blur, his voice distant. Jim not so much saw him as sensed his presence through a haze of fatigue. He was tired of listening, of cultivating clients with potential and dissuading others. Nothing was worse than the client who wanted to climb beyond his ability, especially if he was waving money in your face. Still, he couldn't bring himself to say no or yes.

"The puna is vast," he said. "You don't know what it is like to be alone until you experience it. If there is trouble, there is no one to turn to and no place to hide. What you are asking is probably impossible. Some indigenes might be hostile as hell."

Bartolomé folded his napkin and stood. Jim was surprised at how rapidly he had eaten. "I know that this is difficult for you," Bartolomé said, his demeanor even and solicitous. Extracting a blue envelope from his purse, he placed it in the center of the table. "I'd like to compensate you for your time, Jim, and ask you to give my proposal your full consideration. I'll be staying at the archbishop's quarters if you want to contact me."

They shook hands and Jim watched as Bartolomé d'Annunzio made a stately exit into the lobby. Despite his size, the priest moved with a certain heavy grace. Jim vacillated;

maybe the companionship would help him. He certainly needed the money. With an air of indifference he opened the flap on the envelope and removed its contents: twenty crisp one-hundred-dollar bills, U.S. currency.

Lima, Peru
Sede Eclesiástica Ejecutiva   *July 1965*

Monsignor Alcantara read the missive through carefully, his bushy eyebrows twitching up and down, his dark brown eyes seeming to dart at the individual words rather than smoothly scanning the lines. The wire had been sent by Archbishop Ignacio Diego Ugarte, who was concerned about the presence of a Vatican emissary in Cuzco, Father D'Annunzio. Not only had the emissary's arrival been unannounced, his departure for Chiquian was imminent. This latter piece of information brought the monsignor up out of his chair.

Although the Church had managed to establish some authority and presence in the mountains and valleys of the high puna surrounding Chiquian, it was tenuous at best. Despite centuries of Spanish occupation and religious education, the imprint of ecclesiastical authority on the indigenes was faint indeed. Religious rituals, as practiced by these people, were too often and too easily discernible as thin metal foil beaten to conformance on mandrels of Incan and pre-Incan granite.

The gloss and sheen were a concession to Mother Church, but the form and substance were not.

Hastily gathering his papers together he made it a point to wire his thanks to the archbishop, and at the same time, in his best diplomatic fashion, urge him to be more timely in the future. Only a few minutes remained before his meeting with the cardinal, and it would not do to have His Eminence suspect him of an oversight. Alcantara stepped quickly up the last flight of stairs leading to the cardinal's chamber, the crucifix attached to the rosary at his waist swinging wildly. Across the street in the chapel tower the bell began to sound the hour. He would be just in time for the daily briefing.

Departure

Jim Bridgman dropped his bags outside the entrance to the Turista Hotel and leaned against the wall, waiting for Bartolomé. Night in Cuzco was near and the low crimson light had turned the whitewashed adobe walls a delicate pink.

Across the street, a few indigenes squatted against a wall and snugged their ponchos close. Muttering something unintelligible, one man lurched upright and stumbled to the curb where he urinated unabashedly into the street.

Jim knew they were seeking employment as *portadores,* carrying loads for gringo climbers. As he watched, three taxicabs turned the corner and pulled up in front of the hotel. He noted the fresh faces exiting the cars and the pretentious show of alpine gear. While the concierge summoned the hotel porters, several indigenes approached the climbers.

Jim could not hear what was being said, but the indigenes seemed disturbed. After several minutes of hassling, the discussion ended and they dispersed across the street as the climbers followed their gear into the hotel.

Although Jim was anything but solvent, he felt a need to compensate the Peruvians for their disappointment. A little money would certainly facilitate their getting home. They were not reluctant to accept a few *soles* apiece and each one shook Jim's hand.

This interaction had been witnessed by a figure sitting in a darkened recess of the hotel's foundation. It was an older, heavyset *campesino* dressed as were the other men, except for his wide-brim felt hat and the stout wooden staff with which he pulled himself erect. He walked slowly past the *norteamericano,* looking up into Jim's face as he did so. His hair was gray beneath the hat and his eyes bleary smudges of caramel.

"Buenas tardes," Jim said.

The old man chuckled as he answered. *"Buenas tardes."*

His smile seemed to widen before he turned and hobbled away, his form rapidly becoming vague in the darkness. He could be heard to mutter to himself, the words alternately soft then loud, almost like an incantation. The language was not Spanish, but it did not sound like Quechua either.

Across the street, one indigene still remained. As the old man passed him he quickly made the sign of the cross and departed in the opposite direction.

Dismissing the encounter from his mind, Jim peered down the street. Another taxi was approaching the hotel, the broad face of Bartolomé visible through the windshield. He picked up his bags.

Lima

Charlie Newell contemplated his face in the mirror as he fondled a near empty glass of bourbon. It wasn't his first and the bartender was a little uneasy; Charlie could become loud if the mood lent itself. A door opened and Charlie saw another image appear beside his own: a handsome young man in a well-tailored overcoat. As he approached, Charlie gave a long audible sigh. "My conscience stirs from the shadows," he muttered.

If he heard, Xavier Ruis took no offense. Although too young to be a parental figure for the venerable reporter, he did admirably well. His newspaper provided Charlie's employer, InterAmerican News Service (IANS), with gratis office space for which it received Charlie's counsel on all matters relevant to the United States.

"Management has sent me to find you."

"Really? What do the luminaries of *El Observador* want with a discarded relic like me when they have a Harvard-educated whiz kid like you in their stable?"

Xavier grinned. Charlie was his mentor, had taught him

how the real world functioned and when, where and how newsmen conducted their business; if only he would ease off his drinking.

"They have a story that demands the services of a senior man," he answered, "preferably a politically nonaligned gringo who is bilingual and nobody knows."

Charlie's glass was poised midway to his lips. "In other words," he responded, his words slightly slurred, "the job is suitable for a cast-off stringer whose only claim to fame is that he was twice the runner-up for a Pulitzer prize, but couldn't keep his mouth shut when it really counted."

Xavier grimaced. He hated it when Charlie got like this. "No," he answered, looking around and lowering his voice, "there may be major trouble brewing south of Cuzco near a township called Chiquian. The indigenes there, as you gringos say, appear to be getting restless."

"With reason?" Charlie's demeanor abruptly took on a more subdued tone.

"We suspect so. Word from those who are better connected suggests a conspiracy for profit, a land grab."

"So? It's happened before."

"Not on this scale, not since the colonial days."

Charlie studied his protégé for a moment and motioned to the bartender. "Two coffees," he said, much to the man's relief.

"So," Charlie said. "Who's grabbing who?"

"The indigenes are always getting grabbed," Xavier answered. "Since the conquest, millions of them have died in the mines or been worked to death on the haciendas. All of their good agricultural land has been stolen. Occasionally, they join together and try to 'grab' some of it back; but they always lose. This recent effort was ill-advised."

"Oh?"

"Yes, it seems that certain corporate and commercial interests were reaching out at the same time. Oil, natural gas, minerals, timber, the whole nine yards. They've butted heads and blood is flowing, most of it indigene, of course."

"And who's doing the grabbing? The Peruvians?"

"Yes, and the *norteamericanos*."

Charlie took a sip. "Why doesn't that surprise me?" he said.

Chiquian

Jim awakened to the cold press of window glass against his face and an ache in his shoulder. The first nuance of dawn was slowly diffusing over the eastern rim and, low in the dark western sky, a thin sliver of moon gleamed like an upraised scimitar. Shapes began to resurrect themselves across the puna. *"Diez kilómetros,"* the driver said. Jim grunted his acknowledgment and sat up, pulling the heavy serape over his shoulders. What appeared to be the remains of a small rancho suddenly appeared and was lost in the dust. Jim was instantly alarmed. The bodies of slain animals could soon be seen nearby. There were more burnt buildings, but no people. Had they fled? A chill quite apart from the frost that filled the pockets of uneven earth prickled his skin.

"What in hell is going on?" he muttered.

Bartolomé, who was now awake and looking about, pursed his lips as if to reply and then said nothing.

~~~~~

Chiquian was orderly but subdued. Four weeks prior it had been a bustling community filled with human enterprise. Now its citizens appeared apprehensive, waiting for something to happen.

Leaving Bartolomé at the Hotel del Sol, Jim had set out to procure additional provisions for their trek. On his return he heard raised voices and the apparent groan of a man from an alleyway. Peering into the shadows he saw three soldiers: two, seated on a low wall, drank from a half-empty bottle of Pisco and kibitzed with the third, who, in an indolent fashion, took leg-weary kicks at the prone and semiconscious form of an elderly indigene man. One soldier started to rise, mumbling something unintelligible and pointing his finger. Jim's first instinct was to help the man on the ground but he quickly realized the folly of doing so. Increasing his stride, he pressed on toward the hotel plaza.

His room was occupied. "Jim!" Bartolomé exclaimed. "I'm so glad you're back! Let me introduce you to Lucho, a confidant and friend of the Church." Jim shook the hand of the young indigene man, the sense of unease that he had first felt upon accepting the commission once again asserting itself. Before he could inquire as to Lucho's presence, Bartolomé continued, "Lucho lives here in Chiquian but has spoken with people from the *campo,* who have provided us with a rough location."

"How fortunate," Jim answered, looking directly into Bartolomé's eyes. "Nothing is more welcome than a little timely assistance." Making no reply, Bartolomé unrolled a map upon the bed. The road head, marked with a red X, was at a small rancho some sixty miles distant. "Show me," Jim said.

Lucho took a pencil and carefully drew a light line southeast from the rancho to a cluster of mountains almost due west of Nevado Viracocha. "There is a large *ayllu* here," he indicated. "Even walking, it should take no more than two or three days."

Jim multiplied Lucho's estimate of time by a factor of three and took a deep breath. "Does this place have a name?" he continued.

"Karoma," Lucho answered.

Jim was astonished. "You've got to be kidding," he said. "That's just folklore."

"On the contrary," Bartolomé interjected. "These people say that Karoma predates the conquest; that it has survived because it is high and remote. The Spanish simply never gave it any credence."

There was something unctuous about Bartolomé's words. Jim felt as if his opinion were trivialized. "If these *campesinos* know so much about it," he stammered, "you sure as hell don't need me!"

"Oh no, Jim!" Bartolomé was quick to apologize. "Please don't misunderstand. I need you more than ever. They could well be wrong. It will be up to you and me to discover the truth."

"What is our objective?" Jim asked. "Are we searching for a man or a lost city?"

Bartolomé shrugged. "Both, I suppose."

Jim had long ago written Karoma off as imaginative speculation. Yet, the indigene might be right. He grappled with his conscience; it wasn't too late to get out, all he had to do was get in the car and start driving.

Trailhead

They were under way at 2:00 A.M. "You didn't tell me the man we're looking for was a priest," Jim remarked, having picked up the fact from Lucho.

Bartolomé gave him a sideways glance and began to relate the history of Father Mariano Raimondi. "He was exceptional, Jim, one of the most promising scholars to ever matriculate at the seminary. When he opted for a life of service in the field, many people were dismayed."

"Sounds like he preferred real life to politics."

"Yes. From what I can gather, he was a truly spiritual man. After his disappearance, the Church simply assumed that he had assimilated himself into the native culture, as many other priests have done."

"What is the Church's interest in this man now?" Jim asked. "This seems like a lot of fuss over someone who hasn't been seen in fifteen years."

Bartolomé was slow to respond, as if searching for an answer. "Father Raimondi is still a servant of the Church," he finally offered, "and as such receives the patronage of the Church."

The words seemed to hang in the air. Bartolomé's reply did nothing to assuage that unsettled feeling. Jim let a few minutes elapse before pursuing the subject of Father Raimondi. The fact that Father Raimondi had fallen from a mountain while conducting services with a portable altar piqued his interest. "Did he say anything about his injuries?"

Bartolomé pulled the cork from his flask and Jim could smell the sharp scent of brandy. "Some. From what I've been told he must have been in a coma for over two months"— Bartolomé paused—"and when he awoke he possessed extraordinary mental powers. He was treated by a man they called a Hatun Laika."

Jim reflected on the strange revelation. Suddenly, he longed for the familiar, an American landscape, the friendly faces along the streets of Telluride. In the immense blackness outside the car gigantic shapes brooded and chafed at the forces restraining them. Jim could feel their dark presence and relished the cozy protection of the car, however illusory it might be.

〜〜〜

With the exception of a young indigene who lived near the rancho, the grounds had been deserted. "Espinoza took his family and horses into the mountains," he informed them somberly. "He left the burros for your gear. Wait here and I'll bring them."

A wry smile appeared on Jim's face and quickly faded. The revelation that they had been expected was sobering, although it was pointless to create an issue at this juncture.

Neither man spoke as they leaned against an adobe wall, looking at the massive bulk of Nevado Viracocha in the distance. Detached from the *cordillera,* the defiant massif was surrounded on all sides by a ring of jagged, ice-capped peaks and rocky gendarmes. Even from the rancho, Viracocha seemed to loom over them, its giant, bulging cornices clearly discernible above an enormous fluted wall, which seemed to shimmer and move as if a delicate drapery suspended from the sky.

"Is that your mountain, Jim?" Bartolomé asked after a long interval.

"Yes," he answered, but did not elaborate.

Bartolomé gripped Jim's shoulder. "I will say a prayer for them tonight," he whispered. Jim, tight-lipped, nodded his acknowledgment.

The burros arrived and were quickly loaded. "Are you still sure you want to do this?" Jim asked, shouldering a large frame pack. "There are hundreds of square miles of mountains out there, sliced up with canyons and rivers that no one can cross. There are bogs, black flies and *ladrones* who would slit your throat for a piece of bread. You'll either be cold or hot, but never comfortable. It will take a month before your lungs work."

Bartolomé picked up his outdated rucksack. "Destiny calls," he answered.

Chance Encounter

The *prefecto* rolled his eyes. "Señor Newell, what you are planning is most inadvisable; there is considerable unrest in the vicinity of Chiquian. You would be at great risk."

"Comunistas, you say?"

"*¡Sí!* We are doing our best to protect the people and re-solve the situation. It is really only a minor disturbance in terms of numbers, but unfortunately it blocks access into the region."

Charlie appraised the chief civil administrator for the Cuzco district: fidgety, nervous and obviously lacking suffi-cient instruction on how to deal with the problem of a gringo journalist. Pressing the matter would accomplish nothing. "Well then, thank you for your time," Charlie responded. "I'll cable my agency and see if they have an alternate assign-ment."

"That would be wise." Señor Vargas spoke in his most benevolent manner. "If there is any way we can further assist you, do not hesitate to contact us."

Outside the civil administration building, Charlie paused to consider his next move. Across the street, a burly man with a short crewcut was exiting a cab. Sunlight reflected off metal-lic-coated lenses as he stood erect and looked across the street toward the entrance of the building. Charlie lowered his head and turned away, his heart pounding. In that brief instant, he recognized a man he hadn't seen in twelve years.

Karl Slesser has been a prominent figure in an investiga-tive story he had done involving the CIA. That story was the principal reason Charlie had wound up in Peru, one of the few places his employer could still keep him on the payroll. Within hours of the story's release, it was withdrawn. Char-lie was enraged, much as he was now. Karl was a notorious hit man and operative for the worst elements of the organiza-tion. What in hell was he doing here?

Slesser's presence, in whatever capacity, was significant. The man had made a living wreaking havoc with foreign governments, from the overthrow of Mosaddeq in Iran to the elimination of the Arbenez government in Guatemala. Charlie had heard rumors of his involvement in Bolivia and he wondered if there was a connection. The CIA had a bad habit of working for private interests.

A moment later, Karl Slesser crossed the street and brushed past into the building. Peering after him, Charlie saw his dim figure taking the stairway steps to the *prefecto*'s office two at a time. Karl knew exactly where he was going.

Lost

Jim cursed quietly. They had now been under way for twelve days and there had been no indication of a track into the mountains. Lucho's line on the map had dead-ended on the rim of a small glacial basin into which Bartolomé, overly curious, had slipped, spinning and tumbling for a good seventy feet before a shallow crevasse brought him to a halt. Three days following that episode, they awakened in the midst of a storm to find their tent afloat in two feet of water; their sleeping bags were still damp.

The daily effort of trudging up and down loose slopes looking for any indication of a track leading higher was exasperating, as was Bartolomé's predilection for straying on his own. How the priest managed astonished Jim. No matter how late, Bartolomé always stumbled into camp intact. Still, Jim could see the fatigue build in Bartolomé's face and new notches accrue in his belt. Jim wondered what would happen when the brandy ran out.

One incident had thoroughly frightened Jim. A glacial stream exiting the mountains on their right broke into a criss-cross pattern of lesser streams, although fast running, that carried far out onto the puna. The burros balked. Leaving Bartolomé with the animals, he started fording the various tributaries. It was tricky business, made more so by pockets of deep mud and silt. After thirty minutes effort, Jim made it through, only to turn and see that Bartolomé, attempting to forge a route on his own, had become lodged in the mud beneath a large boulder. The water was welling up over his shoulders and into his face. Only a Herculean effort by Jim managed to save him. After that, they had walked in silence for three days, until at last they had reached the base of this steeply rising slope. Jim fervently hoped that the faint trace of switchbacks led to their destination.

～～～～

Bartolomé collapsed beside Jim and accepted the water bottle. Despite the physical agony, he was ecstatic. "Praise God's handiwork, Jim. This is beautiful beyond belief. It's easy to see why you love it so much!" Jim nodded to acknowledge the remark, but said nothing. Four hours later, the slope vanquished, they were encamped in a high cirque set deep in the mountain flank. A small glacial lake, no more than a hundred yards across, reflected the last glow of sunset and the low crenellated ridge above them.

Bartolomé moaned in his sleeping bag.

"Jim, in the left outside pocket of my pack there should be a bottle of brandy. Will you fetch it, please?"

The priest pulled the bag down about his waist and sat up against a rock. He took the bottle and contemplated the red-and-gold label. "This will help my joints tonight, but it won't help me get there tomorrow, will it?"

Jim shook his head.

In moments, the steeply sloping blue-white ice that protruded over the southwest shore dulled to a glimmer and the still surface of the water became a black cauldron full of stars.

En Route

Charlie Newell knelt in the dust by the disabled van and silently cursed his fate. This was their third stop in the last thirty kilometers to deal with the same flat tire. He estimated that forty kilometers remained to reach Chiquian, which Arturo, the driver, had solemnly informed Charlie and the proprietor of this backcountry delivery service, César Oré, would require at least three more such stops for applications of chewing gum. Charlie waved off César's apology; although well remunerated, smuggling the newsman into Chiquian put César at considerable risk.

The van was loaded with goods for the Quintero family, expensive foodstuffs, wines, clothing and various luxury items flown from Lima and all over the world to Cuzco and thence to Chiquian via truck. Receipt of these goods at Chiquian and their safe delivery to the Hacienda Santa Rosa was the responsibility of César Oré's enterprise. It would not do, either by loss or delay, to arouse the ire of *El Patrón,* Carlos Quintero, the most powerful *hacendado* in the region, who saw everyone as his servant or at most his inferior. He carried a long whip and was not afraid to use it.

"We will get another tire in Chiquian," César informed Charlie. "If you still want to meet Carlos Quintero, you may leave with us in the morning."

Charlie nodded his assent and began to relax. The ailing tire was still holding and their prospects of an arrival before nightfall looked better. *"¡Vámonos, Arturo! ¡Vámonos! ¡Esta noche, bistec y vino!"* he called out and Arturo laughed, depressing the accelerator as they started up a short grade.

From the top they could see the distant glint of white-washed buildings, still removed, but now in sight. The road began a series of switchbacks that descended steeply through rugged rock outcroppings and water-scoured gullies. Although they had traversed this road many times together César could not help but caution Arturo. *"¡Más despacio, Arturo! ¡Ten cuidado con las piedras!"*

Arturo nodded his head politely. *"¡Sí, Jefe!"* He was quite familiar with the road hazards, as they both knew. However, he was not prepared for the obstacle that was manifesting itself at the approaching turn. Moving in their direction was an enormous herd of llamas that filled the road and extended up the hillside. Arturo carefully brought the van to a stop as Charlie and César exchanged glances. The herd was slowly advancing toward them and within a few minutes they were engulfed in its midst. Charlie gaped at the expanse of fleece in varying shades of white, tan and brown and thought of the air slowly leaking from their defective tire. There seemed to be no end to it.

Sheep began to appear amid the llama herd, as well as an occasional goat. Arturo was more knowing of country ways and disturbed by the proceedings. He knew that no individual *campesino* family owned so many llamas, only the *hacendados,* and they would have no reason to be running their animals down the road. Neither would *campesinos* bring animals onto the road, for that matter. Many llamas had been killed on the highway and a typically poor family could not afford to take the risk. Moreover, it wasn't just llamas now; every manner of domestic animal could be seen. Arturo looked in vain for the herders or anyone accompanying them. More minutes passed and César began to lose his patience. He told Arturo to move forward, however slowly. "Don't be afraid to use your horn!" he admonished.

Arturo reluctantly started the engine, but before he could engage the transmission, the doors to the van were abruptly jerked open. A pair of large brown hands grasped Charlie by the collar and left arm and pulled him effortlessly out onto the ground where he found himself looking up at a dozen or more indigenes, who surveyed him silently. Oh, my God, he thought to himself, this is it. On the other side of the van he could hear Arturo cautioning César. "*Jefe,* be calm. Do not raise your voice to these people."

Karoma

The wind that had begun to whisper across the rocks told Jim that they were close. Even so, he was not prepared for the view that was suddenly his. In the distance, what had to be Karoma was clearly visible, only slightly higher than the pass where he stood, and connected by a wide trail. An incredible array of cultivated terraces fell out of sight beneath it. Above, gently rising to the southwest and bounded by an encircling ridge of pinnacles, a large meadow was dotted with grazing animals. The buildings were all stone, protected by a high wall with an opening to the trail.

"You've done it, Jim." Bartolomé joined him, struggling for breath. "It can be no other!"

Jim was incredulous. Distance aside, Bartolomé's intelligence had been highly accurate. So taken were they with the view, neither man noticed the two sentries secreted on either side of the pass. Jim was startled when one of the shotgun-bearing indigenes stepped up on a rock and motioned them past. "*Señor, Padre,*" he said.

As they approached, loaded burros could be seen wending their way upward through the cultivated terraces and footpaths. On a rounded knoll central to the village was situated a church whose silhouette excited Bartolomé. "Blessed Mother Mary!" he exclaimed.

A small group of people were gathered where the trail entered the village. The *curaca,* or village headman, was recognizable by his badge of office, a silver-tipped staff, known as a *vara,* and the silver cross worn around his neck. Two

younger men, one on either side, were identifiable as *ca-
ciques,* or assistants, by the silver stripes on their ponchos. In
melodious, soft-spoken Quechua, their leader welcomed them
to Karoma.

"Father Raimondi has just returned and is anxious to meet
you," he said. "Dinner is being prepared."

~~~~~

In the dimming light, the church took on a spectral cast,
somber and mysterious. Its walls were carved stone, unusual
for their decoration. Situated as the church was on a rocky
knoll, separated from any other building, there was a sense of
exposure in its approach. Bartolomé recognized the carving
which covered the exterior as *churrigueresco,* a Spanish ro-
coco style occasionally practiced during the colonial period.
"This is very old, Jim," he muttered, "maybe even sixteenth
century. Very mysterious. During the conquest, it may well
have been a sanctuary against the Spanish."

As they drew closer, the carved figures began to stand out
in relief, partially illuminated by candles, which had been
placed along the walkway that traversed one side of the building to an entrance in the rear. An old woman was waiting at
the top and motioned them to follow. After a few steps along
the walkway, Jim could not help but stop to examine the wall
more closely. Squinting against the gloom, he ran his fingers
over the stone. "No Spaniard stonecutter ever did this," he
said in a low voice.

The entire wall was covered with what appeared to be Incan and pre-Incan deities. Some were in human form, others
like mythological animals. Intermixed among these were also

Christian figures: angels, saints and representations of Jesus and the Virgin Mary. The entire church was obviously done in the same manner.

"Does this bother you?" Jim asked.

"It shouldn't, Jim, but I have this sudden sense of foreboding. It's as if we've just passed through some portal into a place we don't belong."

Jim, who was not so affected, merely shrugged, saying innocently, "The dark side of the moon."

Bartolomé looked at him silently for a moment. "Indeed," he muttered.

Exodus

The animals had ceased their movement up the road and were now milling about as if awaiting human direction. Despite the proliferation of livestock it was amazingly quiet. Charlie looked quizzically at César, who responded with a slight negative motion of his head. Other than dragging them out of the vehicle, no one had harmed them. Still, Charlie noted machetes dangling from the waists of several indigenes, some of which seemed to exhibit smears of blood, as if hastily wiped off.

One of the indigenes approached César and thrust his hand inside César's coat pocket. César immediately grasped the man's wrist and began to struggle. Arturo yelled at him, *"¡No,*

Jefe, no!" César stopped, his eyes wide with terror as the indigene raised his machete in the air. The wallet was retrieved and handed to a tall, slender man who had just arrived. Looking at Charlie, he held out his hand. *"Por favor, su cartera, también."*

Charlie recognized the man as a mestizo, of Spanish and indigene bloodlines. He appeared on the verge of exhaustion, eyes bleary and hard. Dried sweat left streaks through the dust and stubble of beard on his face. His was the countenance of a man not only driven to his physical limits but to those of the mind as well.

Charlie knew something terrible must have happened. More people were coming around the turn, men, women and children. Horses and burros came next, some dragging crudely fashioned litters. Even from where he stood, he could see that the litters bore injured men. Women walked stoically behind their wounded and cries of pain floated above the crowd.

On impulse, Charlie reached into the van for his camera and, pushing his way through the ring of men, began jogging down the road toward the litters. Behind him the tall man followed, shouting orders back at the indigenes. The horses stopped at his approach. They were Andean ponies, compact, woolly and very strong. When Charlie looked down at the first litter, he felt his stomach convulse. A man, wounded in the abdomen, looked unseeing into the sky. The stench of his ruptured bowel permeated the air and his hands, wet with fresh blood, trembled as they continuously groped about the wound, scarcely disguised by the flap of shirt covering it.

Charlie recognized the work of a hollow point bullet fired into the man's back and expanding as it passed through the body. Probably running away, trying to escape, he thought, as the *campesino*'s life abruptly ended. The tall man touched Charlie's shoulder and motioned him aside. Kneeling beside the litter and closing the man's eyes, he made a brief prayer. Two men then unhitched the horse and carried the body away.

"You are a *norteamericano,* a *periodista?*" the leader asked Charlie, returning his wallet.

"Yes," Charlie answered, his voice strained.

"If you are a good man, you will write of this. Your *capitalistas* are as guilty as the *hacendados.*"

Charlie followed the man back to the van, which had been emptied. César and Arturo were waiting. "Their *caserío* was attacked this morning by some of Quintero's men and about twenty militia," César related. "Apparently, they put up a good fight. The attack party withdrew, but they inflicted serious losses. Many people and animals were slain. They had to abandon the old guns they fought with because there was no more ammunition. Another attack would wipe them out, so they flee to a valley higher in the mountains. They are refugees, Señor Newell!"

The tall man interrupted, "Our people are innocent. We have no part in the rebellion! We live by ourselves and ask nothing of other people. Why do they do this to us!"

Charlie shook his head. "I am sorry, señor. It is a great and evil wrong. Do you have good land?"

"We did! We were rich in land and food until this morning!"

With that he spat upon the ground and left, shouting commands to those assembled nearby. In response, there was more shouting and cries as the animal herd began to move.

Charlie motioned to César and Arturo and the three men stepped to the opposite embankment to watch. The setting sun illuminated the dust, creating a golden aura through which the column moved into the shadows beneath the cliffs. Man and beast, on their pilgrimage together, Charlie mused. The procession was somehow magnificent, the sound of it, the drops of blood consecrating its passage. It was religious in scope, he thought. No, more than that. It was part of an even greater procession, the endless procession of all those who had been persecuted and tortured in this lonely, forsaken land.

Old Friends

The open doorway was illuminated by a lantern from within. As they entered, a black-robed priest could be seen seated with his back to the door. The priest was conversing with an elderly man who wore a battered straw hat and leaned forward from the edge of his chair on a cane. Jim felt a rush as the old man looked in his direction. It occurred to him that this was the Hatun Laika that Bartolomé had mentioned. The priest slowly arose and, grasping the chair back, turned to face his visitors.

Bartolomé edged forward; his voice quavered, "Mariano?"

Mariano could manage only a few steps, raising his arms to beckon Bartolomé, who then rushed across the room to embrace him. "This has been no welcome for an old friend. Please forgive me, Bartolomé, I have had duties . . ." Bartolomé engulfed the older man, then held him at arm's length.

"Seeing you alive again proves God's magnanimity!" he exclaimed. "I am filled with joy!"

A nervous disorder caused some facial muscles to spasm and Mariano's speech slurred slightly. "No more than I," he managed.

Jim watched the reunion in silence. Behind him more visitors were crowding into the room. He could not avoid noting that several left weapons at the doorway.

"Mariano, let me introduce you to my guide, Jim Bridgman."

The frail priest clasped Jim's hand with both of his and held it to his chest, the faintest trace of a smile slowly manifesting itself. Jim looked down into the watery gray eyes and saw the feverish light that burned there. He felt the clammy skin pressing against his. For a moment, Mariano turned his face aside and studied the *alpinista* with his peripheral vision. Then, turning back, he released Jim's hand. His smile broadened. "We are indebted to you, Señor Bridgman, for bringing Bartolomé to us."

A stew of some sort was being prepared in a large cast-iron pot straddling a depression in the floor filled with glowing coals. Bread was also being baked in an adobe oven set into the wall. Several women tended the food and cast glances toward the visitors. One in particular drew Jim's attention. Her face was flushed with the heat, and strands of damp, black hair clung to her forehead. She turned abruptly away from his gaze and began to stir the stew with a large ladle.

"Rosa." Father Raimondi stepped up behind her. "Our guests have arrived."

Rosa turned and fixed him with a hard stare, peeking at Jim over his shoulder as she did so. "Do I appear blind?" she snapped. "Sometimes I think that it is the devil speaking through you, not God! Tell them the food is ready!"

The gathering seemed strange to Jim. There were maybe twenty indigene visitors in the room who ate where they stood or managed to squat. Bartolomé shared a small table with Mariano and Jim secured a spot at the far side of the room. He tried not to stare at Rosa, but couldn't help himself. The lamb stew was delicious, and as he surveyed the room, he took careful note of its occupants. They were mostly men who paid him little attention and ate with gusto.

Although few smiled or laughed, the din was almost oppressive. Jim felt disoriented and out of place. The men who crowded into the small room shared something that he was not privy to. He was relieved that his task was done and that the morning would see him on his way home. Bartolomé had been more than generous. Despite his concerns, the job had been worth it.

The Hatun Laika sat by the fire with Rosa, staring at Jim. The man seemed familiar, but Jim couldn't remember from where. Occasionally, his eyes met Rosa's and he could see a momentary flicker of light deep within. He wanted to speak with her but dared not risk being forward.

Mariano and Bartolomé were deep in conversation. Jim wished he could hear what was said but the noisy room prohibited it.

~~~~~~~

"Despite it all, you seem serene, my friend. In the midst of such uncertainty, how do you manage it?"

"Uncertainty is a state of mind, Bartolomé. Life is infinite in all its variations, but every variation is defined by immutable law."

"Doesn't that kill the spontaneity of it? It seems that you would reduce our existence to something no more complex than a stone."

Mariano looked at Bartolomé with benevolent condescension. "We must accept what we are. Even though these scripts are written for us, we must still act them out. Pain and joy are no less real or life less beautiful. We simply must have faith in God's plan."

"Why has God given you the crystal ball, Mariano? Does possession of that ball give us license to tamper with what has been ordained? Is it God or our manipulation that has brought this man here?" Bartolomé's voice was heavy with fatigue.

"I cannot speak for God," Mariano answered. "I can only do His bidding as He has revealed it to me."

At this point in the dialogue, the Hatun Laika came to the table and was introduced as Huaman. Bartolomé felt a deep sense of hostility from the old man, who ignored his extended hand and simply stared at him before shuffling off.

Rosa snickered. She could not hear what was being said but was certain that the big priest from the Vatican was having reservations over a very important matter and she could not blame him. Her eyes drifted to where the *norteamericano* sat watching the proceedings. His face turned to hers, but this time she did not look away. The man moved her, to be sure. Close to forty, yes, but still bearing the aspect of a boy. She could feel an attraction between them, yet his look seemed to be asking another question. One she could not, dared not, answer.

As if on cue, the men finished their bowls of stew and began to file out the door. Jim rose and looked about, uncertain what to do. At that moment, Father Raimondi, seeing Jim's indecision, motioned him over. "Please forgive me, Jim," he said. "It was not my intention to exclude you; please join us." Mindful of the fact that Bartolomé had said nothing, had, in fact, not even turned around, Jim grabbed a chair and sat down.

"I understand that you wish to leave in the morning," Mariano began. "To avoid some of the problems you encountered coming, I have an alternative route . . ."

On the following morning, Bartolomé was somewhat contrite. "Jim," he intoned, "please accept my apology for not fully informing you. It was a condition of my coming to Peru that I not reveal my relationship with Mariano to anyone."

Jim hesitated before answering. He was not used to duplicity. In the back of his mind, he sensed something else hanging over his head but could not bring it into focus. Best to take the money and get the hell out of there. "Put it out of your mind," he said. "The trip's been worth it."

Bartolomé saw the suspicion in Jim's eyes as he handed him the familiar blue envelope. "Jim, I will make this up to you; I promise. In the meantime, you won't have me to burden you on the way out."

An indigene approached the pair, carrying a rifle and an old cartridge belt, which, to Jim's surprise, was placed in his hands. "Take it," Bartolomé admonished. "God forbid that you should need it, but if you do . . ."

Jim stared at Bartolomé's face and made no reply. It was as if a cloud had momentarily darkened the sky. Bartolomé watched him exit into the sunshine and stride down the street, his tall, broad frame incongruous amid the smaller villagers. It was only with great effort that he suppressed the urge to call him back.

On the hillside above, Father Raimondi leaned against an old stone column and watched. Standing beside him, Rosa shared the view. "So that is the brave *norteamericano?*" she asked, observing Jim's movement toward the pass.

"Yes, Rosa."

"Does he look like the man in your vision?"

"Oh yes. I'm sure."

Rosa looked wistfully up at the sky. "Why did you not tell Bartolomé that you were alive sooner?"

"For our purposes it was better the world thought me dead. Now events are beginning to converge toward a crisis that will demand all we can give. I only hope that I live long enough to witness our victory."

"Do your visions offer any hope?"

"They show me a long and bloody struggle."

Rosa de Melgarejo removed her cloak and slipped it over Mariano's shoulders. "I hate it," she said, "all this talk of blood and death. You will live to baptize my children and see them grow. Come back to the kitchen now; María has the tea ready."

Mariano dutifully obeyed, noticing, as he took her arm, her lingering glance behind. "You must leave for the hacienda now," he said sternly. "Carlos Quintero is a curious man and must not be made suspicious of your whereabouts. Remember he is *El Patrón!*"

Indeed, she thought to herself, looking back once again toward the pass. The trail was empty; Jim Bridgman was already descending the old Incan pathway which would place him in a highly contested area of the altiplano. It would take the gringo a lot longer to reach the rancho than it would her, if he ever got there at all.

Executive Caucus

From her station in the kitchen Rosa listened to the unending palaver of the *hacendados* gathered in Carlos Quintero's living room. She was sure that either General Valesco or Colonel Rohem would have mentioned a gringo captive or casualty by now. The image of Jim Bridgman being pursued across the puna held increasing sway in her mind.

Sensing the discussion had stalled, Rosa stepped outside to escape the heat of the ovens. As she did, a late-model sedan turned down the drive and parked. An officer beckoned to the stocky, strong-looking man who exited and pointed to the house. As he approached, their eyes met and Rosa felt a surge of fear that this man somehow knew her. The door opened and he entered without a word, taking a seat near Carlos. No introductions were made.

Karl Slesser's jaw was set. He did not like dealing with these weaselly bastards; but it had to be done. His superiors were uptight about this one and the repercussions of failure could be serious.

Victor Soriano was feeling the wine. "I do not trust our faceless friends in Lima any more than I trust *yanquis*. Where is the piece of paper that guarantees our interests, our future?"

Except for a faint tremor in one eye, it was as if Karl Slesser had not heard the slight, but he had.

General Valesco did his best to cover up. "Victor," he responded, "copies of the concords have been sent to all of you. Everyone shares equally. You will be paid a duty on every liter of oil that flows down the pipeline, on every cubic meter of natural gas, on every truckload of ore that goes to the crushing mill. Every load of produce brought from the selva will be hauled in your trucks and the contracts for the harvesting of timber from the *montaña* will be shared by all of you."

Octavio Villanueva was next. "That is what we are told, General. But how and when are we to be paid? The *norteamericanos* are a fine people to lunch with, but when it comes to money they never smile. What is the mechanism, the fiduciary arrangement for the processing and transfer of funds? At present, we only have a contract with a Peruvian company that is yet to be legally registered."

"RDC was registered yesterday," Carlos interjected. "Our

partners have made a substantial deposit with Banco Federal. You should stop whining like old women. Remember, the resources rest in Peruvian soil. If something sours, there is a world full of customers waiting for our summons. In the meantime we'll be rid of the *campesinos*."

Karl stood up and made his way across the room toward the kitchen. Behind him the conversation stopped. Rosa barely made it back to the stove before he appeared in the doorway. For an instant the hard and knowing face looked into hers and then the door was pulled shut.

Turning to the landowners, Karl was blunt. "Look, I'm not here for policy. It's not my department. I don't negotiate deals; I implement them. Now, we have a problem. This fucking area is supposed to be sealed off—it's not."

The outburst of mumbled indignation and denial was short-lived. Karl continued, "As we talk, there is an American newsman nosing around Chiquian who's very much interested in talking with you, Carlos. I'd advise you to keep him at a distance until we get some direction on the matter."

Carlos' temper flared but he controlled it. He was the master of an estate nearly three hundred years old, larger than many countries. He would respond to this insolent bastard at the appropriate time.

Karl remained on his feet. "That's not all. A priest from Rome, in the company of an American mountain climber, is wandering around the puna somewhere just south of us."

"The Church does what it's told in Peru," Carlos replied. "He's just another buffoon sent from Rome on a paid vacation. We'll make sure he's removed. As for the roads, they are closed. We'll have the *guardia* deal with the newsman."

Karl made no reply. His confederates in Arlington were concerned. They, like he, never took anything for granted.

~~~~~~

In the kitchen Rosa's anxiety mounted. What were they talking about? Handing the heavy wooden spatula to one of the servants, she took off her apron. "Check the bread in ten minutes," she said. "I'm going for a walk."

Misdirection

Jim turned off the Primus stove, plunging the early morning camp into silence. His tent was pitched in a small arroyo where hopefully it would be invisible to *guardia* patrols. He had been on the puna a week now and was almost out of supplies. The return route had placed him in an area of intense military scrutiny, necessitating maneuvers which more often than not found him lost. He cursed himself for not taking the same route back to the rancho. What in hell had Father Raimondi been thinking of?

He had scarcely adjusted to the quiet when a distant drumming sound began to manifest itself in the the west. Initially it was barely audible in the arroyo, but rapidly became louder. Soon other sounds could be heard, the crackle of small arms and shouting. Another minute passed and Jim could distinctly hear men and women screaming and the agonized neighing of horses.

He began to run toward an overhanging bluff split by the arroyo, but had not made twenty feet before a wave of fleeing *campesinos* and choking dust spilled over the lip and dropped onto the sand. Gunshots sounded around him as people frantically sought protection under the arroyo's walls or cringed frozen with fear. From the embankment above, shadowy figures on horseback fired down into the confusion. A massacre was suddenly in the making as Jim groped on all fours for his rifle.

Bullets narrowly missed him as he screamed at the *campesinos* to run for the bluff. Aided by Jim's fire, they quickly scurried into the dust. Jim grabbed the rifle of a soldier who lay groaning in the sand. Two others, also victims of his marksmanship, lay nearby. Above him the *guardia* pulled back from the lip of the arroyo. Taking advantage of the moment, he ran after the *campesinos*.

Urging and pushing, he managed to get the last of the people into relative safety as firing began anew. Taking one man aside whom he perceived as a leader, he told him to take the people as far as they could go up the defile and find a way out. Jim, with some of the weapons they had scavanged, would provide a rear guard action. The indigene did not hesitate. Taking one long look at Jim as if to fix him in memory, he began instructing his people in Quechua. Within seconds they had turned a corner and were out of sight.

Carrying two rifles and a bandolier of ammunition, Jim managed to establish a vantage point on a ledge about thirty feet above the arroyo floor just inside the bluff. This enabled him to see the soldiers beyond the bluff, crouched on either side of the arroyo, as they began to creep forward. He estimated about forty men and wondered where he should fire first. Deciding that the soldiers to the right presented the most imminent danger, he took a deep breath and aimed carefully.

The return fire was ferocious, but Jim adjusted and kept firing until his ammunition was nearly exhausted. He had hit ten or twelve men, he wasn't sure; the important thing was that he had bought time for the fleeing *campesinos*. Now he had to escape himself. As he clambered down from his perch, he was surprised to find himself bleeding from fragments of rock dislodged by near misses.

The arroyo was completely in shade both inside the bluff and outside. Jim could hear the sounds of soldiers carefully advancing, but the cadence of their movement was increasing as they gained confidence in his diminished capacity to return fire. Jim was now running, afraid to waste any more ammunition to slow his pursuers. A towering abutment rose before him and he stopped at its base, perplexed. The arroyo forked and there was no indication of which way the *campesinos* had gone. Their tracks were swept clean.

He was at the point of nervous exhaustion, drained by the demands he had suffered. There was no time to reconnoiter. Jim chose the left fork and continued on. Scarcely seventy-five meters ahead he realized his mistake as the route ended in crumbling vertical walls. Behind him he glimpsed a shadowy figure dart behind a protruding rib. There was no turning back; he was trapped.

Several minutes ensued in bleak silence. The soldiers had stopped their advance and seemed to be waiting. Jim's mind was in turmoil. Should he surrender or fight, the result would be the same; of that he was certain. The only question was whether or not the prolongation of his life for a few more miserable minutes was worth the struggle.

He sat in the sand with his back against the rock. Better to savor these last minutes and let them come to him, he thought. He hoped the end would be abrupt, one last flicker of consciousness and then the end of all pain. Despite the problems, he was proud of the life he had chosen. Too bad that old age and the pleasure of comfortable reflection would be taken from him. An involuntary shudder passed through his body. He lowered his head. It was over; he had nothing left.

"*¡Gringo! ¡Norteamericano! ¡Hola!*" Jim looked up, but saw nothing. The voice sounded again, "Let's talk, eh? There is nothing to be gained by more shooting!" With that Major Joaquín Zamora stepped into view, holding his hands shoulder high, palms forward. He advanced a bit further and stopped. "What do you say?"

Jim came warily to his feet and stood where the officer could see him. He could see no one else, but they had to be there watching, ready to shoot. Whatever their plan, he had no alternative. Jim moved out into the middle of the defile, still clutching one rifle and wearing the bandolier. As if by unspoken agreement the two men walked slowly toward one another, careful not to stumble in the loose sand. At two meters separation they stopped, standing face to face in silence.

Zamora looked up at the tall gringo. Jim's unwavering gaze and lean, muscular body impressed him. *Un hombre formidable,* he thought. There was something in Jim's bearing that made him hesitate. Given his normal *modus operandi,* the major would have simply signaled with a twist of his wrist and Jim would have fallen dead at his feet before the sound of the rifle reached them. But the gringo intrigued him. He would not die today. Before he decided on the details of Jim's fate, he would bring his prisoner to Carlos Quintero. He would show the arrogant *hacendado* how strong men could be made to behave at the hands of Joaquín Zamora.

PART THREE

The Crucible

Captive

It was late the following day when they arrived at the Hacienda Santa Rosa. Still tied over a horse, Jim was in a state of excruciating pain and nausea with no sense of where he might be. They had stopped moving and he was dimly aware of sliding downward, of striking the earth. The upper part of his body and legs were chafed and bloody from unrelenting contact with the horse. His neck ached and the sound that he struggled to recognize was his own voice, the involuntary moans of agony.

Still bound hand and foot, he was picked up and carried into a room. The rope which had been used to bind him was exchanged for iron shackles. Not long thereafter an indigene woman was sent with a small portion of food and water, but she could not rouse him. Laying the tray by his side, she left. The door was slammed shut behind her and locked. Jim could smell the dirt floor and feel a cold draft coming from somewhere. Somehow, it was soothing. He slept.

In the morning, the door was jerked open by a uniformed soldier who knelt by Jim and tilted his head upward to ascertain if he was conscious. Jim blinked his eyes against the harsh light and tried to speak, but could manage only a hoarse groan. Satisfied, the guard rose and left. Jim could hear voices and then a shadow filled the doorway. It was Rosa.

In the contrasting light, she could barely make out the prone form on the earthen floor. As her eyes adjusted she could see that it was Jim and that his lips were split and crusted with blood. There were also contusions on his face and neck and a gash in his head above the hairline. Jim moaned as she helped him to a sitting position; there was at least one cracked rib.

"Listen," she whispered, "I am a friend, Rosa. Do you remember me from Karoma?"

Jim groaned and shook his head. "Yes."

Rosa was horrified at his condition. In the gloom, Jim could not see her reddened eyes. She took his face in her hands and kissed him lightly on the forehead. "Oh, God," she said, "I am so sorry."

"Not your doing," he mumbled.

At that remark, tears began to stream down her face. "We must feed you," she managed.

With Rosa's help, Jim finished a bowl of cooked cereal and some bread. Outside, the loud sound of an unmuffled motor could be heard over the shouts of a number of men.

"Listen to me!" she said. Jim blinked his eyes and looked at Rosa, trying to focus on the urgency in her voice. "Yes . . ." he stammered.

"They are going to send you to Condoroma. It is a mine

where they hide political prisoners. You must try to escape as soon as you can. If you linger, the mine will kill you. They want you to die there."

At the sound of the guard returning, she quickly slipped a small loaf of bread into his hands and stood up with the tray. "For tomorrow," she whispered.

The vehicle was vintage Third World transportation, painted blue and red, and strewn with tassels and religious artifacts around the driver's compartment. A cargo rack ran the length of the top and was loaded with wooden boxes and items of metal construction that Jim did not recognize. *"Vamos,"* one guard said, prodding him with a gun barrel. As he staggered forward he noted that the rear windows on either side of the vehicle were permanently covered with plywood sheeting; he felt his stomach tighten.

Three men were already in the back, their hands shackled to the framework of the seat back in front of them. Jim was pushed down the aisle and ordered into a seat by himself on the opposite side. All of the seat backs in that area were fitted with shackles and chains looped through the seat-back frame and welded to prohibit lateral movement. Despite the morning cold, he began to sweat.

One guard ordered him to place his hands on the seat back, as the other guard stepped behind him. They had obviously done this before. When Jim did not respond, the man behind placed the barrel of his revolver against Jim's head and cocked the trigger. The ominous sound shocked him into sensibility. He dropped back into his seat, wincing from the pain in his chest. Both guards patted him on the back as they left, laughing.

Carnage

Ever so carefully, Charlie pulled the curtain aside and peered into the predawn gloom. He had been awakened by the unmistakable sound of automatic weapons fire and the heavy thump, thump of a large-caliber machine gun. Except for a few sporadic shots following, the outburst had lasted only three or four minutes.

The firing emanated from the other side of the Plaza de Armas in the vicinity of the church. There had been no human outcry, nor could Charlie discern anyone moving about. This did not surprise him. In the days he had been sequestered at the Hotel del Sol, in effect under house arrest, the quaint, colonial township of Chiquian had been transformed into an armed camp. Normal traffic into the town had ceased and the marketplace was closed. Indigenes from the countryside were not to be seen.

What small excursions Charlie did make around town were carefully monitored and his anxiety grew as his presence became increasingly awkward. César Oré was strangely unavailable and the interview with Carlos Quintero had become a moot point. Still, the newsman had hung on in the hope of a break.

He stared out the window for several more minutes trying

to build up his courage. The hotel was practically empty; there were only two other guests and they were on the opposite side of the building. Grabbing his coat and camera, he left the room, heading for the fire exit at one end of the hallway. Something terrible had happened. He knew it.

~~~~~

Outside the streets were deserted. Taking the alleyway behind the hotel, he walked briskly north two blocks before turning left back to the main thoroughfare. Surveying the intersection carefully, he dashed across the street into the shelter of an empty lot, which had been partially walled off. Just in time. Two large military trucks filled with soldiers turned into the intersection right behind him and sped down the street in the direction of the plaza.

The sky was getting brighter and Charlie felt an urgency to move. Quelling his nerves as best as he could, he climbed over the low wall at the rear of the lot into a narrow street which led to the plaza. As he did so, he could hear more vehicles approaching the center of town. He made one block, the shrubbery of the plaza coming into view, when he heard the synchronized tramp of soldiers jogging at doubletime somewhere behind him. Ahead, two Jeeps moved slowly past the plaza. Was he trapped? He stepped into the recess of a storefront to gather himself together.

Off and on in the distance he began to hear voices. He was about to despair when a soft, rapping sound attracted his attention from the storefront directly across from him. A door opened and a small, wizened man motioned to him. "Señor," he said, *"por favor."*

It was a jewelry store and Señor Arriaga had been awakened as had Charlie. "I live above the store," he said. "When the guns go off, I come down to put my best pieces in the safe. One never knows anymore. You are the *periodista*, true?"

Charlie nodded. "Yes, and thank you very much. Do you know what's going on?"

The small man hesitated; his eyes grew moist. "I do not know, señor. But late last night, many people came to the church. *Campesinos*."

Charlie froze, his mind spinning. "Can I get near the church without being seen?"

Señor Arriaga thought for a moment, then he pointed upward. "You might try the roofs. I could send my nephew with you."

Charlie smiled. *"Gracias, señor."*

~~~~~

The sun had just risen behind them, illuminating the eastern wall and rear courtyard of the church with a soft rosy glow. Charlie and Ramón lay behind the roof cornice of the building and peered over. The area was entirely cordoned off, including the block in which this building and Arriaga's shop were located. Most of the windows of the church had been shot out and the large door on the eastern wall lay in splinters.

Charlie's heart began to pound. At least a hundred indigenes were being herded into the courtyard. Some of the faces seemed familiar. With a start, he recognized the tall man, the refugee leader, arguing with an officer. He could hear the man's raised voice and saw the officer strike him with a rid-

ing crop. Two soldiers subdued the leader and shoved him toward the courtyard with the others. Charlie was aghast. The
indigenes were being bunched against the rear wall of the
church. Along the low wall which formed the courtyard, soldiers with automatic weapons were beginning to assemble.
"Oh, my God," Charlie cried. "No!" But there was nothing
they could do.

Condoroma

Jim awoke to a dark void and an aching chill which racked
his body with shivering. In the dim aura of starlight diffusing
through the recessed opening in the ceiling he could make out
the still forms of his four newfound friends huddled about the
concrete floor on straw mats. The night cold helped to suppress the stench emanating from the open latrine which ran
along one wall, but could not entirely eliminate it.

He rolled over on one side, drawing his knees up together,
and snugged the serape close about his neck. Although he had
been incarcerated at Condoroma only two months, he knew
that his survival, quite apart from an execution, was already
in doubt. He found himself taking whatever small advantage
he could find to conserve warmth and energy or manage an
additional scrap of food. To minimize contact with the lead
ore, he rinsed his hands as frequently as possible and kept a
dampened rag over his face to protect his lungs. His companions had been working the mine as political prisoners for

over two years and coughed constantly. Two, Simon and Gerardo, complained of abdominal pain and appeared anemic.

Jim worried about a lack of vitamin D. He spent almost twelve hours deep in the mine and only briefly experienced sunlight, at dawn and day's end. He was becoming a creature of the dark whose world consisted of the labyrinth of tunnels and galleries spread within the nameless mountain above and the cold, dank blockhouse in which they were confined each evening. Vicente told him they were lucky; the shifts used to be eighteen hours.

The windowless adobe blockhouse was built into a deep hillside excavation and thus most of three walls were contiguous with the surrounding earth. It was originally designed to store explosives, but water seepage became a problem. As a consequence, the explosives were moved to a shed some one hundred meters distant and the blockhouse was converted to a large cell for the confinement of special people brought to Condoroma by the *policía secreta* or the *guardia*. The mine owners took credit for performing a public service and boasted of their no-nonsense handling of dangerous criminals.

Jim watched the starlight dim and heard the sound of increasing wind across the roof. Soon snowflakes would be winnowing their way downward through the square-cut opening in the ceiling. In the morning, they would sweep the snow into the latrine and walk gingerly about the room to stimulate blood circulation. Eventually the door would be unlocked and they would be marched under heavy guard to the *cocina* where they would receive portions of a watery porridge made from oats or quinoa. If they were lucky, there would be bread.

Jim made sure to use as much sugar and powdered milk as possible without risking the attention of his jailers.

Outside the door he heard the guard cough and spit. It was their one consolation that at least some of their tormentors had to also endure the night cold, although Jim wondered why a guard was necessary on the other side of a one-inch-thick steel-plate door. His fellow prisoners called it La Ciudad de Perdición, the City of Doom. An apt name, he thought, for the sickly wraiths who worked and died in its depths.

It was nearly pitch black now and the wind began to roar. He could hear the clanging and banging of loose metal driven by the gusts. The onset of the storm had the psychological effect of making the interior seem relatively warmer. Dawn was still hours away and he rolled back to his other side. The vestiges of a dream still scampered about his mind—waterfalls gushing beneath brilliant blue skies, pine trees sparkling in the sunlight, a blue tent pitched in a high meadow. He struggled to draw them together again, to re-create the images and the comfort they brought him.

Request and Denial

Mariano knelt before the small altar and tried to compose himself. The mélange of images that had so inflicted his mind after the accident had returned and he struggled to retain his composure. He prayed for God to bring order to his thoughts so that he could divine the Holy Will without error. Behind him, pacing back and forth, was Rosa de Melgarejo, no respecter of sanctums, religious or otherwise. She was voluble and highly agitated. Mariano turned and motioned her to one of the pews where he joined her.

"When are we going to get him out of there?" she demanded, her voice reverberating in the small church. "Twenty more men came in yesterday, with horses."

"Please, Rosa, you must be patient. Nothing we can do will alter the divine will. Soon the accumulation of events will guide us and we will learn what our role is to be."

For a moment Rosa was silent, wrestling with inhibitions toward religious authority nurtured and reinforced since childhood. Her tone became somewhat more modulated, but the sting was still there. "What is the *norteamericano*'s role, to suffer in that miserable pigsty until he's dead? What did he do to deserve that? Is it some part of God's will that we are not party to, that we take on faith?"

Mariano did not respond; he knew where Rosa's emotional impetus came from. The woman had been attracted to the *alpinista* and somewhere in the fragments of Mariano's visions, there were hints of what might happen between them; but it was too soon to discuss that with Rosa. One thing though was clear. "It won't be long now, Rosa. I promise you."

"I don't want promises, I want action, Father. We could take him out of there easily with thirty men and have him back here within a week."

"No!" Mariano uncharacteristically snapped. "No! There will be no more talk of this until the voice of God is heard!"

"As he speaks through you, eh, Father!" Rosa shouted back.

"It is His will, not mine!" Mariano replied.

Rosa was already stalking away. "I would prefer," she shouted from the entrance, "that He speak for Himself!"

The door closed behind her with a boom and Mariano slumped in the pew. Except for the rasping of his breath, the silence of the sanctuary reasserted itself. Tears welled in his eyes. "Oh, Rosa," he moaned, "it is not that simple."

A Plan

The lift rattled and shook as the five men were lowered through the final staging to the bottommost level of the mine, eighteen hundred feet below the surface. Jim clung to the supports and watched the black rock walls go by. A few secondary tunnels off the main shaft appeared and disappeared; but none offered a route to freedom. A sharp squeal from the rigging signaled the end and they jolted to a stop. As each man stepped out, he was handed his tools and directed to the "gallery" to be excavated that day. They were escorted by men bearing shotguns.

Every trip down was the same, an entombment. Jim fought against his rising panic. I'm going to die like a poisoned mole, he thought. The air was foul with dust and gases from lack of ventilation, and the temperature stifling. His mind was constantly beset with a sense of impending disaster. In the dim light of a few low-wattage bulbs he and Vicente made their way through knee-deep water and muck. Their only relief during the ensuing twelve-hour stint would be a twenty-minute break for stale bread and dried cheese.

Jim carried a long metal bar, over one inch in diameter and weighing close to sixty pounds. Today he would be a driller, boring holes for dynamite charges by slowly twisting the bar, or "star" drill, in the grasp of one hand while bringing a sledge to bear with the other. Vicente would work the ore carts with the three other men, two pulling with ropes slung over one shoulder and two pushing. Ore excavation was done by hand and chunks too large to be lifted were broken up with sledgehammers.

Placing one hand against the wall for balance, Jim immediately withdrew it in disgust and plunged it into the muck to remove a gooey substance from his palm. Sputum, tinged dark red with blood, marked the passage of men whose lungs were failing. One grim consolation for confinement in Condoroma was that no one lived to old age.

Arguments and fighting were frequent and Jim worried constantly about being struck from behind with a shovel. Some men, suffering from lead poisoning and fatigue, became demented and had to be watched. He had seen a miner beaten to death by a man so afflicted wielding a short-handled shovel. It took the efforts of six men to restrain him and bind his limbs. As he was being hauled up the tunnel, he had screamed, *"¡Madre de Dios! ¡Madre de Dios!* Save us from the devils!"

Jim stumbled on, immersed in his thoughts. It would be another rough day. He was deliberately being assigned the "big

drill" in an effort to break him and he had to admit their
scheme was working. They were midway down the adit when
Vicente screamed in his ear and grabbed him. Jim looked
down. One more step and he would have plunged into a black
gaping hole. "Thanks," he murmured.

~~~~~

Jim lay on his straw mat looking blankly up at the ceiling,
his sense of hopelessness increasing with the fading light. His
wounds had mostly healed, although his ribs still ached.
However, the pain meant nothing compared with his longing
for the wide, open sky, the freedom of movement over virgin ground. Freedom to breath, to exult, to reach upward into
clean air. But every day his world grew smaller, more con-
fining; the senses dulled and he subsided into a listless apathy that Vicente recognized as the prelude to total submission
and ultimate death.

"Jaime," he whispered. "Come on, talk to me! Let's make
a plan, what the hell!"

Jim mumbled something indecipherable and closed his
eyes.

Vicente shook him by the shoulder. "Come on, *alpinista,*
figure a way to climb out of here."

Jim managed a smile, pointing to the hole in the center of
the twenty-foot ceiling. "You mean there? I would need to
have wings like the condor, my friend."

"Maybe you do," Vicente answered.

Jim studied the rectangular opening which protruded
through the roof like the stump of a chimney. Some flat iron
that previously held ventilation equipment for the explosives

stored there was still bolted in place. Also, he noticed a length of electrical conduit reaching from the edge of the opening to within three feet of the wall. It had been painted over, and although flush with the ceiling, was well secured with oversize bolts and hangers. If it could hold his weight, he might be able to traverse the ceiling and reach the opening. It would be a very difficult set of moves, but given the incentive, well worth the try.

Jim rose to his feet and crossed the floor to the section of wall beneath the end of the conduit and ran his hands over the surface.

"We need something sharp . . . like a chisel." Jim's voice was distant.

Silence ensued and then Vicente stepped forward, taking Jim's arm. Looking up into his face, he said, "We will get what you need, my friend."

Jim's smile was wan. "I don't know who I am any longer. Maybe I can't do this. I'll fail and get you all in trouble."

Vicente snickered. "Oh no!" he said. "We know who you are. Your problem is that you don't know who you are. You have already become a legend to the people. The gringo alpinist who fought off an army and saved a whole village!"

Jim had said nothing of his battle with the militia. "Where did you hear that?" he asked incredulously.

"Ah, Señor Bridgman. That type of news has wider wings than the condor. You are one of us, my friend, and we are bound to support you."

Jim turned away momentarily, not daring to look at Vicente.

"Jim"—Vicente spoke again—"there is one more thing I

must tell you so that you truly understand. "Did you ever hear of a man called El Halcón?"

"No."

"He was a fighter for justice and famous throughout this region. He fought the *hacendados* and the soldiers for years before they captured him and brought him here. His real name was Luis Tirado."

Vicente paused to collect himself before continuing.

"He was a difficult prisoner from the start. They tortured and starved him, but could not break his spirit. One night, despite the debilitations of this treatment, he escaped. On the next morning, he was recaptured and brought back."

Vicente was silent again and Jim turned to face him.

"Did you notice that fifty-gallon drum lying in the weeds across the road, the one with the small rectangular opening high on the side?" Vicente held his hands about eight inches apart.

"Yes," Jim said softly.

"First, they cut that hole with a torch. Then they forced him inside and welded the top on. They continued to provide him with food and water. Every day the guards would come to torment him by banging on the drum with their rifle butts and urinating through the opening. No one stopped them. Within a few months he went insane and died in his own excrement."

Jim closed his eyes. "Where did they bury him?" he asked.

"They didn't," Vicente answered.

Aftermath

Three hours had elapsed since the last shot had been heard. The sun was approaching its zenith and the heat was building on the exposed rooftop. Ramón peeked over the cornice and ducked back beside Charlie. "Señor," he said, "I think we can move back now."

Charlie nodded, beads of sweat beginning to form on his brow. He lifted himself to his knees and hesitated. "Ramón," he hissed, "can we get down beside the church courtyard somehow?"

Ramón's eyes widened. "There are still soldiers there," he answered. "That would be *muy peligroso!*"

Charlie stared at the young man in silence, expressionless.

Ramón sighed. "All right, Señor Newell. We can try."

After considerable backtracking and passage through private property, Ramón brought them into position behind the church property. Eucalyptus trees, planted along the low wall's interior, gave them a measure of concealment. As they drew closer, the bullet patterns of automatic weapons fire upon the doors and walls from the initial assault on the church could easily be seen. Shattered stained-glass windows on the eastern wall were patched with remnants of cloth and paper tacked to what remained of the window frames.

Seven *guardia* soldiers could be seen strolling about the courtyard with rifles slung over their shoulders. They were overseeing the work of a dozen or more *campesinas* engaged in cleaning the rear wall of the church and adjoining pavement. The church wall, up to a height of seven or eight feet, had been totally defaced by weapons fire and an inundation of human blood.

On the pavement women worked on their knees with putty knives and other implements to scrape up the mess. Others pulled buckets of red foam after them as they scrubbed both pavement and wall with stiff bristle brushes. The stench and large black flies were almost unbearable. Charlie lowered his head and fought to control himself. Ramón's face was blank, except for the trembling of his lips.

Charlie took several pictures and pointed down into the small ravine behind them. Careful not to make any dust, they crept down the slope and away from the orchestrated massacre.

Execution

Jim's back and shoulders ached. Dark gray dust and sweat formed a thick scum on his brow and face that seemed impossible to wipe away. He blinked his eyes against the irritation and tried to take a deep breath through the dampened rag tied over his nose and mouth. Vicente sat on a pile of rubble beside him. Two guards at the entry to the gallery watched over them and another stood behind the shift foreman who was kneeling before an undercut in the adjacent wall. The roof of the undercut was only about five feet above the floor and underneath it, at least fifteen feet in, their cellmates, Luis and Gerardo, swinging short picks to deepen the penetration.

Tension among those present was high. "This is deliberate planned murder," Jim whispered to Vicente, "a goddamned execution!"

The process was called caving, a technique in which a block or column of ore is undercut, allowing the weight of the ore and overburden to cause a collapse and breakup of the deposit. Normally timbering was used as a temporary support and blasted out after the area was cleared. In this instance, no timbering was provided.

Simon had been sent on an errand, leaving Jim and Vicente to witness the unfolding tragedy. They could readily feel the terror that Luis and Gerardo were experiencing. *"Jefe,"* they were constantly calling out, "we are far enough, yes? We should stop here? Please, *Jefe,* let us have some water and we'll talk it over. We can't work without water!"

The shift foreman ignored their repeated pleas, directing them back and forth within the cut. Jim could tell they were no longer swinging with any effect, trying not to increase the undercut any more and stall the foreman for one more day—a day which might save their lives.

"Put some strength into it!" the foreman shouted. "You are not working. I cannot help you if you do not help me." Thus speaking, he laughed and the guards laughed with him. Something was transpiring that neither Jim nor Vicente immediately divined. They could not know that in distant Lima a decision had been made and that the plant manager, over a bottle of Pisco with friends, had designed this accident for Luis and Gerardo. It was much more entertaining than simply shooting them and permitted the perpetrators to speak convincingly of the terrible accident that claimed the lives of so and so. Given the license, the plant manager would have made it much more entertaining, but his directions were otherwise and with an air of resignation he complied.

It had become silent within the undercut. They could hear the low sobs of the two men. "Please, *Jefe,*" Luis' voice issued from the dark shadow, "no more, we don't want to die!" The sound of someone starting to move out from beneath the overhang could be heard. Quickly, the guard moved in front and worked the action of his shotgun. The clear menacing rattle sounded in the chamber like the snap of an overseer's whip. Jim heard the scrape of iron on rock as someone took his pick in hand. There were two sharp strikes against the rock and then a dull cracking sound as the enormous mass fractured from the wall.

The gallery filled with dust and the low rumble of falling rock. Jim and Vicente lay face down, holding the wet rags tight against their faces. When it was over, a massive mound of ore lay at the base of the wall. They were too numb to cry. The horror of Condoroma had bludgeoned them into silence. The shift foreman kicked Jim in the ribs and spat on Vicente. "Your shift is over," he growled, "when you get the bodies out." With that, he and the guards left.

Time-Out

Charlie needed a drink badly. Entering the hotel via the kitchen, he went directly to the bar where he was poured a double bourbon, neat, and slipped a small, folded piece of paper. Carrying it to a booth which afforded a view of the stairway leading to the second floor, he sat down and waited for his nerves to subside. The bourbon was warm and delicious, a stark, solitary rush of pleasure in the dark heart of a starless night.

Charlie was now in serious jeopardy. Karl Slesser had to have learned of his whereabouts by now and the thought of what he might do hovered like a black cloud in the newsman's mind.

He unfolded the scrap of paper, read it, and closed his eyes. Opening them again, he saw two men, a military officer and a civilian, start up the stairway in the company of two soldiers. He turned toward the bartender and nodded. The bartender walked into the office behind the bar, followed shortly by Charlie. There were two bags on the floor.

"When did they first show up?" Charlie asked, handing the man a twenty-dollar bill.

"About two this afternoon. They didn't seem to disturb things in your room. I packed up your stuff as fast as I could. Do you have a place to go?"

"Yeah," Charlie answered. "Any idea on how to get out of town?"

"Join the army!" the man said and unlocked the side door.

~~~~~

The following morning, Ramon guided Charlie to an old abandoned *tambo* north of town, where he was picked up by a produce truck and secreted in its load of potatoes. Shouting at Charlie through the open rear window, the driver cursed the dust and the fate of all born to the altiplano. As the vehicle lumbered down the road, Charlie could hear him singing between draughts from his bottle of Pisco. With each swallow, the man's spirits seemed to lift higher above the hard baked adobe road that pointed straight to a horizon he was destined to never reach.

Escape

Jim and Vicente sat on a pile of rubble, numb to their circumstances. After a few minutes, the older man began to cry. Jim wrapped one arm over his shoulders and held him close. Finally Vicente pushed himself erect, avoiding Jim's eyes. "-I'm sorry," he rasped.

They were alone in the bottom of the mine with no way out except the tunnel that traversed the floor of the mine and sloped upward through two levels to the vertical lift. It was there that the lower guard station was positioned.

"How long will it take us to get the bodies out?" Jim asked.

Vicente shrugged. "In our condition, probably two days, if we're lucky."

"So," Jim said, "with no food, this is our execution, eh?"

Vicente was thinking. "The guards are relieved after our shift is over. I have seen the next shift waiting."

"So?"

"Well, why don't we just take a nap, no digging at all. Then, we'll go up to the guard station and ask to be taken up."

"And they will say, 'Where are the bodies?' "

"And we will say, 'They're in the tunnel by the gallery entrance.' "

Jim studied Vicente's face and matted hair. Tear streaks showed beneath his eyes as if he were made up as a sad clown. "And they will say," he countered, "go down and get them."

Vicente managed a smile. "Yes. And I will say that no one told us to carry them up, that we are too tired. And then you will say, 'Don't you remember, Vicente, we're supposed to bring them up in the morning.' "

Jim looked at his hands, encrusted with scabs and sores and black from contact with the ore. "We have to do something. It's worth a try, Vicente. If we don't escape tonight, we'll never leave this place."

"I know," Vicente said. "Do you have the strength to climb out of the blockhouse?"

The handholds had been cut with a discarded ax head and masked with handfuls of dust scraped from the building's walls, wet with water, and "troweled" over the notches. Jim forced thoughts of Luis and Gerardo aside. "I am not as strong as I was a few months ago," he answered. "On the other hand, I am much lighter."

~~~~~

They played out their skit at the lower guard station. The guard, behind his cage, did not know what to do. He was uncertain that he had properly understood his instructions. What the prisoners told him made sense. After all, they had been working for fifteen hours. Signaling the upper station that the lift was coming, he let them leave. With proper obsequious-ness, the weary miners stepped into the lift and were hoisted upward.

The upper station knew nothing of what had transpired and sent the two men to the *cocina,* accompanied by two guards. After eating, they were escorted back to the blockhouse. Jim could not make out Vicente's face in the darkness. I'm the cause of this, he thought. They're killing everyone who's come in contact with me. It was escape tonight or death for the two of them.

~~~~~

Jim squatted in the darkness and looked up at the dim open-ing over his head. A few feet away, Vicente waited expec-tantly. "Can you do it?" he asked.

Jim shook his head. "I don't know; I can only try."

For three weeks, they had been preparing the escape; chis-eling holds into the adobe wall and pasting them over with adobe powder. But, for fear of leaving evidence of tampering, they could not test the electrical conduit's ability to hold Jim's weight.

Jim rose and padded silently to the wall. Vicente had cleared the first half-dozen holds. He could now only watch and pray. Outside, a guard dozed against the door as Jim worked his way upward. A fall would be catastrophic, the end for both of them. From the last hold, he wedged the ax head they had scavenged from the mine between the conduit and the ceiling to force a separation. Next, he fed his looped belt through the separation and inserted his arm into the two re-sulting loops. Taking a deep breath, he then surrendered his weight to the conduit. It held. To reach the opening it remained only to repeat the process ten more times, a seemingly impossible feat, but he forced his rational mind aside.

With Vicente whispering encouragement, he persevered; but the six-foot-deep recess to the roof remained. Jim struggled, hanging by first one arm and then the other. He had to commit to the move or fall to the floor. The first two swings yielded nothing, but on the third try he allowed more slack from the belt and his left hand found a section of steel angle from the old mounting. Clutching that, he released the belt and swung beneath the recess, where, with his last remaining strength, he pulled himself up into a chimney position, his legs and back taking the load from his arms. A minute later he felt the cold night breeze wash over his face as he wrestled over the lip and onto the roof.

Vicente was delirious, but the job was not over. The building was built into a hillside where its sturdy roof now served as a convenient boneyard for discarded mining equipment. Jim hefted a heavy triple pulley and secured his grip. Carefully, he edged his way across the roof until he looked down at the sleeping guard. The one-hundred-pound implement crushed the man's skull, killing him instantly. Jim quickly descended from the roof and opened the door for Vicente. Together they dragged the guard inside, taking his shotgun, ammunition and serape. Locking the door behind them, they ran down the steps and across the road into the darkness.

An impulse caused Jim to stop at the abandoned fifty-gallon drum. He knelt, closing his eyes, his hand over the tiny four-inch by eight-inch opening that was once a man's only window on life.

"You are a wonder, my friend," Vicente whispered. "Per-haps an *espíritu* as they say."

"What are you talking about, *amigo?*"

"The men in the mine think your presence is an omen. They say no gringo could swing a sledge as you do. They say that Viracocha lives inside you, otherwise you would be dead on the mountain with the others."

Jim grimaced and followed Vicente into the darkness.

Fugitives

Time was running out. They had decided to move east, the least likely direction their pursuers would anticipate, and then turn north toward Karoma, wherever that might be. During the march they had not seen one person, only the burnt-out remains of huts and the signs of human exodus into the hills. There seemed no hope of rescue by friendly indigenes.

Twelve nights had been spent walking trails and overgrown dirt roads that only led to dead ends or worse. Early in the mornings they would seek any ditch or declivity which hid them from view. In the late afternoons they would rise, care-fully survey the landscape for soldiers and begin to scavenge for food. The staple was raw potatoes, rotting in the fields un-harvested or cast aside as unsuitable. Twice Jim found hand-fuls of dried corn in abandoned homes and once a small metal canister partially filled with quinoa. Hunger was a serious problem now and his strength was waning fast, the rest stops longer and more frequent. Vicente fared better, but he, too, was in serious decline.

On the afternoon of the thirteenth day, Vicente went in search of food, leaving his partner to sleep. Not long after, Jim was awakened by the sound of a small, high-winged plane bearing military markings. A surge of fear quickly subsided as the plane droned off into the distance. Within minutes, he was dozing again, oblivious to the warm sun upon his face or the quickening breeze which skipped across the altiplano.

～～～～～

Two men stood above Jim's sleeping form. "Señor," one said.

There was no response. The man who had spoken knelt, touching him lightly. "Señor."

There was a faint murmur.

At the sound of horses arriving the man arose and turned. "Señorita, is this the man?"

Rosa de Melgarejo dismounted and dropped to her knees beside Jim. "Oh, thank God, yes," she said. "Quickly, we must get some nourishment into him and get out of here. Go and bring the other man here."

On the Mend

Four days elapsed before Jim Bridgman came to. During this interval, the Hatun Laika rarely left his bedside. Poultices and compresses made up of exotic compounds were applied to the wounds inflicted by the army. Incense purified the air and incantations were spoken in a low voice. A dried llama fetus buried beneath the threshold guarded against evil spirits, and various talismans, carefully arranged atop a wooden crate, worked their magic. They included a silver amulet, a packet of dried seeds, a "cat's eye" made of crossed sticks and string, two hand-polished gemstones of topaz and garnet and a small gold figurine of a man wrapped in brilliant feathers.

The whole business offended Bartolomé's religious sensibility, but there was no alternative. Moreover, there was such an air of confidence in this Hatun Laika, such a professional bearing, that Bartolomé could not help but grant him a certain measure of credibility. The old man, in turn, maintained an attitude of tolerance, slightly tinted with condescension, toward Bartolomé, who shared the nightly vigils with him. An unspoken relationship, a concession for one another's estate, evolved through the dim candlelit nights.

It was late on the third day when Jim's fever began to subside. The old man motioned to Bartolomé, who sat in a quasi-stupor at the foot of the cot. Rousing himself, he placed his palm gently against Jim's forehead. It felt cool. The old man nodded his head emphatically and laughed, a deep laugh of self-satisfaction that rumbled within his chest. Bartolomé grasped his crucifix and offered a short prayer in Latin. When he was finished, the old man took the crucifix which dangled from Bartolomé's waist and held it in his hand as if examining it. *"¿Jesucristo?"* he said, looking up at Bartolomé. Bartolomé nodded in the affirmative, at which the old man released his grip on the object and shuffled out the door. As he went, he could be heard repeating the name, *"Jesucristo . . . Jesucristo . . ."* followed by the same low laughter.

Jim awoke the following morning, clear-eyed and alert. At his bedside were Rosa, Mariano and Bartolomé. Rosa smiled. "Welcome to the living," she said.

"Where am I?" he asked.

"Karoma," Bartolomé replied. "You've been here for four days now."

Jim seemed confused by this revelation. "We made it," he said incredulously. Then with a start he remembered his compatriot. "Vicente!" he cried out. "Where is Vicente?"

"Easy, Jaime," Rosa said, coming around the bed to restrain him. "He is all right; he'll be around to see you later. Now, lay back and rest. Someone will bring you breakfast shortly."

~~~~~~

Outside, Rosa and the two priests turned up the street toward the church, no one speaking. Finally, Rosa broke the silence.

"Well, it looks like you got your wish, your hero, your martyr . . . your vision. Word has spread all over the countryside about Jaime. They also know about him in Cuzco . . . and Lima!"

Mariano stiffened, but made no reply. Bartolomé had his own thoughts. "The *guardia* could be here soon," he said. "Karoma cannot remain a secret forever. Perhaps we should think of moving him . . ."

"Bartolomé," Mariano interjected. "All that I have foreseen has come to pass. I have no reason to believe that tomorrow will be any different."

Rosa stopped and grasped Mariano by the sleeve. "You talk about him as if he were a thing that God has given you to do with as you please. I don't want that man hurt any more. He has gone through hell; it is a miracle that he's still alive!"

Mariano managed a pallid smile. "I know, my dear. I know."

Cuerpo de Paz

The Peace Corps office gave the impression of being vacant. After several unanswered hellos, Charlie was about to leave when a young woman, paintbrush in hand, stepped into the room. He had met her at the hotel, but didn't remember her name. "Mr. Newell," she said, displaying an endearing smile, "come on back. We're painting our radio room." Charlie followed, desperately hoping these people might be allies.

"Radio room?" he queried. "Yeah," she responded, "we have a shortwave set for communication with the embassy in Lima." Charlie had surmised correctly and his eyes widened when he stepped into the room. "Good Lord!" he exclaimed. "You can communicate anywhere with this!"

A young man whom Charlie also recognized was introduced as Robert DeVoto. After a clumsy inquiry, he learned that the girl was Ann Stevens, a graduate student in economics. She departed to prepare tea, leaving Charlie alone with Robert. Robert seemed tense and Charlie was certain that he was apprehensive over something Charlie might know.

Suddenly he remembered having seen the young man deliver a parcel to a residence a few blocks away. The seemingly innocuous event had struck him as odd. Charlie decided to gamble. "Robert," he said, placing his hand on the young man's shoulder, "I am your friend and not your enemy. Do I have your confidence to speak privately?"

For a moment Robert DeVoto was mute. He stared at Charlie and swallowed. He had the appearance of a sophomore accused of cheating on a midterm exam. "Yes . . . yes . . ." he stammered. Charlie held up his hands. "Relax, Robert. I'm sure that my interest in what's going on is pretty much in league with yours. I'm a newsman, here to cover a story. You, if I'm not mistaken, are part of that story. In that respect, I assure you, your participation will never be revealed by me."

Another awkward moment followed before Robert responded, "You're not really here to do a story on Andean alpinism?"

"No." Charlie smiled. "I'm here to cover and uncover what we suspect is a *campesino* rebellion being brutally suppressed by the government, which is hiding the fact from the public. Are our suspicions on the mark?"

"Yes."

"Robert, that package you were delivering yesterday, what was in it, medical supplies?"

"No. We do smuggle medical supplies as they become available, but yesterday, that was ammunition. Ammunition is more difficult for them to acquire than guns, although they need more weapons also."

Charlie was taken aback at the frankness of the admission. "I won't ask who's supporting you, but how did you get involved in the first place?"

Robert ruffled his hair and sat down, relieved to have a confidant. "We were taken on a tour when we arrived, to acquaint us with the situation in the *campo*. It was bad: dysentery, disease, malnutrition, people being treated like slaves and worked to death. It was appalling. The only redeeming factor was the people. Despite their oppression they smiled and shook hands with us."

He paused, blinking his eyes and nervously working his lips, before beginning again. "We were at a big hacienda, seeing how a progressive farm works. But all we saw were buildings, no heavy farming equipment. They told us it was either in use or out for maintenance. We had just started, but it was obvious that they were being very careful about whom we talked to or what we saw.

"We had just boarded a big truck for a tour of the fields when we heard a gunshot. Carlos Quintero yelled something at the driver, who started the motor and headed for the front gate. Halfway down the driveway there was a regular fusillade of gunfire. Several bullets hit the truck and we dropped down on the bed. The truck then swerved around and headed in the opposite direction. We ran over bushes, lawn furniture and right through a back fence where the truck slewed into a ditch. How the driver got that far I don't know; he was shot in the throat and unconscious when we pulled him out. There was nothing we could do for him, so we ran into the field behind the house."

Robert paused to gather himself; his voice had softened and he was looking down at the floor.

"The gunfire was increasing, so we decided to retreat a little more. Right away we found this gully with tire tracks run-

ning through it and we followed it, moving cautiously. After a
hundred feet or so we heard a sound and stopped. A minute or
so went by and we heard it again. I went ahead alone to check
it out, staying close to the side of the gully." Once again Robert
stopped, struggling with his composure. "It's all right," Charlie said. "Take your time."

Robert nodded and began again, "The gully narrowed for
a short distance and then opened out. Right in front of me
were four men, naked and chained to an iron pipe over their
heads. At their feet a small rivulet of water ran through a
drainage ditch. Of course, they couldn't reach it. Three were
dead; all had been horsewhipped. Two of the bodies were
bloated and swarming with flies. The stench was awful. I had
to dip my kerchief in the water and hold it over my face to
approach the one man still alive. The others joined me and we
tried to free him, but we had no tools. The supports were set
in concrete and the shackles were heavy chain and steel. The
man was unconscious, but for one moment he came around
and looked into my face. I could see his eyes try to focus.
'Señor,' he said, *'por favor* . . . kill me.' He died within seconds of that remark."

Tears were streaming down Robert's face. "After that we
edged toward the hacienda. The fighting had stopped and
there were bodies and bleeding people all over the place. Nobody spoke to us. Our van had taken several rounds but was
otherwise operable. So, we hot-wired the vehicle and headed
back toward Chiquian. After about two miles we were stopped
by a cart in the road. In an instant we were surrounded by
armed *campesinos* and pulled outside.

"When they found that we were *norteamericanos* there was

some shouting and a strange-looking priest was brought forward on a pony. He dismounted and held up a photograph of
a group of men. Pointing to four of the men in the picture, he
asked us, in English, if we had seen any of them at the hacienda. The face of the last man to die was unmistakable and
I told him of our experience. He was greatly moved and told
us to remember this day. He said that the blood that flows
here, flows from all of our hearts, that until every man is free,
no man is free. Then they let us go. It wasn't long after our
return to Cuzco that I was approached by some people. After
that, I couldn't say no."

Charlie was at a loss. Robert's experience would have sent
most people packing, but he hadn't run. "Look," he said, "for
my part, I need a radio on a regular basis."

Robert nodded. "It's yours."

"And that hacienda, did it have a name?"

"The Hacienda Santa Rosa," Ann answered from behind.
"And the owner's name is Carlos Quintero."

PART FOUR

Servant of Fate

War Room

The *curaca* sat down by Jim and held his hands out to the fire. Rosa looked over from where she was kneading bread dough and smiled. "When you become older," the *curaca* said, "each morning is colder than the last."

Jim contemplated the face so seamed with age, sun and toil. He noted the hands, large and thick-fingered, slowly massaging the silver inlay of his *vara*. The man spoke infrequently, but Jim knew that he listened intently. Intelligence, well polished with time and the burden of life and death decisions, made for a man with little tolerance for superfluous chatter.

"Jaime," he said, grasping Jim's wrist. "Today, I want you to sit by me."

His meaning was obvious. Jim glanced toward Rosa, saw her pale and look away. "I would be honored," he answered.

~~~~~

Bartolomé waited for the scouts to dismount and motioned them toward the kitchen where the principals waited. It had been four hard days of riding for the men and everyone was anxious to hear their report.

"There has been much suffering among the people, but their spirits still shine. Most of the women and children are hidden in the *montaña*. It is too dangerous for them to cross the altiplano."

"What of the casualties?" the *curaca* queried.

The two scouts looked at one another. One, who wore a silver condor on a leather thong about his neck, spoke. "Most of the serious casualties have been removed to the *montaña*. People from the *montaña,* the selva and other locations are providing what assistance they can."

The *curaca* digested this for a moment. No one else spoke. "How many fighters do we have and how many are mounted?" he asked.

"Our best estimate is about five hundred," the second scout responded. "Maybe about half have horses."

The *curaca*'s face gave no indication of his thoughts. "And weapons?" he continued.

There was a joint sigh from the two men and the first speaker responded, "Mostly machetes and farm implements. Maybe one hundred of our men have guns. There has been some increase recently. Thirteen of Zamora's men were killed in two ambushes. Each man carried a pistol and a rifle."

"You will go out again tomorrow," the *curaca* announced. "We will steal and ambush, steal and ambush until all of our men are armed. It will be important to create many diversions at the same time. Zamora's men must be divided. That will give us the opportunities we need."

The scouts acknowledged their understanding.

"One thing more," the *curaca* said. "Tell them that Jaime walks the same path with us. That when he speaks, he must be obeyed."

Behind them, the door opened quietly and closed as Rosa left. Jim saw that Bartolomé was staring at him. Something momentous had occurred that Jim was not sure he fully grasped. No one had discussed anything with him. Mariano, who had seemed detached from the proceedings, came over.

"It's all right, Jaime," he assured him. "Our fortunes are linked together and we must make the best of it."

〜〜〜〜

Except for Bartolomé, the room was empty. He reflected on what had just transpired. Like it or not, he was part of an armed rebellion fueled by the anguish of a people and the psychic visions of a vagrant priest. To save himself he should leave. But how? And what was this feeling stirring within, this growing sense of exhilaration that seduced his will? It was time to be alone for a while, to think and ponder the sublime agony that was Peru.

Invitation

Charlie awoke to the chill of an unheated room and wondered if this meant there was no hot water. A loud knock on the door brought him upright. "Just a minute!" he shouted. Struggling with his robe he opened the door to find a hotel maid. "Mr. Newell?" she said, scrutinizing his face. Realizing he had overslept, Charlie groaned. "Yes," he began, but before he could continue, she had pushed her cart into the room and latched the door. Placing her finger over her lips, she whispered urgently, "We don't have much time; you must do exactly as I say."

Charlie was dumbfounded. As she spoke, she was hurriedly removing articles of clothing from the hamper. "Do you have trousers and boots for walking?" she asked impatiently. Charlie nodded and turned for the closet. "You have cameras, film?" she asked. He managed a "yes" and pointed to the camera bag on the settee. Throwing a wide brim straw hat onto the pile, she added, "Wear that low on your forehead. Hurry!" Charlie stumbled into the bathroom, changed, and returned to find his remaining clothing and other belongings disappearing into her linen hamper. "We will keep these for you. See Roberto when you get back."

She looked at her wristwatch. "In two minutes Señor Prado will receive a call on the inner office phone. We will wait above the stairwell. When he answers, you will quickly descend the stairs and turn right at the bottom. Go around the stairs and leave the building by the service entrance. You will exit into the alley, turn left and keep walking until you come to an open garage."

Charlie followed her to the stairwell landing, his heart pounding. For all his experience, he was not prepared for the suddenness of events nor the commitment required of him with virtually no word of explanation. From their vantage, he could see the concierge surveying the lobby from his roost.

The remaining minute seemed interminable, but Prado's eyes never left the floor. Finally, Charlie saw him turn abruptly toward the open office door and slip from his stool. "Now!" Charlie heard the maid's voice rasp in his ear and he plunged down the steps.

Charlie walked slowly up the alley, wondering if this wasn't just a scheme to eliminate him. As he approached the garage, uncertainty began to claw at his will.

Ever so cautiously, he entered to find a *guardia* courier waiting astride a motorcycle with a sidecar attached. Pointing to the sidecar, the courier said, "Get in."

〰〰〰

It was nearly sunset when the motorcycle stopped and the mail sack was jerked away from Charlie's face. "Get out," the driver said. With considerable effort, Charlie managed to extricate himself from the sidecar. His legs were unsteady and he clung to the low windscreen. They were on a high undulating plain, not far from Chiquian. The driver, brusque and imperious, lifted Charlie's camera case and jacket from the vehicle and set them on the ground. Charlie began to panic. What the hell was this?

"Do you see that large rock?" the driver asked, pointing to a tall boulder a short distance away. "Yes," Charlie answered.

"You'll be picked up there. Wait on the other side, away from the road."

As Charlie started off, the driver yelled after him, "*¡Un momento!*" Taking a water bottle, a small paper bag and a blanket from the saddlebag, he handed them to Charlie. "You will need these," he said. Then, with the only sign of civility offered through the long day, he squeezed Charlie's shoulders and turned back to his motorcycle. Suddenly, Charlie was alone, the scent of road dust in his nostrils and the sound of motorcycle exhaust barely audible in the distance.

The base of the rock was black from campfires. A pile of twigs had been gathered there and he found a box of stick matches in an old tin can. Charlie realized with a feeling of forlorn resignation that no one would come until morning. He had to make the best of it. Inside the paper bag were two bread rolls, which he devoured. Saving the paper for a fire starter, he leaned back against the rock to await nightfall.

A Confidence

"Where did you get the firewood?" Jim asked.

Rosa wiped her hands on a towel. "It is brought up from the *montaña* on burros. There is an old trail behind us which runs all the way down into the *selva*."

"An escape route?"

"Not really. It is very narrow and exposed. It would take forever to move this *ayllu* down it, if that's what you're thinking."

Jim shrugged. "Just a thought."

"So," Rosa said as she placed two steaming cups of tea on the table and sat down, "how are you feeling?"

"Very good, thanks to you and Huaman. I am in your debt, Rosa."

Rosa looked into his face and then down into her tea. Jim sensed that there was something she wished to say. This wasn't the first time she seemed on the verge of some disclosure. He would wait.

"Vicente left this morning. I told him to delay, but he could not wait to see his family again."

"He is a good man," Rosa offered.

"Yes," Jim agreed. "You can trust him with your life."

The conversation was awkward from the beginning. Rosa exhaled and looked around the room. "Jaime," she said, "are you going to stay here?"

"I don't know. I don't know what I'm going to do, if I can do anything. I'm a wanted man. There's a price on my head and I'm sure the U.S. consulate would rather I conveniently disappear."

"Do you understand what's happened to you?"

Jim's eyes narrowed slightly. "I know I've been manipulated."

"Yes, Jaime. The route you took out from Karoma and your capture were deliberately planned. Father Raimondi saw you in one of his visions. He saw you as surviving a terrible ordeal and becoming the champion of these people, defeating the *hacendados* and returning the *campesinos* to their land."

"And Father D'Annunzio was sent to fetch me. That much is obvious now, but this vision business . . . Oh, Christ, it all makes sense. That meeting yesterday. I thought they might be just looking out for me. I'm no soldier, Rosa, much less a commander."

"You'll have to make up your mind soon or circumstance will decide the matter for you."

"This is crazy. I know what horrible crimes have been committed here. I've had my own personal experience. Peru has turned Raimondi into a madman. As for Bartolomé, I'm sure if he had known what would happen, he would have been straight with me."

"Regardless, Jaime, these people and their suffering are real."

"I know that."

"I am the last person who wants to see you involved but do you know what I think?"

"What do you think, Rosa?"

"I think that leaders are born, not made. Mariano, mad as he may be, sees the same thing shining within you that I do."

A Passing

Charlie Newell was in trouble, too frightened to even think. He lay face down in a shallow depression, his head and shoulders partially covered by the still-warm corpse of a young woman. Thirty minutes earlier, as he and his guide Alfredo were investigating the site of a recent battle, gunfire had broken out on the low rise just above them. Shouting something indecipherable at Charlie, Alfredo broke for the horses secreted near their campsite. As Charlie frantically gathered his camera equipment and notes, this woman, whose lifeblood was now congealing over his upper body, appeared on the skyline and stumbled down the slope, nearly falling at his feet.

Mustering strength that only panic could provide, Charlie managed some vestige of a fireman's carry but fell after only a few steps. The sound of soldiers' voices as they descended the slope precluded any further movement. He had no idea if he had been seen carrying her or not. The field was strewn with bodies from the morning's conflict and he could only hope they would take him as an earlier casualty.

Two soldiers argued in a jocular manner over whose shot brought the peasant girl down. Prodding her body with a bayonet, they concluded she was dead and sauntered off. One of the bayonet thrusts grazed Charlie's arm, drawing blood. It was a miracle that he had not cried out.

Charlie thought of his satchel and notepads and wondered why they hadn't yet been seen. The photographs and notes thoroughly documented each atrocity and would guarantee a search for their owner and his execution if found. Scarcely breathing, he prayed for darkness to descend.

Mercifully, the light finally dimmed. Soldiers who had been searching corpses for gold or silver artifacts shouted to one another, and then there was silence. Still Charlie did not move until the silent form of Alfredo appeared beside him and whispered his name.

Struggling from beneath his sorrowful burden, he took Alfredo's hand and noted that the shadowy figure had found his satchel. A small campfire burned about seventy-five yards away. Alfredo motioned him to follow, but Charlie could not leave quite yet. Through her dying, the young woman had saved his life. Gently rolling her over, he composed the figure, closing the eyes and folding the arms. In a final gesture, he took one lifeless hand to his lips, kissing it, and gently laid it back. "Wherever you are now," he whispered, "may you find happiness and peace at last."

Intelligence Report

Jim, Bartolomé, Mariano and the *curaca* sat at the little table in the kitchen. Except for the crackling of the fire and the sounds of Sylvana cooking, there was silence. Jim stared in awe at the young indigene man who sat by the hearth, devouring his second bowl of stew. As best as Jim could figure, he had run forty miles nonstop over mountainous terrain to bring the envelope that now rested on the table. "*¡Esto es un recado urgente!*" he had shouted before collapsing into Jim's arms.

"What is his name?" Bartolomé asked.

"*¿Como se llama, usted?*" Jim shouted toward the fireplace.

"Lino!" came the answer and the young man resumed eating.

Bartolomé looked at Jim. "Please read it again," he said.

"It won't change the contents," Jim responded, picking up the letter.

KAROMA IDENTIFIED BY MILITARY. SPECIAL MORTAR COMPANY IN TRANSIT TO CUZCO. ARRIVE TO-

DAY/TOMORROW. NUMBER OF SUPPORT TROOPS
UNKNOWN. ORDERS ARE TO MARCH ON KAROMA
ASAP. MJR. J. ZAMORA TO COMMAND.

"When was it sent?" the *curaca* asked.

"It's not dated," Jim answered and closed his eyes.

"They could be *here* tomorrow or the day after," the *curaca*
said. Jim noted the faltering voice and felt the power of the
whirlpool begin to assert itself. The indigene leader had spent
a lifetime in crisis. No one needed to say it; the old man was
failing. Jim's gaze took in those seated around the table. How
in hell did they get this far? he thought. Other than himself,
the only other viable candidate was Rosa and she already had
too much on her plate.

Damn it! He nearly cursed out loud. This wasn't his fight.
How dare they do this to him? There hadn't even been one
stinking word of apology over Condorama. In the corner of
the room, he noticed Lino had fallen asleep on a scrap of old
carpet. Jim rose and draped his serape over the boy. What
American youth would ever be called on to do what Lino had
done today?

Sylvana motioned him over. "He didn't want to interrupt
you, so he asked me if you were the famous *alpinista* who
lost his friends on Viracocha."

"What did you tell him?"

"I said yes, of course. Then he told me that he always
wanted to be an *alpinista* and that if you needed a new friend,
he would be glad to climb with you."

Jim swallowed and made no reply, returning to the table.
Bartolomé and Mariano exchanged glances.

"Well, gentlemen, any suggestions?" Jim asked. "No? Then, let's begin with an inventory of what we have."

New Arrival

They were still several switchbacks below the pass, but it was obvious to Bartolomé who they were. The first rider was Alfredo, one of Karoma's men, the second would be the newsman, Mr. Newell. He nodded to the young man beside him, who immediately set off to inform the others.

Charlie, swaying on the back of his horse, clung to the saddle pommel and wondered when the agony of blistered thighs and back spasms would end. He had never been clear on their ultimate destination, but was certain the pass they were climbing led to something important.

They reached the summit sooner than he expected. Charlie had let his attention drift and did not see Alfredo drop from his horse and walk to where a man was sitting against a rock. As Alfredo approached he stood up and Charlie was astonished to see an enormous priest, the habit of his order cinched with a wide leather belt, clutching a double barrel shotgun in one hand as if it were a child's toy.

Bartolomé appraised Charlie as Alfredo helped him from his horse. "Welcome to the *ayllu* of Karoma, Mr. Newell," his voice boomed. "We are appreciative of the risk you have taken on our behalf." Charlie looked up into the dark bearded face. "My efforts are small, I'm sure, compared to yours," he responded as his eyes dropped once again to the shotgun.

"Please do not be alarmed," Bartolomé said. "It has been my turn for sentry duty today. I use this only for an emergency signal where a runner would be too slow."

Charlie nodded and smiled. "You present a formidable figure, Father. May I know your name?"

Bartolomé hesitated, looking down into the reporter's eyes. "Around here, call me Bartolomé; in your stories, use something else!"

Bartolomé handed the shotgun to an indigene who had just arrived and reached over a rock to rouse another young man who had been napping. "This lad will take you in," he said. "Go ahead now; I won't be far behind. Please excuse us if we are not up to our usual level of hospitality. It has been trying for all of us the last few days, but I assure you at the least there will be food and shelter."

With that Alfredo and Charlie remounted and set out following the indigene. Charlie's mind was spinning. This priest, who weighed three hundred pounds if he weighed an ounce, must be the man that he had heard about. What was this place? For a moment he decided to question Alfredo, but put the notion aside. It was too late and he was too cold, too tired and too hungry to press for more information. A light flickered into life ahead of them and he heard voices. Whatever this place was, they had arrived.

Incursion

The village was extensive, yet amazingly well hidden. On a knoll in its center was a small church, alongside of which was the priest's home. The light they'd seen from the trail the previous night had shone from his door, and the silhouette of the man who had stepped before it was none other than the much pursued gringo *insurgente,* Jim Bridgman.

"Are you the *periodista?*" he had demanded. "I hope to hell you're worth the trouble it took to get you here." Charlie thought that Bridgman was laughing quietly when he asked, but his fatigue made him uncertain. Now, somewhat recovered, he found Jim to be amiable enough, but even more formidable.

Charlie had been interviewing Jim and the others when the church bell began to toll for the lives lost in the struggle. They listened respectfully and, as the last echo receded, an odd silence descended, only to be broken by a distant shotgun blast, followed immediately by another and cries from the village below.

"The bastards!" Jim muttered and grasped Charlie by the arm. "Come on," he said, "let's get you to safety."

"Wait a minute," replied Charlie. "I've got a job to do."

Jim studied his face for a moment. "All right," he said, "but if all looks lost, take your pictures and notes and clothing and get out of here. Climb the wall and look for a place to hide. We'll come looking for you."

Charlie returned to the church as the bell began to toll again. All along the low wall that fronted the *ayllu* men and women were forming their first line of defense. Others tra-

versed the upper slopes behind the *ayllu* and climbed into the
rocks. That puzzled Charlie and he wondered what Jim's
strategy could be. There was nothing to see along the trail
leading from the pass other than the hasty return of two sentries on horseback. He found it curious that no attempt was
being made to defend the pass or, apparently, the trail.

Other than the two warning shots, there had not been another sound for several minutes. Charlie surveyed the trail with
field glasses. He saw nothing at first and then, abruptly, a double column of men came into view around a small abutment.
They were an imposing-looking group, but worse than that, he
noted ten or twelve soldiers carrying mortar components and
ammunition. Dear God, he thought to himself, they'll set those
pieces up behind some rocks and level this place without risking a man. Below him he saw Jim Bridgman in the company of
several young men climbing toward him. He motioned them to
hurry.

Jim had chosen this position to direct his defense. The
youths who had followed him would serve as runners. He
quickly dispatched two of them for the high fields above the
ayllu. Charlie relinquished his binoculars to Jim, but even
without them it could be seen that the columns had stopped
and were deploying into positions for support of mortar emplacements.

Jim studied their movements for a minute or two and summoned another runner, whom he sent on a circuitous path
downhill to the left, over a wall, and on into the terraces beneath the trail. For a while Charlie caught glimpses of a furtive
figure snaking along the stone retaining walls which formed
the terraces and then he was lost from sight.

Not long thereafter a mortar was fired, but failed to reach

the *ayllu* from that position. The villagers remained quiet and poised as they watched the *guardia* form in columns again and begin to move forward. Two hundred yards closer they set up new positions. This time their range would be suffi- cient. Not one shot had been fired by the defenders. Charlie looked anxiously at Jim, who seemed very calm and intent.

More soldiers, heavily burdened with large packs, were just reaching the new mortar positions. Through the glasses, Jim could see his men on the rocky ridge above the trail waiting for his signal, while below the trail others crept into position. It was his hope that all or most of the *guardia* would be on the trail, eager to ravage the *ayllu* once the mortars had done their work.

If he was right, they would have presumed that resistance was possible and thus committed most of their troops. So far, he counted two hundred and fifty men in uniform. That was good. Success would now depend on timing, the discipline of his people and the wind. He nodded to one of the young men, who began waving a black cloth tied to the end of a stick.

Within seconds, gunshots were heard in the vicinity of the pass—six, seven, eight shots and then there was silence. Jim observed the *guardia* looking toward the pass and their *co- mandante* in animated discussion with his officers. The fol- lowing minute seemed like an hour's recital of the Rosary to Bartolomé, who had joined them. Finally, Jim picked up the white flag that lay at his feet and waved it at the church tower. At once the bell began to toll, stopping after three rings, at which time gunfire broke out from atop the ridge.

As the bystanders watched, the mortar men fell to the

ground as if cut with a scythe. More troops fell in the exchange as they searched for shelter. Then smoke began to rise
along the trail. Soon the trail was immersed in it and the loud
concussive sound of explosives broke out all around them.
"What in hell is that?" Charlie yelled at Jim as debris began
to fall from the air. "Dynamite," came the reply.

Father Raimondi had silently joined them. Charlie observed
the priest as he took in the battle scene. A strip of cloth ban-
dage was tied about his head, a slight stain of red showing
where a fragment of glass had opened his scalp. The man
seemed exultant and charged with emotion. Charlie, too,
could feel a wild sense of elation. Before them and above,
columns of smoke billowed into the dark blue sky. Charlie
Newell quickly stepped back and raised his camera.

A muscular indigene entered the room and approached Jim.
"Jefe," he said, "what will we do with the prisoners?"

"There are not that many," Jim answered. "Let them go
with a message to their leaders that, unless they withdraw, this
is the last act of mercy we will show them."

Charlie's jaw dropped. Jim Bridgman was speaking as if he
commanded a vast army. "How many casualties did you have
today?" Charlie asked.

"We lost none."

"What about the *guardia?*"

Jim thought for a moment. "Six survived," he answered.

"May their souls find peace," Bartolomé intoned, making
the sign of the cross.

"We have captured a lot of weapons and ammunition, including four mortars with a total of one hundred two rounds left."

Bartolomé grunted. This had been a major effort by the *guardia* to destroy them. How long would they wait for revenge after suffering a catastrophic defeat? "What do you think?" he asked Mariano.

With great deliberation, Mariano lifted his gaze from the fire to Bartolomé. "The war is not over," he finally said, "it is only deferred. We must prepare to leave, cache the mortars and everything we do not need. The next step is theirs. There is still food here and we have all of our horses. But we cannot stay too long."

"I will never leave this place," the *curaca* said from his seat near the fire. "The spirits of my people live here and I will die where they wait for me."

The *curaca* looked at Jim across the table. Their eyes met and Jim motioned to a number of fighters waiting outside the small room. He stood as they crowded into the room and began to speak.

"Father Raimondi says it is time for us to flee, so that we may fight another day. But, that is not what we must do. We must stay here as long as we can and take the battle to the *guardia,* to the *hacendado*'s doorstep. We can't waste our time and resources chasing small patrols across the puna while we wait for our enemy to pay us another visit. That is not a strategy for victory. I ask you now, are you with me?"

As they nodded their assent, there was a rap on the door and Sylvana opened it to find the Hatun Laika leaning on his walking stick. Before she could restrain him, he had pushed his way through the door.

"It's all right," Jim called out, "I sent for him."

The old man made his way across the room to Jim. They conversed quietly for several minutes, the Hatun Laika nodding his head emphatically as Jim spoke. He then accepted a cup of tea from Sylvana and sat down by the fire.

Charlie didn't understand exactly what he'd just seen but he knew it was important. He also knew that tomorrow he'd have to leave to get out the story of the indigenes victory. He remained seated, watching as Jim Bridgman walked away. How in hell did the climber get mixed up in all this? The man possessed instincts that no one could have guessed; he had kicked the government's ass today.

Behind Charlie the two priests sat talking together. Bartolomé leaned across the table. "Do we have a problem?" he whispered. A small smile appeared on Mariano's face. "No, Bartolomé, we have a leader!"

On the Carpet

Joaquín Zamora moistened his lips and breathed deeply. He sat erect in a straight-back chair and waited for General Valesco to read a note handed him by Colonel Rohem, his aide-de-camp. Carlos Quintero, in whose home they met, was conversing with members of other families in the region. For the moment, Major Zamora was being ignored. "I am not only worried about your competence," the general had told him, "I am also concerned about your sanity. You have taken actions far beyond those necessary and in the process lost two hundred men, not to mention armaments and horses. You will immediately desist from all advances until you are directed otherwise, and you will respond to commands from Señor Quintero as if they came directly from my lips!"

Joaquín swallowed. *"¡Sí, General!"*

As General Valesco stared venomously at Major Zamora, he thought of millions of dollars of carefully negotiated contracts going up in smoke and his own military career being thrown on the pyre. Relations with the United States were delicate and the only safe thing was total suppression of anything potentially harmful. Turning, he placed one hand on Carlos' shoulder. "This Bridgman, his very existence must remain an absolute secret. Understood?"

"Understood," said Carlos.

After General Valesco had retired to his room, Carlos called for the houseboy. "Take the girl to the general's room," he said. The boy padded off and shortly returned with a slim young girl of about thirteen years of age. This was the household's latest *pongo,* a peasant house servant—brought this morning by her parents—whose titular duties would include housecleaning and help in the kitchen, but whose real utility would be to grace the *patrón*'s bed or the bed of whomever he designated. The parents in their oblique way understood this, the girl did not.

Carlos surveyed her appearance and nodded. Taking her by the hand, the boy led her off. Who knew, some day the girl might learn to appreciate her duties. If she became pregnant, it was understood that Carlos Quintero, as an honorable man, would stand as godfather for the child.

Strategy Meeting

Mariano and the *curaca* sat opposite Jim as Bartolomé prowled around the room. "We are agreed then," Jim said, "that we must break the will of the *hacendados* and that to do that we must first deal with Carlos Quintero." It was more of a statement than a question. There were no objections and he proceeded to unroll a large topographical map on the table.

"This lake, Laguna Quilacu, is almost fifty kilometers long. Look at its drainage here; the outflow runs through a narrow defile for about three kilometers and enters the valley, which runs down the altiplano across the road from Chiquian. The structures indicated here are those of the Hacienda Santa Rosa, correct?"

"*Sí.*" The *curaca* nodded. "The valley was farmed long before the Spaniards came because the earth is rich where the water floods. The hacienda was built in the valley to provide access to the water and the fields. If the hacienda were placed on the puna above the valley, crops and equipment would have to be hauled a long distance up, which would have been expensive and time consuming."

"Weren't they concerned about flooding?" Jim queried.

"The hacienda is built on a slight knoll, about the height of a man, and the road to it elevated. The valley is wide, and flooding, when it comes, is only a fraction of a meter, nothing to be concerned about."

Jim pointed to the outlet of the lake. It was very narrow. "Have you been here?" he asked.

"Yes." The *curaca* looked puzzled.

"This is a dam formed by rocks and debris falling from mountains on either side?"

"Yes," the *curaca* answered, beginning to understand the line of questioning. "The *laguna* is very deep. I remember now, it was told to me by my father that centuries ago, before the Incas, the earth leaped and tossed in the night. The Supreme *Apu* was dreaming of the future and became angry in his slumber. Without his knowing it, he caused the rocks to fly through the air and the waters to gush across the land. Many people were killed. When he awakened, he was very sad. It was many years before the lake rose again."

"Would the Supreme *Apu* of Viracocha be angry if it happened again?"

The old man was silent for a while. "I will ask Huaman to speak to him," he replied, "but I don't think he will mind."

Pointing once again to the map, Jim spoke. "There are four mines indicated in this area. Silver mines, I presume?"

"Yes," answered the *curaca*.

"Do they use dynamite, and if they do, which mine would have the most?"

"I worked in the mines," the *curaca* replied; "they store hundreds of kilos. But I must tell you, it might take all of the dynamite from each to do what you are thinking and then it might fail."

"I understand," Jim said. "We cannot stand a prolonged effort against the *guardia*. We have to do something which will totally discourage our opposition, make them go away. Is Carlos Quintero still at the Santa Rosa?"

"Yes."

"Is he still the leader of the *hacendados?*"

"More than ever," the old man snorted.

"Then here is what we must do." Jim exhaled and leaned back in his chair. "First, we get more dynamite, all we can, move it to the *laguna* and prepare the charges. Second, we pick one hacienda, the most vulnerable, and destroy it, raze it to the ground. That will get their attention. During this, the Santa Rosa will be kept under twenty-four-hour surveillance. Whatever sources we have on the haciendas will be alerted for anything they might hear regarding a meeting of the *hacendados*. We must be informed immediately. If the *hacendados* panic, as I'm sure they will, they will convene at the Santa Rosa. Quintero is their leader, a man with a large ego. They will have to come to him for assistance. Plausible?"

"Yes," came the chorused reply. Jim looked quizzically at the Men of God and raised his eyebrows. "To ensure that they do what we want, we will raid them, not putting ourselves at great risk, but enough to keep their nerves jangling after we hit the first hacienda. When the meeting we hope for convenes, the hacienda workers will quietly slip away and we will blow the dam."

The *curaca* lifted his seamed and weathered face to Jim's. Jim had presented the plan in the form of a large question. It was ultimately the *curaca*'s decision, his people at risk. Jim returned his gaze and waited. Finally, the old man spoke.

"You cannot bargain with these people. They take what they want and they want everything. They slaughter and denigrate our people. They could never suffer enough to repay their debt. If ever we are to be whole again, we must act now to drive them away and reclaim our land. The gods are acting through you, Jaime. This is either a new beginning for us or the end. It cannot be anything else."

Mariano had been strangely silent through the proceedings. "The mines," he said, "will they have surplus food?"

"Yes," the *curaca* answered.

"We will take that, too," Jim noted. "Tomorrow night we will strike the first two mines and see what we find."

〰〰〰

Mariano left the meeting to seek some respite with nature. He noted the small birds that frequented Karoma, the red, yellow and blue effulgence of their life force expanding and contracting about them. He felt their ecstasy at being alive and the sublime green and blue aura of the shrubs, trees and grasses. Yes, something was taking form at last, but it was still vague in his mind. Mariano knew that such intricate structures could not be forcefully probed; prescience was a window in the mind that opened of its own accord and through which passed only what fate ordained.

First Blood

The two mines, Cerro Plata and Mina de las Cavernas, were owned by the same corporation and located on opposite sides of a high, rounded ridge rising nearly four thousand feet above the puna. When the trucks brought the miners up that day, no mention was made of the strange indigenes who joined them, four men crowding into each truck and squatting on the floor. They spoke to no one and no one spoke to them. The miners exchanged glances and kept a knowing silence. When the trucks descended that evening, they knew that the visitors would not be with them.

On the following morning, miners waiting for the trucks would notice a wisp of smoke above the mountain. Those who leaped from the first transport would be met by stillness. They would notice the absence of sound from winch systems and generators, the absence of guards or anyone moving about; then they would notice the bodies. The plant manager would enter the guard shack, stepping over a lifeless form lying in a pool of congealed blood. With a shaking hand, he would grasp the land phone connecting Cerro Plata to Mina de las Cavernas. There would be no answer.

Hesitation

Rosa blinked her eyes against the growing darkness and tried to see amid the jumble of boulders scattered across the *quebrada* floor downstream of camp. A pale, saffron light lingered over the jagged skyline, and beyond the canyon's mouth, the vague shape of a distant glacier glimmered feebly.

"Señor Bridgman!" she called out.

"Over here, Rosa," came a response as the figure of Jim Bridgman rose up out of the gloom to one side and motioned to her. Jim watched Rosa pick her way toward him and felt that familiar surge within his gut.

"You must eat, gringo, or you will become food for the condor. We cannot afford to lose you."

Even in the dim light, Jim could make out Rosa's dimpled cheeks and the graceful curve of her lips. Extending his hand, he pulled her up beside him and for a lingering instant felt her body's warmth, relished the scent of her hair in the clean mountain air. As he accepted the parcel of food, he mumbled his thanks, the moment suddenly awkward. Rosa looked up. She smiled, her lips pressed tightly together, and grasped his wrist.

"Sit down," she said softly. "You eat and I'll talk."

The bread was slightly stale, but palatable, and the beef ribs heavy with meat.

"Where," he croaked, his mouth full of food, "did you . . ."

"Carlos Quintero is minus one cow," Rosa answered. "He won't know it for a week, and then he'll accuse his foreman, who is probably stealing from him anyway."

It had been an arduous day and a hunger, too long suppressed, finally asserted itself. Rosa watched as Jim unabashedly devoured the food; within minutes it was gone. He wiped his mouth and hands with the cloth and lay back upon the ground.

"I'm sorry," he said. "I'm becoming a wild beast; Condorama didn't help."

"Don't be," Rosa answered. "When you have an appetite, you must satisfy it."

Jim looked over at Rosa's now nearly indistinguishable

form. "We are like two disembodied spirits talking to one another," he said.

"Soon, we may very well be, Jaime. Life is short enough, but ours could be very short. Tomorrow night we leave this camp to raid the Colquemarca. Maybe we won't come back."

The ache in Jim's gut returned. Was it just physical deprivation? The awful isolation of the altiplano? Or . . .

"Rosa?"

"Yes," she replied, the subtle hint of anticipation in her voice.

"This is probably . . ." he began and trailed off.

As silence fell Rosa could hear the seconds exploding in her heart.

"It's . . . it's starting to get cold. Maybe we should get back to the others."

"All right," she said.

Escalation

Thin clouds hung low in the twilight sky. From a hillside vantage point Jim and Rosa watched the raiding party carefully disperse around the Hacienda Colquemarca. Below them, the Villanueva family awaited dinner, the dining room brilliantly illuminated and already casting shadows over the grounds. Jim could see that his partner was tense. The infamous hacienda had been carefully chosen as the most protected and belligerent in the region. Victory had to be total; this was key to Jim's strategy.

The light from the windows occasionally flickered, indicating people within moving blithely about, unaware that their sentries had already been immobilized.

The attack was designed to leave an escape route to the road. Several outbuildings were fired first and then the shooting began. The overseers and hacienda toughs ate by themselves in a bunkhouse. Relying on the sentries, they were taken completely by surprise. Two windows were suddenly shattered and a grenade thrown through each.

When the rear of the house came under fire, Octavio Villanueva, his wife and two daughters bolted for the black Mercedes parked in front, followed shortly by Luis Villanueva and his wife. As they dove through the doors, a carefully placed shot into the trunk spurred them on.

Two hours later, everything of value had been loaded onto a hacienda truck and all buildings completely engulfed in flame. All of the hacienda's men and soldiers, a total of twenty-four, were dead.

The indigenes who worked the hacienda watched stoically from their *chozas* on the hillside. They neither resisted the invaders, nor came to the aid of their *hacendado*. In the morning they would pick through the debris and step indifferently amid the corpses.

Intermission

Despite the long faces of his comrades, Jim relished the chance to rest. Rather than scurry to the sheltering arms of

Carlos Quintero, the *hacendado* families had dug in. Even the Villanueva family ran only as far as their nearest neighbor. Until the *guardia* was recalled in force, fleeing to the Hacienda Santa Rosa only meant abandoning their holdings to certain destruction. Obviously they were willing to gamble individually that they could hold out until the strategic situation changed. This could only mean one thing, that arrival of reinforcements was imminent.

This did not bother Jim. Despite inferior forces, he had forced the *hacendados* to retrench. The psychological edge was his; the high puna was relatively safe. If all worked as planned, more soldiers would only mean the government would pay a higher price for its own defeat.

Bartolomé entered the kitchen and closed the door against the morning cold. "It would seem," he announced, "that our commander has set up his field headquarters in *la cocina!*" Jim could see Rosa blush across the room. "In here, I am the commander, priest!" she shouted back. "And if you wish to be fed, sit down and behave yourself!"

Bartolomé sat down. Jim read the expression on his face. He had seen it all before. There were a lot of guys who talked a good climb, but when it was their turn to lead that hundred-fifty-foot section of almost flawless granite, they developed the strangest maladies. Bartolomé and Mariano were now in the active business of taking lives and he could see the hesitancy creep into their speech and actions.

"Any word?" Bartolomé asked.

"They're still sitting on their eggs," Jim answered.

"Jim, the charges are all emplaced in the dam, the wiring and all that. Is there any chance they might go off by accident?"

Jim took a deep breath. It had taken his men a week to tunnel into the face of that great rock and earthen bulwark and place over two thousand pounds of satchel charges. Thanks to the mining interests, several of his men were experts. "No, Father," he replied. "Nothing will happen until we push the plunger."

"What do we do in the interim?"

Jim tried to be patient. "Just what we're doing now, Padre. Harassment of traffic to the haciendas, setting fires in the fields, digging ditches across roads, just shooting up the landscape in general."

"Innocent people could be hurt."

Jim's temper flared. "Worried about your vows, Father? Remember, this was your idea! You want to free the people, you pay the price!"

Bartolomé rose slowly from the table. "I'm sorry," he stammered and left. The man was visibly shaken and Jim felt terrible for reproaching him.

Rosa came over and began to massage his shoulders. "Oh, Jaime," she said. "When will it be over?"

Reinforcements

It was three weeks before the telltale dust cloud of a military convoy appeared on the road above Hacienda Santa Rosa. Soldiers spilled from the troop trucks, aching and dispirited.

For many, this was the second tour of duty and they didn't relish the idea of engaging indigenes again. The mood of the land had changed; the puna now seemed colder and more hostile. Not even the rumble of a distant avalanche interrupted the hiss of an ever-present wind.

Patrols were promptly sent out, but there was nothing to be found. Only the myriad tracks that crossed and recrossed in a meaningless tangle gave sign of human presence. But for the occasional sniper, whose warning shot quickly turned the pursuer about, there was no contact at all. The indigenes had effectively disappeared, leaving the isolated haciendas to wait beneath the sullen glower of the mountains.

A large area had been cordoned off for military vehicles and an armada of buses and trucks to be used for the relocation of indigenes. Tents for the soldiers were set up in an orderly array around a central mess tent. Latrines were then dug with *campesino* labor at one extreme of the encampment and a communications tent set up close to the driveway. In the course of a day, the Santa Rosa was transformed from a rustic hacienda into a military outpost. Carlos Quintero viewed the proceedings with some misgivings, more so because they were conducted without even the formality of asking for his permission than for the cleanup he knew would fall to the hacienda when the military left. He simply shrugged and went about his business.

News Bulletin

The inside of Bartolomé's legs were blistered and sore. The circuit that he had ridden through indigene camps and *caseríos* had taxed the cleric to the limit. Dismounting at the pass, he walked the remaining distance into Karoma. One final draught remained in his brandy flask and he debated whether to drink it standing up or sitting down. As he struggled with the decision, he noticed two figures descending the hillside toward him, and observed Jim's arm slip from Rosa's shoulder as they drew near. Rosa ran ahead and threw herself into Bartolomé's embrace. "I'm so glad you're back!" she exclaimed.

"I would come any distance to hold Rosa de Melgarejo in my arms," he replied, clasping her diminutive figure in a bear hug. After releasing her, he turned to Jim, who stood waiting silently. Neither man spoke. Finally, Jim extended his hand. "Welcome back," he said. "We need every good man we can get."

"Thanks, Jim," Bartolomé answered. "Perhaps later we can talk."

Jim nodded. "That would be good."

"One other thing of importance."

Jim came alert at the intonation in Bartolomé's voice. "Yes?" he said.

"One of our watchers intercepted me below the switchbacks. The meeting has been called."

Jim could feel Rosa squeezing his hand. For an instant he became lightheaded, almost dizzy. Rosa's voice seemed distant. "I'll have to get back; they'll be looking for me."

Jim nodded his assent. The rehearsals were over, it was time to take the stage.

Omen

General Valesco was flown from Cuzco to Chiquian in a light surveillance plane and driven from there to the Hacienda Santa Rosa in a faded green, four-door military sedan. The accompanying escort included two Jeeps and an open truck loaded with troops standing at the ready. They did not travel unseen, but were not interfered with. Long before the general arrived, a sense of anticipation had been growing in the camp. The standoff between forces was drawing to a close.

Umberto Valesco sat in the middle of the backseat, his feet flat against the floor, one hand palm down against the cushion. He endured the jostling without his customary complaint. Uppermost in his mind was the contingency at hand and Carlos Quintero, who, in his view, had displayed a level of incompetence bordering on treason. Luckily, Peru had won the diplomatic war and news leaking out from Chiquian was not regarded as having much substance with those world agencies that mattered.

"A minor problem with some would-be Communists in a remote area near the selva," Colonel Rohem had explained to an interviewer. "Our indigene population does not have an easy life. They are very slow to learn new ways, although we are helping them with every resource at our disposal. Sad to say, but they are very unworldly and susceptible to rhetoric from any firebrand who comes along. It only takes a handful, a dozen or so young people who take Mao's *Little Red Book* as absolute truth, to call themselves a movement and set about fomenting trouble. These perpetrators have been apprehended and placed in an agricultural cooperative for a year where they will learn something useful for their people."

So that was it. Little did they know, Valesco thought, of the real menace out here. He bristled inwardly at the fact that the *norteamericano* had broken out of the infamous Condorama. All this under the suzerainty of Carlos the Magnificent. Still, it would not pay to be too firm with him now. Carlos was connected, as were they all. Time would provide for his retribution. There was great emphasis on relocating these indigenes and he had the feeling that this program was not only related to cooperative development, but some darker side of things.

It would be unwise, he felt, to begin with troop deployment. Word would be sent out that he, General Valesco, would speak personally with their selected leader and offer his solemn vow on all agreements. After all, this was for their own good. They need never be hungry again.

Looking out the window, he mused on what the next few days would bring. The indigenes were obviously organized, a leader must have risen to the fore. He wondered what he looked like. Was he younger? Older? Did he wear one of those stupid-looking hats?

~~~~~

For his part, Carlos Quintero was apprehensive, but not overly so. He stood on his own soil and was lord of the land as far as the eye could see. The recent raids were unsettling. Carlos and the others had been certain that the indigenes were neutralized and that the few who had not fled or been killed would submit to relocation. Still, he was more curious than alarmed. Indigenes could be stubborn, but they were rarely intelligent. The dynamite was most likely already useless, sitting out on the puna somewhere. He and the general would sort out the matter and devise a plan.

Friendly Persuasion

"It is war," she said. "Mankind has always warred and men and women make love in the midst of it. Why not? Why shouldn't life go on?"

Rosa spoke as she smoothed their blanket over the sand and sat to remove her boots. Jim looked at her, but made no response. He sat to one side of the blanket, leaning against a smooth, reclining boulder that disappeared into the sand.

"It will be cold soon," she continued, "and you, my friend, will be more in need of warmth than I. My blood is thicker than that gringo crap."

Jim was forced to smile. Rosa was irrepressible and he had learned that she was more comfortable giving orders than taking them. He caught a momentary glimpse of a well-shaped, pendulous breast as she removed her shirt and pulled the large double sleeping bag over them. For a moment Rosa wriggled under the cover as she removed her trousers and then crept toward him. "Do all *yanquis* make love with their pants on?" she hissed and began to assist him.

"Rosa," he replied and fell silent, groping for words to express himself.

"I know," she said. "People will soon die because of what we do. This bothers you, Jaime, but this moment is no different from any other. These people will die for eternity and for eternity we will have killed them. Shall we never make love again? What is so sacrosanct about tonight? The world is terrible, Jaime, and tonight especially I want to feel your flesh against mine."

The sun's light was reduced to a single scarlet trace on the horizon. Jim held Rosa's naked body against his own and slowly ran his fingers over its contours. His face nestled against hers, immersed in the intoxicating scent of her hair. Her warmth enveloped him and the soft swelling of her breasts against his chest caused him to pull her closer as if he could make her part of him. He could feel the need growing. This woman had insinuated herself into his soul.

Something in the Air

Say what one would about Carlos Quintero, no one could contest the fact that he was a superb host. Dinner was more than a lingering memory; it was a sense of satisfaction that continued on long after the fact of its consumption. General Valesco, his aides, Carlos and the *patrones* of the other haciendas were gathered about the great fireplace, its ample glow filling the room. Cigars and various liquors were provided and an aura of comfort so pervaded the room that no one felt inclined to begin the business at hand. Carlos noted, with some pique, that Karl was not present. Probably playing with his radio set, he imagined.

A fire also burned in the family room. A story was read to some children while others played games. The women chatted or read. María Villanueva was knitting an afghan while maintaining careful surveillance of her two daughters, who became overly excited when visiting. One of the women had gone to find the maid. The progeny were anxious for cocoa and their mothers requested either herb tea or hot milk with honey for themselves. It was nine-thirty before she returned, pushing the serving cart. It was odd, she related, none of the servants could be found and so, not wishing to disturb Carlos, she had prepared the drinks herself.

Outside the house, there was silence. Lights gleamed in the overseer's quarters where the nightly card game was under way, but only a muted laugh or shout gave evidence of the fact. The army encampment was also subdued. Many troops were in their sleeping bags early to escape the cold. Two frustrated mechanics were replacing a truck clutch plate and fervently hoping that some soap and hot water would be left in the field kitchen.

Feeling heady from the liquor, Carlos put on his jacket and slipped outside to clear his mind. Overhead, the sky alternately brightened and darkened as clouds began to pass before the moon. A brisk wind skipped across the puna and whirled around the hacienda, tapping on windowpanes and rattling the metal gamecock on his perch above the roof. There was a scent of moisture in the air, as if a storm was in the making. Carlos stepped down from the veranda. Taking a long breath on his cigarillo, he exhaled the smoke slowly and watched the wind whisk it away.

Carlos felt unsettled, not just over what he perceived as General Valesco's obstinacy, but the incipient sensation that something was lurking in the darkness. He could sense it, though peer as he might into the shadows, he saw nothing.

A Matter of Perspective

Jim and Huaman shared the warmth of a small fire and the teakettle suspended over it. They spoke little as they sipped the hot liquid. Huaman's face was half hidden under the wide brim of his hat. The old medicine man had been missing from camp for several days and Jim had been concerned. "Do not worry about Huaman," the *curaca* had told him. "He is at home wherever he travels in the *cordillera*."

Indeed, it was true. Looking no different from when he had left, Huaman magically reappeared at sunset and joined Jim by the campfire. "What have you told the men at Laguna Quilacu?" he asked.

"If they hear nothing to the contrary," Jim answered, "they are to detonate the charges at ten o'clock this evening."

Huaman said nothing and continued to sip his tea. A few minutes elapsed and Jim felt uneasy. "Have you spoken to the

Apu?" he queried by way of prompting some conversation.

"Yes," Huaman answered.

"And . . . ?"

"The *Apu* says that the *laguna* will grow again."

Jim thought again of the charges set deep into the accumulation of rock and debris beneath the outlet of Laguna Quilacu. Wherever possible, men tunneled into the dam with short shovels and hand picks, forcing crawl spaces deep into the jumble of boulders that constituted the basic structure. Large caches of charges were emplaced and the tunnels backfilled. Now, within a matter of hours, innocent women and children were on the verge of execution. There was no other word for it.

"You worry about the families?" Huaman asked matter-of-factly, reading Jim's mind.

"Yes," the climber barely managed. The night around him seemed suddenly cold and alien. Despite his zeal for the indigene cause, he had never anticipated that events would take such a turn.

Huaman rose and emptied the dregs from his cup. "You worry about nothing," he said and disappeared into the darkness.

Huayco

The first two buildings were empty, as was the horse corral. All of the workers and livestock were gone. Carlos began to panic, running from building to building. What did it mean?

Had they simply run away and took what they could? Or was there an impending attack? No, not with the army here, they wouldn't try that . . . or would they? How many of them were out there under arms? His mind was crazed with fear and questions he could not answer. Rousing his men, he told them to come to the house and bring their weapons.

As he waited, his attention was taken by a bright orange flash in the southern sky, followed shortly by a second, equally bright, the afterglow lingering for two or three seconds. Over a minute later two distant, but distinct booming sounds were heard, connoting great energy. Carlos stood transfixed, wondering what it was. Lightning strikes? An airplane crash? By then his men had joined him and he posted them around the house. No one in the army encampment seemed to have noticed. With a snort of disgust, he spat on the ground and mounted the steps back onto the porch.

Inside, the party continued and he heard General Valesco asking after his little *pongo,* much to the delight of his audience. Carlos pulled a chair into the shadows and sat down. There was little comfort in the semiautomatic shotgun one of the men handed him. Only the dawn could bring him cheer.

〜〜〜

A huge subterranean roar reverberated around the *quebrado* walls as if a river were being disgorged through a tunnel. On the stream side of the dam two huge bulges had formed, one above the other, and then burst outward. Immediately thereafter, thousands of tons of rock, sand and compacted earth cascaded down into the gorge below, followed by a gigantic waterfall sluicing through a wide fissure.

The sound grew in intensity as the fissure eroded, displacing more material and increasing the flow of water. The grinding and crashing of boulders hundreds of feet below were soon overcome by the cataract's roar. Further downstream, where the canyon began to twist and turn, the flood rushed hundreds of feet up a granite wall, surging over and under a glacial terminus. Large sections of ice broke free and slid down into the foaming torrent. Each time the canyon turned, the waters surged high on the opposite wall. Within a few minutes the canyon was choked with a turbulent slurry of water, rock, ice, dirt and sand, which scoured its walls, flushing out the accumulation of centuries.

At the canyon's exit, the angry flow expanded into an immense wave filling the narrow river valley and hurtling down across the puna. As the flood channel narrowed further, the liquid accumulation rose in height until an eighty-foot wall of black, semiviscous fluid loomed out of the night over the Hacienda Santa Rosa.

〜〜〜〜

Carlos heard the roar of its approach, well before it could be seen. The half-realization of what was about to occur brought him to his feet. Screaming at his men he leaped from the porch. The moon had reappeared and in the distance a strange disturbance was taking life. The earlier breeze had suddenly reappeared as a wind, which quickly grew stronger. A heavy, rumbling sound began to manifest itself and he felt a vibration in the ground. Shouts and cries began to issue from the army encampment.

Three of his men joined him. *"Patrón,"* one said, "we

should . . ." A sharp cracking sound split the air and the massive rumbling abruptly escalated in scale, drowning out their speech. They could not know that the sound was caused by the drumming of immense boulders against the earth as they tumbled along in the flood. Dust was now literally rising from the soil and faces appeared in the hacienda windows. Glass panes began to break and screams came from within. Carlos ran.

The wind was now a gale and the ground shook violently. Carlos' men staggered backward toward the house as their leader disappeared. Tiles came loose from the roof and cracks appeared in the walls. One pillar supporting the veranda roof collapsed. People began to exit through the front door and run in a confused fashion for shelter elsewhere. General Valesco appeared on the porch, a look of stupefaction on his face and a bottle in his hand. He gasped at the monstrous liquid wall gleaming in the moonlight, its ebony facets sparkling like black diamonds. A eucalyptus tree snapped like a twig and was gone. In the last instant of his life, he raised one arm as if to ward off the inevitable and screamed.

Satisfaction

Jim sat apart from the small group of men at the lake's edge, listening to the lighthearted banter. Their low voices suited the early morning mood, he thought. Leaning back into the slope, he relished the warm sun upon his face. Above, horses grazed idly and made soft neighing sounds. It was good to be there and share the historic moment.

Each individual seemed a little more poised and deliberate in speech. After all, as Huaman had said, "Without land, a man was nothing. Without pride, he was less than nothing. Without fidelity to his ancestors and their legacy, he was a traitor."

Huaman, who waited below, looked out from his vantage by the canyon's mouth; he could see the wide ribbon of devastation that extended north across the puna. Clenching his heavy walking staff in one hand, he pounded it savagely into the earth, his face distorted into a great comedic smile. The dissonant intonation of a language long forgotten burbled from his lips as he fell back on the grass, his stomach and chest heaving, and laughed silently at the sky.

Survivor

Major Zamora had been late for the meeting, and as his Jeep passed through the cut, was astonished to see all of the hacienda lights abruptly go out. At the same time an ominous sound became clearly audible below them. Feeling a sudden sense of urgency, the wary officer ordered the driver to pull over.

Leaving the Jeep, they had proceeded ahead on foot. The

flashlight's illumination revealed nothing, but they felt a definite vibration through the soles of their boots. Further on, the sounds became distinct: cracking and snapping, the flow of water, and a strange rumbling like a distant volcano. Something was terribly wrong and as the moon reappeared from behind a cloud, he saw it—an immense and rapidly moving flood, a flowing mass of curdled earth, glossy black in the moonlight. Before him, the road had disappeared and he realized that the flow, only a few minutes ago, had been much higher. "A *huayco*," he had whispered in awe.

In the morning, they had investigated the site as well as the terrain permitted. Buried forever beneath many feet of muck and stone, nothing of the Hacienda Santa Rosa remained. Several kilometers downstream they could discern what appeared to be the mangled remains of trucks and buses. Everything in the *huayco*'s track had been totally obliterated. Even the callous Joaquín Zamora was numb.

It was time to go, but the major had been unable to resist one more scan of the terrain. Raising his glasses, he was astounded to detect movement in the layer of muck near the embankment's edge. At first he thought it was an animal trying to free itself. Then, to his further amazement, like some biblical miracle, he saw someone struggle upright. Although otherwise unidentifiable, the tall, lean figure in high boots suggested only one man.

Summing Up

Jim handed Bartolomé the dispatch from Charlie Newell and waited for his reaction. Lima radio had reported the incident as a massive *huayco* which stuck the Hacienda Santa Rosa during the evening hours, two days prior, and claimed the lives of General Umberto Valesco, some visiting families, and an unspecified number of soldiers stationed nearby. The commentator confirmed that although the *huayco* was one of the largest in recent history, the loss of life was significantly less than otherwise possible. Colonel Rohem was to assume General Valesco's responsibilities in the area.

It was also noted that hacienda owner, Carlos Quintero, miraculously survived the flood and was presently en route to his home in Lima. Plans for any future construction on the estate would be contingent on engineering and geological assessments yet to be performed. No mention was made of an indígene relocation plan or the possible involvement of unnatural forces.

Jim had not expected any concession speech from the government; the government had no one to concede to if it avowed that the disaster was the work of God. However, the ball was clearly in its court. Quintero's unexpected survival was significant and the simple fact that no hacienda workers perished would be more than enough to arouse suspicions. No matter, Jim had done his bit and had now given his notice.

He looked up as Huaman entered the kitchen. The Hatun Laika joined them, pulling a stool to the table and sitting down. They had grown increasingly close since Jim had come to Karoma. "Jaime, you are confused," the old man said, "like a bird motionless in the sky, fluttering its wings and not knowing where to go."

"I want to go home," Jim responded. "I've made it clear."

"Hmm . . ." Huaman rubbed a pebble between his fingers. "Perhaps. But I don't think you should rush back until you're through here, until you have fulfilled the demands of your soul. It would be very sad to feel the land calling you back and not be able to come. Without fulfillment, you will never be happy, never be able to rest. It will persist in your mind until you die."

Bartolomé looked at the Hatun Laika sharply, opening his mouth to speak before thinking better of it. Huaman continued, his voice low and authoritative, "Jaime, we have talked. We want to send you to Aricoma. You will be safe there and can rest. You will need to clear your mind for what trials may come."

Jim tried to read the face that was looking so intently into his. It was maddening to try and decipher the oblique language that flourished amid these mystics. "How many times do I have to say it? I have nothing more to give," he said.

Huaman looked away. "I don't know. Maybe I'm just an old man hearing voices, Jaime. But something tells me your future is being determined now."

Aricoma was to the east and bordered on Bolivia. Jim's mind raced; he had been manipulated, nearly killed, and yet he could not function without these people. "How far away is Aricoma?" he asked.

"Just a few days," came the joint answer. "I'll let Rosa know," Bartolomé added.

Overflight

The overflight of Laguna Quilacu brought them in from the south. Charlie and Xavier were in a state of high excitement. The two newsmen were secured with harnesses and safety lines by the partially opened cargo doors. Both were heavily bundled with clothing and lay prone on the deck, looking out with cameras at the ready. Pablo, the pilot, flew as low as he could, carefully monitoring his airspeed.

"*¡Jesucristo!*" Pablo's voice was suddenly heard through the headsets, followed by a low whistle. "Get ready! Coming up on the starboard side!"

Xavier scrambled across the plane and knelt beside Charlie. A few seconds passed and then the southern end of the lake began to appear, slightly outboard; the view was perfect. A dark broad band ran around the lake's perimeter, clearly indicating a large drop in level. It was difficult to estimate the amount, but one hundred feet would have been conservative. It was a big lake and a vast amount of water had been lost.

As they progressed toward the outlet, a light overlay of gray material began to appear above the original shoreline. The closer the north end of the lake became, the more pronounced was the effect; to the extent that, as the ruptured outlet came into view, much of the grass beside the lake was completely covered with overburden. The contrast was startling and Charlie wondered what it meant.

Abruptly, a huge fissure in the dam came into view. Both reporters gasped at the deep, jagged cut through which the release had occurred. Charlie looked at the canyon wall where the stream made its first turn. He could see where the tremendous surge of water had scoured the granite. In that same glimpse, above the waterline, he observed a swath of light gray over the darker granite, as if it had been spray-painted. It was the same material as that above the lakeshore and Charlie instantly realized that it was mud, simply dried mud.

"They've blown the dam!" Charlie shouted to Xavier. Jim had to have been involved. But how had he put an effort like this together? Charlie could hardly concentrate on taking pictures. Somewhere down there amid the labyrinth of mountains, he imagined Jim Bridgman looking upward. "God help me!" he exclaimed.

The mouth of the canyon passed beneath them and they followed the water course north toward the Hacienda Santa Rosa. The flood had overrun the riverbanks by a wide margin, cutting into the neighboring hillsides and gouging out great volumes of earth. Its path lay stretched across the altiplano like an elongated tendon, its width changing randomly with the terrain. They were nearly past the hacienda before they knew it. Only the severed road from Chiquian gave a clue as to its previous location. A few minutes later they reached the terminus of the river valley where it intersected and fanned out into the Cañon de Matibamba. The mighty river, which flowed through the canyon, had been temporarily dammed by the output from Laguna Quilacu. Giant boulders and other debris were strewn throughout the area.

Xavier took pictures as Charlie surveyed the area through binoculars. His heart was pounding. Beneath them lay the mangled remains of buses, trucks and other vehicles, some with wheels and axles jerked awry like broken limbs. A mountain ridge passed beneath them and it was over. Charlie slumped back against a bulkhead. He fervently wished there was something to drink.

Campesina

At the urging of Huaman, Jim set out for Aricoma in the company of six armed indigenes. No military threat was visible, but the Hatun Laika insisted, maintaining that there was always the possibility of rural *policía* who didn't understand the government's de facto policy. He did not voice his real concern. Evil was like a weed that kept springing up despite the most diligent attempts to eradicate it. In the history of his people there had been too many seeming victories.

They traversed the puna southeast of Karoma in good weather and Jim's spirits elevated as they went. Everywhere along the way *campesinos* came out to meet them. Word of their coming spread mysteriously ahead. An old woman from one village met them with two loaves of bread and grasped Jim's saddle. Her worn and wrinkled countenance confronted his and a shiver ran through his body. "The people of our *ayllu* thank you," she said, thrusting the bread into his arms.

Jim took the loaves and tossed them to the man riding beside him. Leaning down, he took the woman's hand and felt the strength still resident in her grip, the hardened calluses. He could see the dirty, broken fingernails as she tugged at her scraggly yellow-white hair. Red lesions and welts from lice showed through the thinning strands. She stood barefoot, dressed in coarse woven cloth, long unwashed. Yet there was such an aura of nobility about the woman, such a compelling fascination, that Jim could not take his eyes from her.

No doubt this woman had done nothing but labor for her whole life and had accumulated nothing. She had every right to surrender to the unrelenting and merciless forces which shaped her existence. But here she stood by the roadside waiting for them, still a part of the struggle. Always shouldering the burden, even where men failed, women like her carried on.

It was difficult to leave. Mustering his best Spanish, Jim thanked her, holding her hand to the last. From the outskirts of the *ayllu* they waved back and he could see the old woman still standing there, watching. It was more than the bread, he realized as he rode on. What she had intended and accomplished was to give them her strength. No one had ever paid him so great an honor.

Executive Decision

Presidente Ruiz began the meeting with a few brief words and then asked Colonel Rohem to present the findings of his investigation into the *huayco* and surrounding events. The colonel had longed for this exposure for years and was well prepared. He read from a set of carefully compiled notes.

There were few questions; the salient facts spoke for themselves.

"The *huayco* was clearly man-made, the work of indigene saboteurs using dynamite stolen from two mines. They were led by a *norteamericano* named Jim Bridgman in . . ."

"Enough." The *presidente* interrupted the summation. "You have done well, Colonel. I think we all understand what has happened. The question is what should we do now."

"General Cardenal and I have a plan of action," Colonel Rohem answered, careful to credit the new chief of staff. "If you . . ."

"Proceed! Proceed!"

Colonel Rohem spread a composite topographical map of the area over the table. Everyone rose and crowded to one side. From the opposing side Colonel Rohem indicated various features with a pointer.

"First, we recommend that the *huayco* is officially seen by the government as an act of God." Rohem paused; there were no objections.

"If our evaluation of these people is correct," he continued, "they will probably assume the conflict is over. Although we are informed that the *norteamericano* has not served in the military, he obviously cannot be underestimated. We hope he will simply wait until an opportunity to escape the country presents itself."

Rohem looked about the room for any dissenting views. There were none. "I—we—propose a strike against their stronghold at Karoma. It will be difficult to surprise them there, but we can destroy their base of operations. There will be no repeat of the last debacle."

"The *norteamericano* was involved with that, too?" Ruiz asked.

"Yes," Rohem answered resignedly. "The man possesses animal-like cunning and strength. His escape from Condorama was impressive; but still he is nothing more than a itinerant mountain climber who will soon find he is in over his head.

"The enemy will be forced south from Karoma. To eliminate them we propose a pincer movement beginning at Puno in the south and Chiquian in the north." With a pointer, he indicated the salient details on the maps.

Presidente Ruiz walked around the table to separate himself from the others. It bothered him to turn such an important task over to Rohem. The damned Nazi, who made a career out of being in the right place at the right time, was brought in to provide expertise and much-needed discipline for their lax army. True, desertions and unrest among officers had been virtually eliminated; but he wondered if Rohem really understood that he could never be a general.

"The terrain is perfect for such a strategy," the colonel was lecturing. "We can end this uprising and never leave a trace."

The *presidente* continued to pace. Rohem's remark about Bridgman being in over his head bothered him. Still, if this damned *alpinista* could be eliminated now, it would save enormous cost and risk. In addition, if the issue were allowed to sit, the politics could become exceedingly difficult. He turned his gaze upon the Secretary of Education. "Señor Arneo."

"Yes, sir."

"You will be my liaison with Colonel Rohem to minimize presidential visibility with the military."

"Yes, sir."

"Colonel, begin your preparations. This effort, I needn't say, is top secret."

"*Sí, Comandante.*"

Presidente Ruiz dismissed the meeting, remaining behind while his secretary escorted the visitors out. None of the participants tonight fully understood his political problems, nor the complex accommodations that had to be made to achieve and hold office. The forthcoming election was going to be difficult. Javier Duarte was a reformer who championed land redistribution and was rapidly gaining strength. The indigene uprising would have to be harshly dealt with, but quietly. None of his constituents wanted to share their wealth with indigenes. Neither did they want to lose the umbilical cord to world finance and support. Moreover, the specter of a military candidate was constantly with him.

Jardín de Aricoma

It was difficult to read the lettering. Vines and overgrowth had covered much of the wall and a yellow-green moss had begun to inch its way up the water-stained granite blocks. Jim stood back and looked questioningly at his imperturbable guide. The other men were spread out behind him.

"Jardín de Aricoma," the guide said.

What a beautiful name, Jim thought to himself. Behind the wall some distance, an old building looked resignedly down the valley through a small forest of oak, elm and various fruit trees. Birds flew about chattering and chirping in great profusion. Despite its obvious decay, the hacienda was less sad than serene and Jim felt an instant attraction to the place.

The building was a massive, single-story, adobe structure, set parallel to the road. An arcade ran along its full length, open to the outside, and supported by thick rectangular pillars surmounted by bell arches and a plain entablature that mated with the red tile roof. Access was through the central arch, larger than the rest, from which a flight of steps fanned down and out onto the grounds. A large masonry fountain, beset with moss and cracked stone, still bubbled cheerfully—its sound, not obvious at first, wending its way beneath the trees to surprise the visitor.

A gust of wind rustled the leaves and Jim looked up through the branches to the sky. "Tell me, *guía,* that this has been our destination." Juanito merely smiled and signaled the others to unload the horse. When they were finished and the animal tethered, he walked up to the hacienda entrance, leaving Jim behind. Jim could hear the sound of a metal door knocker and the loud squeal of a very heavy door being opened. Voices could be heard faintly for a few minutes and then Juanito returned.

Jim was about to ask him what had transpired when he again heard the door squeal. An elderly couple stood on the top step looking out and then began to descend. Jim saw them cross the open space in front of the building and then enter the shade of the trees, following a stone pathway. They walked arm in arm, moving very slowly, as if in procession. The man was slightly taller than the woman and his hair was white, flecked with black strands. Her hair was snow-white and combed straight back into a bun. Despite their obvious age, they walked erect, faces uplifted, comporting themselves with an innate dignity. As they drew close, Jim could see that the man was dressed in a suit coat with matching trousers. He wore a white silk shirt with a string tie and black, square-toed boots. His wife wore a long, black, brocaded dress, modestly cut above the bodice, with a fine gold necklace of unusual design. She also wore black boots, although low cut with narrow, pointed toes.

"They have been expecting you," Juanito said in a low voice. "A shepherd saw us coming over the pass last night and so they have dressed formally today to greet you."

The couple passed beneath the rusting wrought-iron arch which spanned the entrance to the hacienda and approached them. Jim stood motionless, fascinated by what he saw. This was a model of Castilian aristocracy long past, of deposed royalty in full dress, standing before the ruination of a former time. Politely, almost shyly, appraising him with their eyes, they gazed upon this strange American who had come across the mountains. A minute, perhaps, passed in silence. Finally, the woman extended her hand. "Welcome to our home," she said. "We are pleased to have you as our guest. I am Violeta Castellon and this is my husband Sergio."

Family Squabble

Rosa confronted her father across the table. Her large, dark eyes were moist, defiant. The fire that had been smoldering for two months had erupted into flame. "How can I not be outraged!" he shouted from his wheelchair. "I am put to bed each night, a helpless *lisiado,* while this *insurgente,* who would destroy our people, finds his pleasure between my daughter's thighs!"

"I sleep with the one I love," she responded in an even voice. "In these difficult times, you take what you can from life. You once loved my mother. If you can remember what it was like to hold her in your arms, then perhaps you can understand my feelings."

Octavio's lips trembled. "Rosa, please. We have gone too far with this. We have cared for the indigenes, protected them. But this is different. This man makes war against our kind. If the others find out he is your lover, we are doomed. There will be nowhere to go . . ." He struggled for breath. "Rosita . . ."

"No, Father," she answered. "I worked for El Patrón and for ten years I have served this hacienda well; but the *hacendados* are your people, not mine."

"But, Rosita," he pleaded, "after what has happened at the Santa Rosa, there will be soldiers everywhere!" Octavio de Melgarejo lowered his head and sobbed. Rosa came around the table and knelt beside him. She lifted his face to hers and stroked his hair back. "Please, Father," she whispered, "you must understand. My love for you is no less. But no matter how much you deny it, my mother—your wife—died at their hands. I will never forgive them and I will never dishonor her name. If the loss of your love is the price of revenge, I am willing to pay it."

Respite

Sergio's voice was low, but clearly audible, almost melodi-ous. An old man and his wife, alone on this remote moun-tainside, Jim thought, with every passing day drawing their memories closer about them. Their remaining life was a dim-ming candle, more nourished by the past than the present. He saw their need for reassurance, for affirmation that it all had been real. He saw it in their eyes, in the subtle urgency of Ser-gio's speech and in the unspoken question posed by Violeta's smile.

As they conversed, Jim let his gaze wander about the ex-pansive living room. It was filled with ornate furniture, objets d'art, paintings with heavy gilt frames and various memora-bilia. Dust was prevalent beyond the sitting area and an at-mosphere of decay pervaded the recesses, a sense of time grown stale. Once this hacienda was a place of social focus. Jim wondered what had happened.

"Are you still working the hacienda?" he inquired.

"No, no! Violeta and I have become too old and circum-stance has not been kind to our enterprise. A number of years back we suffered a terrible drought. It lasted five years, even the mountain snows could not help us enough. Then there were torrential rains, which destroyed our roads. What crops we had could not be transported to market. Many *hacienda-dos* left. We did not have enough help to work the fields when things became better. Most of the indigenes had gone to work in the mines and couldn't get back."

Jim shook his head, understanding that situation all too well.

"So we retired and let the indigenes work our land for themselves. After all, it is more their land than ours. All we ask for are vegetables, fruit, some meat and flour to satisfy our needs. We receive more than we can ever use."

A rap on the door announced the arrival of an indigene who would carry a letter for Rosa down to Otorongo, eight thousand vertical feet below. Taking the letter from Jim, he handed him in turn a scrap of heavy paper torn at the corners. Jim unfolded it with a start. It was a handbill announcing his escape from federal custody. Jim was cited for crimes against the state and a substantial reward was offered for his capture.

The handbill was recently posted. He handed it to Sergio, who said, "Best you stay close to the hacienda, out of sight."

~~~~~~

The day Rosa's letter arrived, Jim found himself at a loss, unable to open the missive for over an hour. The sight of her handwriting on the envelope was somehow tantamount to her actual presence and he could feel the floodgate strain within.

"Was it a good letter, Jim?" Violeta asked.

Jim nodded.

Violeta noted the moist eyes and made no further inquiry. It had not always been easy for her and Sergio either, fighting the jungle creeping up from below and the mountain storms from above. Despite it all, they kept things together and were still around to enjoy the sunrise out of Bolivia. A relationship was more than just holding hands, she thought.

Casualty

The moment César Oré recognized Joaquín Zamora approaching from the Jeep, he had a sense of foreboding. The major fixed him with a black stare that denoted nothing but malice. The back doors of the van were already open and two soldiers were busy emptying the contents onto the ground. Across from him, sitting on the ground, Arturo's face was blank with fear.

César watched as two of the crates were ripped open. He held his breath as Major Zamora examined the contents. "Medical supplies!" he heard the officer exclaim. "Now where in the hell are they going with these?"

Joaquín Zamora hissed through his teeth and turned toward Oré. Inwardly, he was smiling at this opportunity. *"¡Conspirador!"* he said quietly and Oré began to feel faint. "No, Comandante, no . . ." César's pleading was cut short by a scream from Zamora. *"¡Silencio!"* Twisting the leather quirt he habitually carried, he positioned himself directly before César, his unwavering eyes only inches away. *"¡Embustero!"* he muttered, the menace in his voice increasing. "There are only revolutionaries out here now. The Santa Rosa is buried in the mud. So who are you working for?"

Oré was not even a momentary match for such a confrontation. His throat and lips felt dry and his feeble attempt at speech was undercut with fear. *"Comandante,"* he managed, "it is nothing. Carlos wanted us to distribute . . ." *"¡Mentiroso!"* Zamora shouted as he shoved César toward the Jeep. César stumbled backward, his face sweeping in an arc, his lips moving soundlessly. "Please, *Jefe*," he almost whispered as he dropped to his knees beside the Jeep.

By now more soldiers had arrived and gathered about the scene. There was silence among them as the drama ensued. Zamora's whip lashed through the air and lacerated César's left cheek. It was so quick that for a moment César didn't know what happened. He felt numb and wondered at the taste of blood in his mouth. Again and again the whip descended. Those who watched fidgeted and grew nervous. Now, totally in a frenzy, Zamora resorted to bludgeoning César about the head and shoulders with the whip's butt. Still conscious, César tried to ward off the blows, but to little avail. Tired at last of the game, Major Zamora stepped back and surveyed the man groveling on the ground. Lifting the flap on his pistol holster, he grasped his Colt .45 revolver and raised it in the air. At that instant, there was a cry from behind and a thud as Arturo's body hurtled into him.

Zamora lay sprawled in the dust while his men subdued Arturo, shackled his hands behind him, and lifted him to his feet. The major then slowly rose, his pistol still in hand, and walked with great deliberation toward the waiting figure. As he approached, the soldiers released their grip and stepped aside. Arturo knew what was coming and did his best to shrug off the rush of fear that tugged at his entrails. He could take this for himself, but the thought of his broken family consumed the very fiber of his soul. If there were only some way to bargain, but he had nothing to bargain with, and it would not matter if he did. Major Zamora was not given to bargaining; his only coin was the suffering of other people.

"Speak," the major commanded.

Arturo stood erect, his eyes fixed on Zamora's, and tilted his chin up ever so slightly. "You are unmanly," he said softly.

"What?" snarled Zamora, who stepped closer.

"You are a coward," Arturo said in a loud voice and spit in the major's face. The major responded by lifting his pistol to Arturo's forehead and pulling the trigger.

When the dust from the last truck settled, Oré struggled to a kneeling position and tried to orient himself. His swollen face was red and black and his vision obscured by eyelids crusted together with dried blood. He did not know of Arturo's fate until he finally made out the still form lying by the roadside. Staggering and crawling to the dead man's side, he looked down and collapsed, sobbing. "Arturo!" he cried repeatedly, his hands grasping and caressing the dead body as if he could bring it to life. Finally, he surrendered to the horrible inevitability and lay clutching his old friend. His moans and cries were finally heard by a group of indigenes who were crossing the road a short distance away. Placing César on a burro, they took him with them. Two of the men stayed behind to deal with the body.

Summons

Jim stood by the rain-streaked living room window, peering into the gloom. The dull thud of the door knocker, unexpected and authoritative, startled him and he looked quizzically at Violeta. As Sergio rose to answer, Jim stepped back toward the darkened kitchen.

Two indigenes stood there, dripping with rain. At first they said nothing, then one spoke tentatively, *"¿Esta Jaime Bridgman aquí?"* Sergio asked them in and called for the maid, Angela, who soon had them dried off and bundled in blankets.

"We come from Karoma, *Jefe,* where there is much trouble."

Jim could hear the gusts of wind and bursts of rain against the windows. "Call me Jaime," he said in a low voice, knowing full well that they had not traveled such a distance for any trivial matter.

"*Sí,* Jaime," the younger of the two replied. "Padre Raimondi has sent us to talk with you. He is not well. 'Soon,' he says, 'the army will march on Karoma.' "

Violeta rose to caution him. "Don't be impulsive, Jim, think it through. Wait until we can find out more."

"The authorities tell us that the people of the puna must leave for the selva. They say that we cannot feed ourselves on the land and that we must be moved for our own good. Priests have been sent from Lima to convince us that this is the right path, but we know better. There is only death for a mountain people in the jungle. Many trucks and buses have been brought to the highway. There are only a few days left to us."

Jim listened in abject silence. The indigene continued, "The *guardia* are searching for you. People have been tortured, but they tell the soldiers nothing. The padre says to tell you that your destiny is here, with us. He has told the people that the Holy Spirit shines within you."

"The man is mad," Violeta interrupted, knowing the full details of Jim's story. "Stay away from it, Jim."

"Without you, Jaime, the people will not come together to fight. They will scatter across the altiplano and die."

The wind escalated in force. Out on the puna people without homes found what shelter they could, huddling together and hiding from soldiers bent on their destruction. A sense of hopelessness closed about him like a shroud. Yet, there was some solace in the crazy logic of it all. Of what objective value was his life? In some far recess of his mind, an understanding was growing. He would come.

∼∼∼∼∼

They rode five woolly Andean ponies, stocky, ill-tempered and strong. On their third morning out, they began to gain altitude. Many of the puddles and rivulets were frozen and a dark glaze of ice ran over the rocks. Clumps of grass were rimed in crystal and dusted with snow. The condensed breath of their horses lingered in the air. Ahead, Jim was surprised to see figures emerging from the fog. He heard voices and was soon being helped down from his horse. The *curaca* took his hand firmly, but did not waste time on formalities. "We must walk from here," he said. "We will talk later."

After a descent which took an hour a stream was crossed via a natural spillway of tumbled boulders and other detritus. On the opposite side low, scraggly bushes with thick trunks grew in profusion. They wandered through these and down the canyon for another twenty minutes before the smell of wood smoke caught Jim's attention.

Soon he could see flames and a number of men moving

about. A boy was running toward him. Scarcely ten or eleven, he stopped and stood to one side as the entourage passed, his eyes fixed on Jim.

The crowd of men opened as they approached to reveal a low circle of finely cut stone blocks. Jim had seen such pre-Incan formations before, usually at the foot of a major pass. The fire was burning in the middle of the circle. A slight figure in a long, bedraggled cloak and rumpled hat stood close to its warmth. He turned at the sound of their arrival, revealing a face pale and drawn.

"Welcome, Jim," Mariano said, extending his hand. The voice was ragged, yet still soft and compelling. He is dying, Jim thought, as he felt the priest's feeble grip. Mariano saw the concern in Jim's face. "Do not worry over me," he said, signaling to a young girl who rummaged through a cloth sack to produce two battered mugs and filled them with sweet tea from the fire.

They sat for a few minutes sipping the tea in silence. "Should you need me," Mariano finally began, "these people will know where I can be found."

Jim started to respond, but Mariano held up his hand. "You will go to Karoma and get our people out in some orderly fashion. And then, Jaime . . . you will do destiny's bidding."

Jim noted the tired smile that graced the priest's lips. His words were neither a command nor a request, only a simple statement of fact. For a moment Mariano and the encampment seemed to disappear. Jim felt himself uplifted and somehow directed toward something he could only dimly divine. There was no fear, only a sublime acceptance of the fact and in that acceptance, substance. He was no longer drifting.

Strategic Withdrawal

Everywhere Jim went, he felt their eyes upon him. He hadn't expected this when he set out from Aricoma; he wanted time to reflect and put something together, but there was no more time. From a vantage in the meadow above Karoma, he had watched the exodus begin, men, women, and children filing through the arched stone gateway toward the pass. Before them, a line of llamas, horses, and burros, heavily burdened, extended for over a kilometer. More women, carrying children on their backs, urged sheep and livestock along from behind.

Karoma could not be defended, he had argued. It was a trap; the military would simply bottle them up until they starved to death. Most of the men who had crowded around him in the small church kitchen were solemn and said nothing. Their homes would be lost, destroyed. The agony was in their faces. Those who had argued soon gave in

〰〰〰

Jim still could not shrug off the guilt, the pain. In the room with him were Bartolomé, Rosa and Charlie Newell, who had managed to rejoin them. Within the hour they would follow the others. "What have I done?" Jim asked. "Have I brought this calamity upon them?"

Bartolomé, who rose and shuffled toward the fireplace, had made no reply. Jim's voice, all at once harsh and demanding, followed him.

"Did you figure on this when you set me up?"

Charlie could see Bartolomé flinch with the accusation. He looked sharply at Jim, wondering what was going on.

"I know that my presence here was planned from the beginning. I don't know why or how! But, goddamnit, you singled me out for some reason. Who tapped me on the shoulder in Cuzco? Who maintained such a judicious silence on what was going on and laid those crisp new one-hundred-dollar bills in my hand? Admit it, damn it! Through your manipulation and lies, we have a disaster on our hands!"

Bartolomé's face was a mask of grief. "It is true, Jim. I am so sorry. I thought we were doing the right thing, that the circumstance, the cause we were serving, somehow justified our actions. Mariano's visions led us to believe . . ."

"Mariano's visions!" Jim was near collapse from the unrelenting pressure. "So Rosa told me. What else did these visions say? Do I ever escape from Peru? Do I live through this?"

Jim stalked toward the doorway where Rosa waited in anguished silence. He could feel the weight of destiny slowly descend like a stage curtain. There was no way out now; the fate of thousands depended on him. Stopping, he turned toward Charlie, his voice charged with emotion.

"We need you now, Charlie. But if you come with us, you risk either getting your head blown off or death by starvation. If you don't want to continue with this, it's all right."

Charlie looked up, his expression both bemused and curious. He had taken considerable risk for this story, never imagining he would become part of it. His dispatches were being carried to Cuzco by a system of couriers and transmitted from there to Lima by radio. As they accumulated in the editorial offices of *El Observador,* the story of the Chiquian conflict slowly spread and government officials, weary of the growing inquiries, became more taciturn.

"You know I'm coming, Jim. You don't have to ask."

Looking at Bartolomé, Jim continued, his voice authoritative and cold. "You must return to Cuzco, even Lima. Continue your fight on the political front. I want you to pressure that archbishop in Cuzco to exert some influence. Talk with the cardinal, if you can. Write your superiors in Rome. Anything you learn, send it by courier, written in Quechua."

Bartolomé opened his mouth as if to protest and then thought better of it. "What of Mariano?" he asked.

"Mariano is well hidden," Jim answered without elaborating. "Rosa will . . ."

"Ride with you, my love," she interrupted. "Remember, these are my people. This is my fight."

"You've done enough," Jim nearly shouted. "Let them do their share!"

Rosa smiled, her voice suddenly soft. "No, Jaime. I alone will decide when I have done enough and that will not be until my mother's land is free and roses blossom at her graveside. Not one day sooner."

Her dark brown eyes looked steadily into Jim's and did not waver. "All right," he said. "But you will ride a horse."

"And you?" she asked, eyebrows raised.

"I will walk."

Staff Meeting

If Colonel Rohem was anything, he was circumspect. His new field headquarters was established near the airstrip just outside of Puno, sufficiently removed from the scene of operations to remain unnoticed and yet possessing ready access to field intelligence sources. His presence was not made public.

As Colonel Rohem entered the hangar at precisely 0700 hours he noted with satisfaction that his staff was assembled and waiting. The building had been commandeered principally for the concealment of armament, but also served for staff meetings. Two folding tables, piled with papers, occupied the center of the floor and were surrounded by four M-48 tanks and six Jeeps mounted with recoilless rifles. There were no chairs; all attendees stood.

"Gentlemen," he murmured, returning their salute and motioning the men to stand at ease. Where General Valesco had "chummed" with his officers, Colonel Rohem was formal and distant. Raised in a Nazi youth camp, he had long since abandoned life's diverse pleasures for singularity of purpose. Mostly bald, of medium height and lean, he was not an imposing physical presence; but these same characteristics served to accentuate his intense focus.

"Rodríguez, you may begin first."

Each officer was required to explain the overall strategy and plan of battle to the others, following which Rohem would challenge the officer with contingencies. The exercise was repeated until the colonel was satisfied that any of them could assume command under the stipulated conditions. This morning they performed flawlessly.

"Patience, that is the key. We are close now, perhaps one week or less. The troops in Chiquian are ready for deployment. Tomorrow, the last of our railcars will be ready. Officers whose contingents will board the trains will place their men on ready-alert status immediately. Those of you who constitute the southern wing of our advance will deploy your troops in the morning and prepare to march upon my orders. You are all advised that these revolutionaries and their supporters are hardened fighters, but undisciplined. It only remains for us to perform as professionals to bring them to bay. Understood?"

"*¡Sí, Comandante!*" The officers' voices sounded in unison.

It all seemed so straightforward at first, Rohem thought as he left the hangar. But glancing up at the mountains north of the airfield, he began to worry. The mountains were big, very big. In the vicinity of Karoma, they would be enormous. The scratchings on their maps, the arrows and lines would have to become real. They were seeking to impose one reality upon another, an older, more vast reality that was not necessarily susceptible to their devices.

Tutorial

Three days had elapsed since the odyssey began. Fortunately, the troops that had been dogging their heels had not detected the files of women and children who left the main track each evening to make their way down to the safety of the *montaña*. The last such party had just left and Jim's fighters were now free to confront their pursuers.

Jim could just make out the shapeless forms of his men scattered across the ground nearby. Rosa sat up by his side, reciting the names of the constellations. "Rosa," he said in a low voice. "Tell me what happened to your mother."

Rosa adjusted the blanket over them. "There is not much to say, love. My mother was a very intelligent woman and not afraid to express her opinions. My father was always begging her to restrain herself, particularly in matters pertaining to the indigenes. She was an indigene and my father, a Spaniard, who suffered because he married beneath his station."

She paused as if to gather herself and Jim placed his arm around her.

"A neighboring *hacendado* was having trouble with five *campesinos* who worked his hacienda. They lived in cardboard boxes, roofed over with scraps of wood, and worked sixteen hours a day. One man lived in the field, sleeping on dirt and covering his body with corn shucks. They began to protest and became belligerent. Each man received one glass of *chicha* a day. After several weeks of this behavior, the *hacendado* lost his temper and poisoned their beer. They all died in agony."

Jim exhaled sharply. "Jesus," he muttered.

"My mother knew what had happened and did her best to see that this man came to justice. It took two years, but she finally forced the *hacendado* into court. The judge heard the case and rendered his verdict in about five minutes."

"Not guilty?"

"Yes, he ruled that the five men had had a collective heart attack!"

"And your mother?"

"Two months later she went to Chiquian and never came back. Her remains were eventually found, the skull crushed from a heavy blow. The police said she was thrown from her horse. Only she rarely rode horses and had driven to town that day."

"How old were you, Rosa?"

"Fourteen."

Jim realized that his left hand was clenched into a fist. "Thank you, Rosa," he said. "I need to understand these people better."

"To understand, all you have to do is imagine a man tilling the one ten-meter row allotted him to raise food for his family, after his twelve- or sixteen-hour shift is through. Then imagine his wife giving birth beside a ditch running sewer water, wrapping the child up and hurrying back to the field to work beside her husband."

"Doesn't the Church in Chiquian do anything?"

"Our Church," Rosa answered in a wavering voice, "my Church! When the first troops came to Chiquian, our local clergy blessed their weapons and offered a mass for their success! The rest Mariano will have to tell you; I haven't the strength."

One Step Too Far

"Mind if I join you?"

Bartolomé recognized the burly man standing by his table as the one described by the *periodista*. "Why not?" he answered, motioning the man to sit. Bartolomé was into his third brandy and the busy hotel bar had little to offer by way of distraction except raucous Latin music. The two men quickly appraised one another. The *norteamericano* smiled. "You're quite an adversary, Padre. I thought that those who took up the priesthood were more inclined to be dovish."

"You must be the agent provocateur from the CIA. I've been told about you."

"Anything flattering?"

"No."

"Too bad, we can be really convivial if given the chance."

"From what I can see, you're not in the business of giving anyone much of a chance."

"Tsk, tsk. Well, I see that your boy got out of Karoma. I thought he might. Valesco used a flyswatter when he needed a sledgehammer."

"You don't think much of our boy?"

"Oh no. We think a great deal of him. That's why we're doing our best to see that he meets with the earliest possible demise. Even Rohem understands the necessity for that."

"You have a great deal of cheek, whatever your name is."

"Karl. You needn't be offended, Father; I'm just talking shop."

"I choose to be offended. The life of a dear man is not a

piece-part to be thrown in a bin, nor the murder of innocent people a subject for chitchat." Bartolomé's voice was controlled, even as his temper flared. One massive hand gripped the table edge. He leaned forward.

Slesser, oblivious to Bartolomé's rising emotion, was confident. He had been waiting for his shot at this fucking, meddlesome priest. With 245 pounds of hard muscle on his five-foot-ten-inch frame, he was accustomed to having his way in any type of confrontation. "I understand your boy has a girlfriend." He leered.

At first Slesser could not comprehend the fact that he was sprawled on the floor and that there was something wrong with his jaw. Blood dripped from his lips and mouth and his surroundings were blurry. He then saw the table being thrust away and felt himself lifted into the air by the front of his shirt. The face of the priest was inches from his; pain gave way to terror.

"There is no fool like an arrogant fool, is there, Karl?" Bartolomé hissed. "May God forgive me for this, but I tell you now, if anything happens to Jim or Rosa, I will find you. And when I am through, there won't be enough of your remains to fill a tobacco pouch!"

Pursuit

Jim watched the last of his men, clinging to the saddle of a horse, emerge from the river and hurry up the embankment to seek cover in the rocks. Across the swiftly moving water he could see the first *guardia* soldiers arrive on the opposite embankment where they would wait for their leader. A moment later, Jim recognized the braided uniform and soft billed cap of an officer. The man's slight form and spirited horse clearly identified him as Major Joaquín Zamora.

There will be no crossing for you today, you son of a bitch, Jim thought. Once again, the mountainous terrain had served as a much-needed ally. It would take only a handful of men, their best riders, to hold this crossing while the remainder of the fighters moved on to the next most advantageous position. They had been playing this game for a week. Each day had had its own unique element of terror as they traversed up and down the sides of canyons on almost nonexistent trails, followed ridgelines, and twice forded muddy torrents.

Zamora, forced to follow Jim, was always stuck with the low ground. At any time, boulders could rain down the steep slopes, crushing both horses and men. In one canyon, where a small stream ran, thirty *guardia* soldiers were pinned down by snipers. Joaquín could see that they were safe behind rocks and boulders and he decided to simply wait it out. Let the rebels waste their ammunition; he knew they were running low. The gringo had proved to be a cunning adversary, but without resupply and reinforcements his capture was only a matter of time.

Too late, he had heard the thunder in the mountains and felt the air suddenly cool. Below, he'd seen the men look curiously around and then he noticed the high-water mark in the canyon, realizing that little if anything grew below it. The water began to rise slowly at first and then rapidly began to cover the rocks. Panic-stricken, the men had tried to wade back across but the current was already too strong. Within a minute, the turbulent flow had swept them away. Five minutes more and the level had returned to a trickle.

Joaquín would not forget that. As he looked across the river and recognized the tall figure of Jaime Bridgman, he could feel the rising flush of anger. You have cost me many men, he thought, but your time is running out. You can hide in the mountains, but you can't survive in them. Before long, you will have to break for the *montaña* and we will deal with you, my friend.

Petitioner

His Excellency Ignacio Diego Ugarte, Archbishop of the Cuzco Diocese of the Peruvian Catholic Church, glowered across the expanse of paperwork covering the dark teak bulwark that was his desk. There was a lapse in the conversation and Bartolomé tilted his chin upward to facilitate brushing away bread crumbs still clinging to his beard from supper.

Archbishop Ugarte winced as Bartolomé produced a corkscrew from the leather pouch hanging from his belt. The last bottle of Tinto Reserva was doomed and at four hundred *soles* per bottle it would be a month before he could resupply. The archbishop was leery of this man, not so much for his ponderous bulk, nor for the graceful ease with which he carried it, but for the intelligence and intensity of purpose that glimmered in those deep-set eyes.

There were problems in the district, serious problems. How much of it was known in Rome or understood by this Benedictine since his arrival, he did not know. However, he was keenly aware of that broad-bearded face scrutinizing his own.

"So, Bartolomé, is your first visit to Peru everything you expected?"

"And more, Your Excellency. I can think of no place better suited for the Lord's work."

"Indeed," replied Archbishop Ugarte, "and what of your work for the Lord in Peru, Father? What exactly is your mission here?"

Bartolomé shrugged and placed one thick, outsized hand atop his head. He massaged his scalp for a moment and slowly began to speak.

"In essence, my mission is best described"—he paused for a sip of wine—"as one of assistance in interpreting and executing the provisions of Vatican II and the recent Latin American Bishops' Conference, which I understand you attended, Excellency, in Colombia."

"Yes," Ugarte interjected. "The official general assembly will be held at Medellín in 1968."

Bartolomé nodded. "My superiors in the Curia, including the Pontiff, feel the applicability of Vatican II to Latin America is readily obvious and fear an inordinate amount of time may pass before implementation begins. Time in which the suffering of many people, which might otherwise have achieved some degree of amelioration, will continue undiminished."

The implication of these remarks was not lost on the archbishop. "Believe me," he said, striking a pose of intimacy and concern, "I fully understand the Church's objectives and am in total sympathy with them. But one must understand the difficulties which apply to these regions . . ."

"Such as?"

"Well . . ." The archbishop floundered for a moment. "Basically, the personal attributes of the *campesinos* themselves. At times we despair of their ability to ever manage their joint affairs without strict oversight, even to the extent of managing their own households. It's possible that their history of Incan and Spanish domination, coupled with poverty, has destroyed them as a viable people."

The archbishop paused to emphasize the gravity of his remarks. His face took on a saintly mien as he concluded.

"It may well be that the proper tack is to focus on saving souls as the Church has always done. The secular side of life in Peru"—Ugarte threw up his hands—"has grown increasingly difficult to deal with through the years, though we have tried our best as the means have been given us to do so. The future role of the Peruvian Church will change; there is no doubt of that, only our uncertainty of God's will."

The archbishop's hands dropped into his lap, connoting finality and resignation.

Bartolomé studied the archbishop for a moment and looked down at the floor. The thought was on his mind that powerful Peruvian families may not be the only entities close to the government. At last he raised his eyes and smiled. Noting his glass was empty, he refilled it and pointed the bottle inquiringly at the archbishop. Ugarte declined, content to lean back in his chair and polish his steel-rimmed spectacles.

"Your Excellency, it is a terrible fact, nonetheless, that a great many people outside these walls do not share the luxury with which we contemplate such quandaries. If you would be so kind as to permit me to relate my experience . . . ?" He paused. Ugarte's eyes widened perceptibly as he nodded his assent. "Please, Father, continue."

Bartolomé cleansed his palate with a deep draught of wine and hunched forward. His demeanor changed and he spoke slowly so as to emphasize his words.

"Are you aware that in the Chiquian district, no more than a hundred sixty kilometers from here, there is a full-scale war under way between government forces and *campesinos* who are fighting to defend and recover their lands? That the government, in collusion with the *hacendados,* is embarked on a course of genocide?"

Bartolomé leaned back in the chair, blinked his eyes and took a deep breath. For a moment he contemplated the magnificent Vesica Picis adorning the wall above the archbishop's desk and wondered if it was a product of native handicraft or if this man ever sought its counsel.

"But that is not the worst of it." His voice rose in pitch. "While hundreds die under the most deplorable circumstances, this country, the world, is oblivious to it!"

There was no sound except for the crackling of the fire. Ugarte swallowed.

"I have walked these battlefields, seen the bodies scattered across the landscape, indescribable atrocities," Bartolomé continued, "people groveling in the dirt bleeding to death from their wounds, beseeching Blessed Mary to save them. No disrespect for the Peruvian Church, but is there nothing we can do?"

Archbishop Ugarte leaned forward; his voice was low and

carefully modulated. "Father D'Annunzio, we had no idea. The civil authorities told us that there was a minor problem with a local group of Communists, and although potentially dangerous for tourists, was of no other significance. I am shocked."

Bartolomé nodded his head vigorously. "They need help, Your Excellency. What can be done? Can you intercede with the local authorities? Or the cardinal? If we could achieve an armistice, perhaps create a dialogue, there would be time to alert other countries, even the United Nations!"

Archbishop Ugarte shuddered within. It was worse than he had imagined. This man, this three-hundred-pound zealot, was involved. The diocese was clearly vulnerable with respect to the new Church mandates and did not need the meddling of an ecclesiastical investigator. These people understood so little of the realities that were faced in the Peruvian hinterland. "It is late, Father," he said. "I will give this some thought tonight and decide what best might be done."

Ugarte saw that the Benedictine, slumping in his chair, had succumbed to the wine. He, too, was tired and felt much older than his fifty-seven years of age. Only the fine appointments of his office still gave him comfort. Arched stained-glass windows with mahogany sills were deep-set into the thick adobe walls and bordered by ceiling to floor velour drapes. A magnificent crystal chandelier, given to him by Carlos Quintero, hung from the open beam ceiling, and a Persian carpet, subtly tinted with purple and red, was a gift from Eduardo Quintero, a cousin of Carlos, who served as the Deputy Minister of Finance. The archbishop relished his possessions and all that they implied.

Bartolomé roused himself at the archbishop's touch.

"Thank you, Archbishop. I am very tired. We shall speak in the morning, then?"

"Yes . . . yes, Father. We'll see what can be arranged. If you're ready, Dominick will show you to your quarters."

"Indeed, I am. You are a superb host, Archbishop, and I am most appreciative."

"Breakfast is at the hour of your choosing."

Rising, Bartolomé bowed slightly from the waist and turned to follow Dominick into the corridor.

Archbishop Ugarte watched his massive frame fill the doorway and disappear. The telephone line to Lima was down; he would have to use the police wireless to communicate with the cardinal's office in the morning. He fervently hoped the Benedictine slept late and liked a long breakfast.

Quarry Ahead

Major Zamora viewed the gaggle of indigenes running over the rise some five kilometers distant with contempt. The cat and mouse game was at last beginning to bear fruit. The *norteamericano* no longer had the resources or strength to take nightly refuge in the mountains and then fight his way out. Indeed, this could be it, the final battle. Joaquín felt a surge of excitement. For several days now, on either side of his column, he had seen refugees, women and children, some with a few goats or sheep, scattering in every direction. He paid them no heed; they would be rounded up later.

Just ahead, two mounted scouts were returning at a gallop.

"Major." One saluted as he reined up. "They are turning into a *quebrada sin salida,* we can see them clearly. They appear to be very tired; there are only a few horses left to them!"

~~~~~

The *quebrada* opened out onto the altiplano, its south wall shorter than the north wall. Jim knew the canyon was a dead-end and that he was concocting strategy out of desperation. Nonetheless, he needed some action that would momentarily stall his pursuers. Clutching a rifle in one hand, he dashed about exhorting his people on into the *quebrada* where they formed a line approximately fifty meters from the entrance. Choosing two of his trusted lieutenants, he had them take a hundred men into the rocks at the base of the south wall with instructions to make their way out of the *quebrada,* unseen, and secure themselves where they could not be observed by the army.

Jim knew that this pursuit was a very personal matter with Joaquín Zamora and that the major had an expansive ego. He guessed that the army would set up a skirmish line across the mouth of the canyon and attack in the morning. That would be as long as Joaquín Zamora could wait.

An Irritation

Colonel Rohem reclined in his desk chair and cast a resigned glance toward the American intelligence agent. Karl Slesser was a burden he had to bear, and it was not easy. Even the man's Germanic origins were little compensation. Karl Slesser was a thug well suited, no doubt, for a beer hall putsch, but hardly fit for the society that Thomas Rohem had known. What was it with these Americans anyway?

"Your guys are too loosey-goosey. They look more like a fucking posse than an army. The recon pilots say they're all over the place."

"Perhaps you could join them in the field and provide the benefit of your experience."

Slesser, oblivious to the sarcasm, continued his thrust. "The only thing that's saving Zamora's ass is the fact that Bridgman is losing men through attrition and he's nearly out of ammunition. You and he should be worried. Bridgman knows your southern troops, for all intents and purposes, are sitting on their asses in a great big line waiting for Zamora to drive the indigenes into them. Likewise, your railroad cadre are going nowhere but up and down the railroad line."

"As we have planned. With the mountains to the west, he is penned in. When Zamora closes in on him, the indigenes will run like rabbits across the altiplano. Our casualties will be next to nothing. Major Zamora is a master in open-field tactics."

Slesser snorted. "Yeah, sure. Bridgman is well aware that he can engage Zamora at any time and not have to worry about an immediate response from the east or south. This man is dangerous, Colonel, a natural genius at this shit. If I were Bridgman and losing men, I'd be thinking the sooner I hit Zamora, the better."

Rohem's eyes latched onto Slesser's without the flicker of an eyelid or the slightest distention of a nostril. But Slesser knew that he had hit the mark and Rohem knew that he knew.

"For you, Colonel," a radio operator called from his station.

Colonel Rohem felt the mixed sensation of anticipation and relief as Major Zamora informed him that the enemy was in sight and fleeing. "Proceed, Major," he ordered, barely able to control his voice.

He returned to his desk smiling disdainfully. "Quarry sighted and your boys are in hot pursuit?" Karl asked.

"Yes, Mr. Slesser. They are running."

Karl Slesser studied the colonel's face for a moment and looked at his watch. "Kinda late in the day," he said.

A Word Aside

Rosa thought about it for a moment and decided to invest the energy necessary to heft her saddle onto the boulder; she didn't want it running with red ants in the morning. Jim watched, too fatigued to rise and assist.

"Jaime, my love, we must talk."

Jim reluctantly pushed himself up to a sitting position. He'd been planning their next move and could little afford the distraction that he feared this conversation would entail. "How about tomorrow?" he responded.

"No, we talk now." Rosa sat down beside him and took his hand.

"Rosa . . ." Jim began to protest.

"You have taken us as far as anyone could. With our depleted forces, all we can do now is flee. That doesn't require a commander; I can see our men to safety. You must take the opportunity to escape. Bolivia is not far away—Bartolomé will help you. You must leave now, before we are surrounded. Should you be captured, it will go very bad for you."

"I won't be captured, Rosa. We're going to win; I believe that."

Rosa studied his face, but couldn't quite divine what she saw there. Her voice softened. "What is it, Jaime? You know what I say is true. Why would you want to stay at such horrible risk? If you're staying for me . . ."

"I love you, Rosa," Jim cut her off. "But I'm not staying for you or for Raimondi or for anybody else. I'm doing it for me. For years, I've climbed and guided on mountains. I've been the big name that others use to build their reputations. But when the climbs are over, they return to their careers, their fancy houses and cars and me, I'm left with maybe some money but that's all. My whole life I've never taken a stand, never done anything important."

Rosa cringed inside. Her lover was a noble man and it hurt her to hear those words.

"Out here," Jim continued, "I feel like I belong."

Rosa's eyes were red and wet. "So what happens next?" she asked.

"We're going to surprise the bastards."

Hiatus

The archbishop's secretary was adamant. "No, Father, he did not say when he would be back, only that he had received an urgent message from the cardinal early this morning. You are asked to make yourself comfortable until he returns."

"That was it, no mention of the nature of his business? Nothing clsc at all?"

"I'm sorry, Father D'Annunzio; I've told you everything the note said."

Bartolomé began to stew. "Can you place a call to the cardinal's office for me?"

"The phone lines are temporarily out of order."

"Then how did the archbishop receive this message?"

"I presume the police wireless. You might try there."

Shadows in the Night

It was 1 A.M. when the first shots brought Major Zamora running from his tent, astounded at the rifle fire issuing from the *quebrada*. Screaming orders, he soon had his men deployed and returning fire. Scarcely had that been done, when firing began behind him to the east. The indigenes were well spaced out, giving an exaggerated impression of their numbers. A few grenade explosions heightened the illusion. Joaquín was close to panic. "How did they get behind us?" he screamed. "Return fire! Return fire!"

The soldiers quickly adjusted their positions and commenced firing when they heard the sound of horses' hooves approaching. Joaquín looked wildly about, but could see nothing. Suddenly the sound was upon him and he caught a glimpse of a silhouetted figure against the brilliant star-filled sky. It was a woman and in the flash from the revolver she was firing he recognized her face, Rosa de Melgarejo. Dumbfounded, he reached for his pistol, but he was too slow.

Another explosion of close-range gunfire erupted from indigenes who had crawled near the army encampment and lain in wait. Joaquín whirled about. "The goddamn son of a bitch!" he screamed again. "It's a trap!" Doing his best to make himself heard, he ran amid his troops and managed to effect a withdrawal out along the northern wall and onto the altiplano. They were not pursued.

Joaquín took the land phone as his operator cranked the generator. "Captain Gonzales," he shouted into the mouthpiece. "This is Major Zamora. They've broken out! They're headed your way!"

〜〜〜

The air was cool, but the radiant warmth of the sun fell in a deluge through the clear mountain sky. The fatigued fighters lay about in a stupor, hidden behind rocks and boulders. While Major Zamora reorganized, no more than twelve kilometers away, they would rest.

Jim sat next to Rosa, who was talking with Huaman. They spoke in low voices in Quechua. Jim surveyed the remnants of his would-be army, scarcely half remaining, and felt his resolve falter. They, in turn, looked at him, unsure of what would happen next.

When Rosa abruptly turned to him and grasped his sleeve, Jim was startled. "Don't sit there on your ass!" she snapped. "Talk to them! Don't be so damned aloof!"

"Aloof?" he asked incredulously. "Didn't I make my feelings clear to you!"

"That's not it," Rosa countered. "If you're going to stay, you must be not only with them but of them."

The terrible strain was in both their faces now. Jim took her hand and pressed it against his heart, kissing her on the forehead as he did so.

Charlie had witnessed the exchange and wondered how anyone had retained their composure as well as they had. He was sick of this war already but he understood his part in it. He also understood that the end could be near. The resistance was being broken by sheer force of arms. Zamora's action was the spearhead of a huge deployment.

When and if they made the *montaña,* he would be given an escort to Chiquian. Jim wanted all of his notes, detailed maps and photographs taken to safety. These people had become his comrades and Charlie's guilt at the thought of leaving was intense. Still, his contribution must not go to waste. He had to let the world know that the level of destruction here was the equal of anything in contemporary history.

Options

"There are two outs," Jim told the circle of men kneeling around him. "Down into the *montaña* or south into Bolivia. If it's Bolivia, we still must reach the high *montaña* first. We can no longer continue to run and fight; there is only enough food and ammunition for one thrust east. That's it."

His remarks incurred a low flurry of epithets and a shaking of heads, although most knew what Jim would say. None of those sitting or lying disconsolate on the grass wanted to leave their land. Still, as long as Jaime would lead, they would follow. It was the test of a man; anything worthwhile required a struggle. The gods had willed it so.

"Zamora will not march today," the *curaca* told them.

"It will take at least another day for him to regain his courage," Huaman chimed in.

The *curaca* snickered and motioned to Jim. "What is your plan?" he asked.

"Tonight," Jim replied and pointed east toward the rail line. The old man nodded his approval.

~~~~~

The dark night offered security from the unmarked observation planes that had been hounding them, but did not lessen Jim's impending sense of disaster. He could hear his fighters stumble and curse in the dark. Come morning, more would be gone: some dead from wounds, others fled. He could scarcely blame the latter.

At dawn they collapsed onto the ground near some rushes

that grew from a drainage ditch which penetrated the rail embankment about a half a kilometer behind them. They had made it. Jim counted the men remaining and was pleasantly surprised. Still, they were too few and Zamora had a national army at his disposal. No doubt the major was looking forward to the acclaim he would receive when the infamous Jim Bridgman was brought in again, tied over the back of a horse.

Missing from Action

"Gone!" Colonel Rohem exclaimed, more with surprise than alarm. "Do you have any idea where they might be?"

"I don't think that they are anywhere," Major Zamora answered. "They lost a significant number of men the other night and the few remaining have probably lost heart. Men have been deserting him ever since they abandoned Karoma. I doubt if he has fifty left."

The major made no reference to his own casualties and prayed that the colonel had not read his report too closely.

"He had enough sting to stop you in your tracks though, didn't he?" Rohem snapped.

Joaquín winced. General Valesco had been so much easier to deal with. This damn German read every single dispatch, over and over. There was no arguing. "Yes, Colonel. I accept full responsibility. Still, the impact of that engagement was far greater on him than us. I truly believe the *norteamericano* has been reduced to the status of a fugitive and should be pursued as such."

Colonel Rohem nodded; it was probably true. Still, revolutions grew from small seeds. One need only remember 1917. By now this gringo was a veteran fighter as well as a demonstrably talented tactician. He would have to be killed to absolutely eliminate the threat. Rohem cursed silently to himself. Lima was pressing him on the cost of the campaign. Perhaps this was the time to retrench.

"Find their track," he said. "Take enough men to finish the job. I will radio Lima that we have effectively destroyed the rebel contingent and that their leader is being pursued as a fugitive. Major, this man Bridgman will be your personal responsibility."

Joaquín flushed. *"Sí, Coronel,"* he saluted. "Thank you, Colonel!"

Respite

Jim sat, leaning against a tree, and relished the scent of pine, the rustling of branches in the light breeze. A small campfire glowed warm and friendly. It had been a long time since he had enjoyed such comfort. Two women from a neighboring hamlet knelt at the fire across from him and conversed in low tones with Rosa. Jim was sleepy from fatigue, food and glasses of *chicha*. The voices of the women seemed melodious in the night, like waves washing over his mind, lulling him to sleep.

"Comandante," a voice rasped in his ear. Jim smiled without looking over. It was Huaman, come to spread his wisdom.

"You have a very small army now, *amigo;* I count maybe a hundred and fifty men, excluding myself and the *curaca.* It is time you gave us guns and taught us how to march."

"You march better than I do, *viejo*—the *curaca* too."

A minute of silence ensued as the two men contemplated the fire.

"Why have so many left, Huaman? Not all of those men had families and many families had escaped to safety before the fighting started."

"It is not your fault, Jaime. The people revere you. But many feel that they have brought this calamity upon themselves for violating the will of the gods. It is not a new phenomenon. If an earthquake had destroyed Karoma, they would have blamed themselves. The women whisper to their husbands that they were born to bear these burdens. But they also believe that, in the gods' own time, a new order will come into being."

Jim shook his head.

"Also, you must remember," Huaman continued, "these men are not soldiers. Attacking haciendas and dynamiting the lake was more like a game to them, but fighting front-line troops is another matter. Add to that, that their families are once again on the verge of starvation and it's a wonder so many remain."

A strange sense of detachment began to slowly envelop

Jim. The fire seemed much brighter than a moment ago, although no one had added any fuel. He smiled at the feeling of separation from his body and the sense of relief it brought. Am I dying? he thought whimsically. He noted Rosa rise and approach.

Huaman paid no heed. The Hatun Laika drained his glass of *chicha* and continued his soliloquy.

"Centuries of subjugation have had their impact. But this is not what the gods want. They are angry because of the people's apathy and the arrogance of their oppressors. They are manifesting their will through you; it is through you that the people will come to know a different future. If it takes a hundred years, this will still be its beginning."

Huaman's voice seemed to emanate from within Jim's head, the words a dance of colors. Something deep inside began to give way; he heard the rush of glacial water somewhere and felt a surge of rising exhilaration. As Jim drifted off to sleep, there was the scent of snow and cool gusts of wind blowing down from the mountain above.

Rosa looked down on Jim's sleeping form and motioned to the two women. Together, with Huaman, they lifted him onto a makeshift pallet of pine needles and covered him with blankets.

Huaman's voice was beginning to slur. "The future is being born in his dreams," he said and stumbled off into the darkness.

Seat of Power

Monsignor Alcantara was more or less as Bartolomé expected, a religious politico in the classic mold, on the surface an ascetic, lean and focused on religious tradition, yet harboring within the deepest sanctum of his soul the love of power and its exercise. Bartolomé could feel it as the monsignor rose from his desk. "We are honored, Father," he almost whispered. "Please make yourself comfortable. There are a few minutes remaining and we can use them to get acquainted." Bartolomé's watch was accurate and he recognized this for what it was, a calculated effort to assess his character before meeting with the cardinal.

Bartolomé settled into the indicated chair and smiled inwardly. The man's grip had been cold, the fingers withheld, the obligatory act of a man who did not like human contact. On cue, a secretary appeared with coffee and pastries. Bartolomé hadn't seen such delicacies in a long time and did not deprive himself. Neither did he allow the monsignor's hospitality to loosen his tongue. His message was reserved for the cardinal.

A few minutes turned into thirty. The monsignor had obviously compiled a list of questions designed to lure Bartolomé into compromising admissions. However, Bartolomé kept turning them aside with bland generalities and slowly eroding the prelate's temper.

"We have heard of serious fighting in that region," the monsignor casually remarked. "Were you anywhere near it?"

"Everyone, I fear, in that region is near it. You should speak with Archbishop Ugarte; his knowledge is far more expansive than mine. In fact, I am certain that bullets have been fired in his direction."

The monsignor blanched. Bartolomé's face was stern and knowing as he reached for another pastry. He had neglected to say that in the fighting one hundred miles away, it was almost a mathematical certainty that a bullet was fired in the archbishop's direction. But why confuse Monsignor Alcantara with technical details.

"Did you by chance meet any of the revolutionaries? They must be a rough lot?"

"No indigene ever confessed to me that he was bearing arms," Bartolomé replied. Why should they, he thought, a man does not confess to his God that he is a man, no more than a child confesses his innocence.

The discourse continued a little longer as Bartolomé enjoyed the last pastry. Monsignor Alcantara leaned back in his chair and observed the visitor from Rome with narrowed eyes. The Benedictine had been involved, he thought, and was therefore vulnerable. His intelligence was in his favor but he could not anticipate the cardinal's power. Nonetheless, they had to be careful with this man.

〰〰〰

Eduardo Rafael Bustamante was tall and gaunt with a thin rime of white hair running the perimeter of his scalp. As he smiled from the doorway, Bartolomé had the sensation of being brought before the Grand Inquisitor of another time and place. There was accusation in that smile and something else, knowledge recently acquired, that lent confidence to its bearer that heretofore had not existed.

His voice was strong, yet soft. "Welcome, Father D'Annunzio. Please come in. This won't take long."

The monsignor closed the door behind them as they sat down at a small conference table. Bartolomé noted the look exchanged between the two men and the subtle nod of the monsignor's head.

"Bartolomé," the cardinal began, "I wish that our meeting had a different agenda. I have summoned you here to explain the Church's position regarding Chiquian and our concern over your activities."

Really! thought Bartolomé.

"The changes envisioned in Vatican II are not accomplished without extensive planning. However, the requisite policies and procedures must be clearly defined and agreed to by both governmental and ecclesiastical authorities. As I informed the Vatican yesterday, we are proud to say that our planning phase is now complete after many months of intensive effort."

"What then are the basic elements of your plan?" Bartolomé asked.

"The sad truth is that the indigene society is no longer viable in the modern world. Our studies show that their land is deteriorating and will soon no longer support even their present lifestyle. So, it has been determined that a two-fold plan of action is needed to save them from themselves and the predations of others.

"First, a significant proportion of their population will be relocated to areas more favorable for farming conditions on the eastern slopes. Second, the government will assume management of all remaining indigene lands, thus assuring up-to-date farming methods and a regular food supply. Those indigenes fortunate enough to have jobs on the haciendas, are, of course, already taken care of."

Bartolomé stood and walked over to the garden window. His face was flushed and he fought against his rising anger. "It has been my finding," he stammered, "that the poor indigene, working for El Patrón, is anything but fortunate."

"The next phase," the prelate persisted, "is implementation. And therein lies the problem. The program is cosponsored, shall we say, by the good offices of our Church and the Peruvian federal government. We cannot move without their approval."

There is no understanding so profound as one thief contemplating another, Bartolomé thought; get on with it.

"There is a hiatus, unfortunately, on the eve of our beginning." Bustamante's voice began to change. "The government is directing us to put our own house in order first." The cardinal was staring directly into Bartolomé's eyes. Bartolomé, for his part, was staring directly back. "Please go on," he said, guessing what was to follow.

"I want you to understand that this is not an indictment, Father D'Annunzio, but the Guardia Civil has identified you and Father Mariano Raimondi, whom we thought deceased, as leaders in the Chiquian rebellion. In two days warrants will be issued for your arrests. Your personal security aside, this represents an attack on the Church and the work we hope to accomplish. The evidence includes photographs and eyewitness testimony and is utterly damning. Our advice and request of you are that you not contest the charges, but take this opportunity to leave the country."

Bartolomé rose to his feet, seething. "So, the role of the

Church in Peru is not to champion justice, but to collaborate
with those who conspire against it. A collaboration that includes the displacement of a people from their ancestral home
under the pretext of saving them, when in fact the motivation
is simply to get rid of them. The plan you are about to foist
upon them will be the Peruvian equivalent of America's Trail
of Tears. You know very well that the selva will kill a mountain people and the scraggly few who remain upon the land
will soon be gone, including those who slave for El Patrón!
Your words are lies, Cardinal Bustamante!"

"Control yourself, Father!" Monsignor Alcantara shrieked.
"Remember to whom you speak!"

Gabriel Alcantara saw that his leader was compromised but
was himself unable to respond, perhaps because he knew that
this huge Benedictine spoke the truth and was not a man to
be silenced with a simple gesture or word.

Rising from the table, the cardinal stalked toward his desk.
Bartolomé watched as the older man stumbled and nearly fell
to the floor. Dear God, he thought, the man is infirm. Monsignor Alcantara restrained him from rushing to assist.
"Please, please, no . . . no," he implored. Looking down into
a face drained of color, Bartolomé growled, "I will have to
contact Rome."

Take Heart . . .

"Do not despair, we will be together again," Jim said to his
assembled fighters. "It is time for us to replenish our strength

and commitment. Most of you have families that you must look to and whose safety you must ensure. That should be done now, in advance of what's to come."

Rosa felt the breeze wash over her face as she watched the shadows from the pine trees move back and forth across the gathering. Huaman, his eyes closed and head nodding, slumped against her. Despite their pain and losses, there was a wholeness to the proceeding, something not of the mind, but from deep within their collective being.

"You have proved yourselves. There is no doubting the fact that man for man you are superior to the soldiers. But we need more help. The time will soon be upon us when all the indigenes of this region will come together on the battlefield."

Jim paused and let his gaze wander over the fighters. He read the expectant looks in their faces, and he felt their love for him. For a moment, he stood transfixed; never had he felt such clarity of mind or purpose. His hands seemed to lift before him of their own accord and he was astonished to hear his voice speaking again.

"Our battle must not be fought here; our strength is in the mountains, which give us refuge and protection. In the struggle to come, we will also need the support of the other *ayllus* above Chiquian. Victory will be ours only through unity. But first, you must rest and replenish your bodies. Until then, I will return to Nevado Viracocha and seek the blessing of the Supreme *Apu*. I will seek his vision on the mountain and if he permits, I will ascend to the summit where no man has stood before. It will be my body, but your pilgrimage. Regardless if I live or die, the future will be yours. Now, until the time is made known, return to your families."

The dirty faces of the men were streaked with tears. Jim was pummeled and embraced by those who had come to love him and did not want to leave. The wind through the pines abruptly escalated until the treetops were bent and debris lifted into the air. Huaman stirred by Rosa's side, his eyes suddenly opened wide. He seemed to be staring into empty space, one hand quivering as if palsied. A light froth came to his mouth and he began to mutter unintelligibly.

A burst of cheers arose as the congregation was thrust into shadow from a passing cloud and just as quickly returned to sunlight. Luminous columns descended through the trees as silver and gold motes of dust whirled through the air. Rosa clutched one hand to her breast and with the other made the sign of the cross.

News from the Front

Charlie Newell had set up an office in an unused garage attached to the Peace Corps headquarters. The slim indigene boy seated opposite him was a courier who somehow managed, through a variety of means, to traverse the vast reach of the back country and bring news of Jim's odyssey. It had taken the young man two weeks to reach Cuzco.

"Lino, are you sure he's still alive?" Charlie asked again.

"*Sí*, Huaman and the *curaca* are with him in the forest; but most of the fighters are gone. Those that remain guard Jaime. Huaman has told them that this is a special time for Jaime."

"Special time? What in hell does that mean?"

"I do not know."

Charlie repressed an urge to scream. "What about the soldiers? What are they doing?"

"They are hunting down our people and putting them into railcars and trucks. They take them to a large compound off the highway. Major Zamora has about thirty soldiers; he is looking for Jaime."

"Has he gotten close?"

"No, they are like wild pigs running through the *montaña*. Major Zamora is a madman. They say that Colonel Rohem will not let the major return to Lima until he is successful."

Charlie slumped in his chair. He wondered if he should summon Bartolomé from the hotel. No doubt the priest was still asleep after his late night radio shift. "What about Father Raimondi? Is he still safe?"

"*Sí,* they will never find him; but he is very sick."

Charlie thought of the mystic priest and worried once again that this uprising might be nearing its end. This would be his last dispatch and it would not be easy to write. "I would like to see Jaime one more time," he half muttered to himself.

The courier shrugged in an offhand manner. "Perhaps, Señor Newell, you could go to the mountain."

"The mountain? Nevado Viracocha?"

"*Sí.* Jaime has told Huaman that he will return there, that he is expecting a vision."

Charlie appeared befuddled. "Lino," he began, his voice raised in exasperation, "why is he going to the mountain for this damned vision or whatever. That place is a trap; can't the *Apu* send it by llama-back or something?"

Lino blinked. "No, señor, such a vision is a sacred thing; one must come to the *Apu*."

"Then what! Why is this vision important enough for Jim to risk his life?"

"It will prepare him for the mountain."

Charlie's eyes widened. "What?"

"Jaime is going to climb the mountain. I want to go with him. It is for our people."

Charlie took his face in his hands. "Oh, my God!" he cried.

PART FIVE

Transcendence

Journey of the Yagé

Huaman waited for Jim upon a slight rise at the farthest extreme of the meadow. Soon, he discerned a vague shape approaching and stood up so that he could be seen. He had reservations about what was to transpire, but there was too much at stake.

The setting sun was well hidden behind the mountains and except for the flare of light along the ridgeline the sky was a deep blue-black. A few stars littered the eastern firmament as rivulets of cool air began to flow across the grass. Above, a solitary condor soared through the last dim glow as the sun relinquished sovereignty to the night.

All of this went unnoticed by Jim, who had been fasting for two days. He shivered in the rising cold and tried to suppress the pangs of hunger. As the moment grew near, he became increasingly apprehensive. Huaman tended the small fire and ignored him. The liquid concoction, made from the San Pedro cactus, had been prepared earlier and poured into a battered, outsized enamel cup where it awaited consumption. Huaman had coached him for the trial to come, guiding his meditation and encouraging him.

"You must understand death to free yourself from it," the Hatun Laika had told him. "You not only fear it for yourself, you fear it for those who have perished about you. Deep in your mind, you fear their spirits and the enmity you think they bear you. You must cleanse your soul and bring your inner self into balance with your mind, with the nature we are part of. Only through this process will you come to realize that death and life are but patterns woven in the same cloth."

His words offered little encouragement. This was no frivolous undertaking; it was a serious adventure that could endanger Jim as easily as a mountain. Many never returned from this journey. He had approached Huaman on the matter and the Hatun Laika had resisted. He well understood Jim's mental state and was concerned over his depression. Jim was not prepared for the Journey of the Four Winds, for the Jaguar Path west where he would confront Death and the dark abyss of his fear. Still, he was motivated to do so and Huaman relented. Perhaps Jim's motivation came from some unseen source. Intuitively, Huaman understood the danger inherent in Jim's darkening mood. He had hoped the land would heal his young friend and that the mountain gods would ease his trial. If not, then there was possibly something he did not know. The will of the Supreme *Apu* might now be manifesting itself through Jim. If so, he would acquiesce—as always.

The liquid was cold and bitter. Jim's innards recoiled at the taste and he grimaced. "Take it all," Huaman urged and Jim did, in large gulps separated by deep hurried breaths. Then it was done; he was committed beyond reprieve. One door had closed behind him, another must open for his return. Huaman continued to speak, intoning each phrase carefully so as to calm his ward. These words are only a palliative, Jim thought, and quietly began to panic. With great effort, he restrained himself. He had asked for the *yagé,* wanted it, now he must see it through.

Something had caught up with him, brought him to earth in the bloody grass of the high puna. Never had he felt so lost, so alone, so ridden with anxiety. He suddenly seemed to flounder, gasping for life like other men gasped for air. Even while he spoke to his fighters, an emptiness was expanding within. Life was too transitory, too fragile to have value.

"How much longer?" Jim asked.

"Very soon now," Huaman replied.

They conversed quietly for a few minutes and then it occurred to Jim that he no longer heard Huaman's voice although he knew that the man continued to speak. Without his noting it, the altiplano had undergone a metamorphosis. The earth and grass, as far as he could see, had assumed a low fluorescent glow, infused with flickering sparks of light, like tiny stars. The light from the grass cast a soft illumination about the campsite, washing over Huaman and the other man sitting before him.

It was then Jim realized that he was suspended in the air, effortlessly floating above the ground. Almost immediately he began to descend, until once more he sat facing Huaman. He noticed that the ground beneath them had become less substantial, that the physical reality of everything, the dark mountains and boulders, lacked tangibility. The campfire had become a wondrous explosion of energy, a beacon from another universe.

He gazed into Huaman's face and felt his first pulse of fear. It had become a surrealistic image that dissolved and reformed as Jim watched stupefied. For an instant the face became his own, then another man's face, whom he had never seen. That, too, disappeared, as did the body. Layer by layer, organs and skeleton were revealed in a rapid sequence of dissolution. Huaman's heart appeared, throbbing convulsively, and vanished. In an instant, it, too, was gone and nothing was left but a motionless silhouette, a cardboard cutout in reality, through which Jim peered into another, inner world.

He gasped as he began to move, drawn helplessly forward through the opening and into the void beyond. There was a momentary start as the emptiness engulfed him. The portal that was Huaman's silhouette disappeared and Jim found himself adrift in space, not the space of human experience, but the manifestation of a superseding reality. Jim understood this, but did not think to question how.

There was no longer a corporeal self. Jim was now pure mind, but his sense of being was undiminished. He was aware of motion, but there was no way of gauging movement. Then the low, shimmering light which permeated the void seemed to brighten beneath him. A moment elapsed and he saw it, an immense glowing object, somehow circumscribed and defined by the congelation of space itself. A feeling, more profound than thought, began to overwhelm him. This visually bounded surface was yet unbounded. Something compelled him to understand that. Its dualistic character did not seem paradoxical at all, simply plausible. Everything that existed or had ever existed was both internal and external to this strange entity. Jim felt it permeate his mind. It was as if he could experience the totality of the universe, as if he could swallow the sum total of existence at will. He was terrified.

Was this the very keystone of reality—that from which time itself began? His composure faltered as the self that was Jim Bridgman began to slowly vanish. He could not scream, there was no body for that. He was the scream, the terror. The process accelerated, probing and scouring the innermost recesses of his being until he was reduced to an essence. Rivers of energy and light coursed across the vast contours of the object but he paid them no heed.

Time disappeared and a presence took form beside him. But he was not startled; it all seemed so natural. The puma had always been with him. He knew that now. The big cat opened its jaws in a silent roar and pawed at the empty space. It looked at him and Jim could see the glow of energy reflected in its eyes. Something was exchanged between them and then the visions started.

He would later tell Huaman that he had become his visions, that he had gone beyond terror, that he needed time to think, to reflect on the ceremony. But Huaman knew what Jim would say. Even as he pulled the serape over his young friend and listened to his breathing, he knew what the experience had been. He also knew that the ego would not die, it would only be purified; that Jim's star was still ascending and would reach its zenith over this land. He smiled at the thought of the cougar who would forever pad silently beside him.

Support Group

Charlie had selected the café because it was out of the main traffic path through Cuzco and mostly served locals. He had scarcely sat down when Bartolomé squeezed through the doorway. The big man was not smiling.

"Any word from Rome?" Charlie asked.

"Not yet," Bartolomé replied. "It's too early and unfortunately I am running out of time. What's this I hear about Jim?"

"It's true," Charlie answered and went on to explain Jim's return to the mountain.

Bartolomé seemed to sag, his eyes red and moist. "He's putting his life on the line to try and pull it together."

"It's a trap," Charlie said, shaking his head. "As I understand it, there is no way in or out of there except over a narrow, highly vulnerable pass."

"I don't think he cares," Bartolomé replied. "Maybe he does have a vision of bringing thousands of these people together. It could prove ticklish for the government; but there are problems. Are there any soldiers there yet?"

"No."

"Can we get there?"

"Well, it would be easier than Karoma."

A waitress brought two liter-size bottles of beer and a platter of fried potatoes.

"Ah," Bartolomé exclaimed, clasping one of the large bottles, "something at last that fits my proportions!"

Charlie Newell was thinking. "If I moved fast, before the

military, and got a film crew in there, ostensibly to film the climb, it might inhibit Rohem from blundering in. The indigenes will come all right. Jim's vision and all that; the Supreme *Apu*. If they come in sufficient numbers we could have a real situation. It would be one hell of a cap to this story. I'll bet Xavier would go for it."

"Where would you get the film team?"

Charlie laughed. "Oh hell, that's no problem at all!"

Compañero

Jim had left camp at two o'clock in the afternoon and begun his ascent of a pass leading to a set of lakes within the confine of peaks surrounding Viracocha. An hour of continuous climbing brought him to a crest from which he could view the west face of the mountain.

The trail was seldom used except for occasional shepherds. It was for this reason that Jim was surprised when he first noticed an old man following him. He was too old to be a *bandido* or a shepherd and was obviously alone.

He was about fifty yards behind and just emerging into view. Jim dropped his pack and made it obvious that he had reached his destination for the night. In front of him every detail of Nevado Viracocha's west face and buttress was revealed in stark relief. An entire route could be traced up the glacier, through the black band that spread across the bottom

of the face, and upward through those airy thousands of feet
to the summit.

For a moment, they surveyed each other across the intervening distance and Jim felt a definite twinge of apprehen-
sion. In the sudden stillness there was a total absence of
movement, not a hint of wind or the flicker of a bird's wing.
Only the reddening sun's rays persisted, with a glow that
seemed to intensify, tinting the air and turning the ancient
boulders into dull molten fire.

He walked barefoot with a long staff and carried his belongings in a soiled blanket slung over one shoulder and tied
across his chest. His loose-fitting trousers, fastened about the
waist with a cord, were obviously the only pair he owned.

As Jim watched, the old man shuffled over to where he
stood. Jim noticed that he was now using the staff for support
more than earlier in the day. His head was tilted downward as
if to study each step. Because of this and the wide-brimmed
hat he wore, Jim could not see his face until he stopped before him and raised his bronzed, wrinkled face to Jim's.

Although this man bore a resemblance to Huaman, he was
much older and smaller in stature. His eyes were similar
though, yellowed ivory with dark brown pupils having no
clear line of demarcation. They were more the eyes of a blind
man than one who could find his way up this lonely mountain trail. Jim would later mention this encounter to Huaman,
who would appear startled and say nothing.

*"Buenas tardes, señor. Me llamo Jaime Bridgman. ¿Como
se llama y por que me sigue?"* Jim asked respectfully.

Without taking his eyes from Jim's, the old man smiled.
Many of his teeth were gone. With his free hand he grasped

the folds of his open shirt and drew them together against the
increasing chill. His chest heaved as if he gathered himself to
speak. When he spoke, his voice was soft and clear, almost
like a caress.

"Soy su compañero, amigo mío."

He said no more and Jim felt no inclination to inquire further. The old man continued to look upward into Jim's face,
holding his gaze. Jim felt mesmerized by a power that with
gentle, but undeniable insistence seemed to be tracing the
very contours of his soul.

At last the thread broke and reality reasserted itself. The old
man knelt on the ground to untie his blanket. Shaking his
head, Jim pondered what had occurred, some subliminal
event that registered on the fringe of his consciousness. For a
moment he tried to gather it into his mind and then shrugged
it off, unaware that time, for some immeasurably small instant, had ceased on this unnamed pass of Nevado Viracocha.

Jim shared his food that evening and used his stove to boil
water for tea. They spoke little, only a few words about the
mountain and the weather. The old man wrapped his blanket
about him and squatted by the small fire. Soon, in the custom
of the very poor, he fell asleep that way. Jim had experienced
it all before. Throwing a few more pieces of dried dung on
the fire, he turned in himself and fell into a dreamless sleep.

~~~~~

Dawn came quietly, treading ever so lightly on the frosted
grass. The sky brightened, clear, with a pale, silver cast. Jim
awoke refreshed, his mind instantly alert with no early morning cobwebs. He felt totally rejuvenated and free of the pre-

vious day's cares. He lay there for several minutes enjoying the morning and the flawless expanse of sky. Glancing to his right, he noticed that his companion had toppled over onto his side during the night and simply remained in that position, curled around the remains of the fire.

Apparently, he had switched hats for warmth. Instead of his rumpled wide-brim hat, Jim noticed he now wore a *chullo* with the flaps pulled tightly over his ears. Jim decided to rise and rekindle the fire. Kneeling by the old man, he placed a hand gently on his shoulder.

He wasn't prepared for the result. Instead of an old man slowly gathering himself to confront the day, Jim found himself looking into the alert face of Lino, their courier, who could be no more than seventeen years of age. Jim felt his heartbeat well up in his chest. What in hell was going on?

"Where did you come from?" he blurted out, a tremor of anxiety sounding in his voice.

Lino sat upright, alarmed by Jim's excited manner. "*¡Jaime! Está bien, está bien. ¿Voy a ascender con usted?*"

Jim motioned the young man to his feet. Lino was relatively slim for an indigene and a bit taller, with fine features, perhaps evidence of Castilian blood. He was handsome and, like the rest, poor. Jim looked down at the little pile of gear he had brought, at the decades-old ice ax with its hickory shaft wired together, at the iron, hand-forged crampons that must have weighed as much as a pair of boots and at the tired and faded canvas rucksack, whose seams were rotten with age.

Making one more survey of the meadow, Jim saw the wide-brimmed hat atop a small boulder only a few feet from the fire. Retrieving it immediately, he showed it to Lino. "Is this yours?"

Lino disavowed ownership of the hat with a vigorous shake of his head. *"¡No, Jefe!"* he barked out. Jim shook his head and slowly exhaled. Above them the sky had brightened as the sun crept above the horizon beyond the mountains. Glancing upward at Nevado Viracocha, Jim observed the summit begin to glow as if illumined from within.

Executions

There were six of them sprawled on the ground, bound hand and foot, filthy, unkempt and starving. They had all been severely beaten, but none had talked. Joaquín's hatred for the indigene bastards was total, as befitting his class and upbringing, although he could not help but admire in a small way their unrelenting, animal obstinacy. Still, he had to move on and this interrogation was going nowhere.

The overcast seemed to be increasing with each day. Winds blew down off the mountains and out of the *quebrados,* leveling the grass and sending clouds of dust spinning everywhere. He spat to one side and pulled his collar up. His men were watching him closely. With an air of casual indifference, he retrieved his shotgun from its saddle scabbard. The large-bore weapon gave him more satisfaction in circumstances like this.

The sound of the breach being worked alerted the captives; they were also watching him closely. Slowly, he walked in a circle around the prone figures. One man suddenly thrust his bound feet out in an effort to kick the major. That man would be first, he decided, but would die last. A gutshot was preferable. As he raised the weapon, several captives began to shout obscenities. Joaquín smiled. The shotgun blast lifted the body from the ground. There was silence and then five more shots at two-minute intervals.

When Joaquín looked up, he saw that his men had withdrawn some distance and glanced away to avoid his eyes. The gun barrel was warm to the touch as he thrust it into the scabbard. *"¡Vámanos!"* he commanded, mounting his horse and setting off at a gallop. Behind him, the soldiers followed, looking away as they passed the bodies.

A Parting

Jim had recovered his cache of climbing gear and Rosa watched as he sorted through it. She had reached a point of near hysteria. His departure was imminent and she felt as helpless as a leaf in a raging stream. Jim watched her face grow pale. The tension had become unbearable; he had to move soon. Rosa was about to depart for a rendezvous with supporters who were bringing them supplies. An indigene handed her the reins to her horse.

"Do not start out until I return," she warned him. "I will never forgive you if you do."

"Rosa." Jim grasped her arms. "Three days may be more than I can wait. The weather is turning in our favor."

Rosa became immobile. Her lower lip quivered and tears

welled up in her eyes. Suddenly, the moment was thrust upon her.

Jim's voice was hoarse. He was incapable of the standard platitudes. "Rosa," he stammered. "Rosa, it will be all right! I know it. Please believe me."

Rosa reached up to touch his face. Her lips parted as if she were about to speak though no words came forth. She shook her head slightly from side to side. "Jaime," she finally managed, caressing his cheek and brushing the hair away from his forehead. "Nothing will ever be more real than my love for you." Her voice dwindled to a whisper. ". . . nor more beautiful."

With that she mounted the horse, and without looking back, galloped out across the meadow toward the pass that led to the outside world. Not moving from where he stood, Jim watched until the tiny silhouette of the wild Andean pony and its rider disappeared into the sun.

Trust Me

The man was clearly deranged. He stared uncomprehendingly at the soldiers surrounding him. An old woman who stood nearby leaned on her walking stick and berated him for being so recalcitrant.

"Speak to them, you fool. They are looking for the *norteamericano!*"

His mouth opened and closed soundlessly, drool dripping

from his chin. "No, *Mamá*," the words finally came out. *"Es un secreto, secreto . . . secreto."*

The old woman pushed her way to his side. "These are nice men; they have presents for the *norteamericano,* but they cannot find him so they can give the presents to him."

The man cocked his head to one side. "Presents, *Mamá,* presents?"

Something of a smile creased his face.

Joaquín stepped forward. *"Sí, Hidalgo, regalos para usted y el norteamericano."*

"¿Yo?"

"¡Sí!"

A minute elapsed as Hidalgo's face underwent various transformations from that of embarrassment, through intimacy, to a posture of sad, childlike authority.

"¿Adónde?" Joaquín almost whispered.

"La montaña."

"¿Cual montaña, amigo?"

"Veer—ah—co—cha."

"Gracias, amiga," Joaquin said as he handed several folded bills to the old woman.

Stealth

It was two o'clock in the morning and the block glacier was starkly illuminated in the brilliance of a full moon at altitude. Jim and Lino moved like wraiths through the surreal jumble.

Only a few hundred feet ahead they could see towering seracs begin to rise where the icefall descended to the block glacier. They were nearly out of the labyrinth, moving slowly and carefully, but with steady progress. Neither spoke in the intense quiet, as if to do so would violate the glacier's sanctity. Only an occasional rasp of breath and the crunch of crampons treading over ice and snow could be heard. The luminous threads of ice seemed like pathways through a mysterious garden or the living veins of the mountain itself.

Jim had carefully chosen these two nights for hauling through the block glacier and establishing a cache above the icefall. Temperatures were low and the loose muck of the glacier frozen. Lino smiled at the shadowy hulk he was following. Jaime was a wise man to climb this glacier at night. He had seen others return from their task of hauling, sweat-soaked, disheveled and muddy. He shook his head. It would be as Jaime said, a bad start if you challenged the sun. To climb the mountain, your mind and spirit must be intact, *armonioso*. You cannot afford to be brushing the hair from your eyes.

Good News

Colonel Rohem was in a good humor as he walked the perimeter of the internment camp that had been established on the bluff overlooking the former site of the Hacienda Santa Rosa. Nearly three thousand faces watched from within as he and his aides made their circuit. Platforms had been erected over the larger trucks to serve as watchtowers; each platform was manned by two men armed with automatic weapons.

Every day more people were brought in and what little livestock they possessed was penned up in a nearby arroyo. Lima had informed him in no uncertain terms of its approval. Rohem paused as a messenger approached and saluted, handing the colonel a sealed envelope. Rohem tore it open and his face broke into a smile as he read. Not the smile of a good story, but rather the smile that accompanied the unexpected acquisition of a secret, one that could be put to good use. Handing the missive to his adjutant, he summoned his communications officer.

"Open a line to Lima HQ immediately. I'll be right there."

Turning back to his adjutant, he spoke in a quavering voice that quickly rose in pitch. "I never dreamed the damn fool would go back to the mountain. Zamora got lucky at last. I'll ask Lima for a division; a lot of *campesinos* are creeping into the area now and many could be armed. As Joaquín has described it, there is only one passage in and out of the basin fronting the mountain. We will seal it tight; no one will be able to enter or leave unless we say so. At last we have that son of a bitch where we want him!"

Baby Steps

Jim and Lino had been patiently picking their way along the base of the mountain since sunrise. Jim made sure they were

moving before the sun's rays began to warm the face and in-
duce instabilities. To their right, the open maw of the berg-
shrund yawned beneath them. On their left, black granite rose
upward for most of a thousand feet, appearing like the bas-
tion of some mythical fortress. Somewhere ahead, obscured
by the jumble of ice, was the foot of Jim's buttress. Lino was
becoming anxious to get there. He felt ill at ease in the chill
blue silence surrounding them.

Indeed, there was a hush beneath the mountain, a peculiar
quiet characteristic of big glaciated mountains. It was particularly noticeable in the morning when the day was fresh and
the senses not yet dulled by exertion and sweat. It was the
stillness of a cathedral, not a human sanctuary, but nature's.
A place of purity, changing with the seasons, yet possessing
an aspect of natural peace that never changed. The distant
thud of a toppling serac sent Lino's heart pounding. Jaime did
not seem to notice, but continued his careful progress through
the ice.

Lino studied Jim's movements as he followed on the trail-
ing end of the rope. He was delirious with joy, embarking on
a major climb, in the company of a great *alpinista.* When he
returned to his *ayllu,* he, too, would be respected as an *alpinista.* Maybe he would still have to plant potatoes and make
adobe bricks for the community, but someone could be hired
to help and tend the sheep. Mama and Yolanda could have a
"casa grande," and people would come for his services and
counsel. Ah, the world would change because of Jaime and
what they were going to do.

"Lino!" The sudden snap of Jim's voice shattered his
reverie. "That is a crevasse, *muchacho!* Watch where you're
going and stay on my track."

Lino flushed beneath his bronze skin and stepped back from the subtle depression in the snow that would have collapsed into a chasm beneath him. *"¡Sí, Jefe!"* he shouted back. The close call had an immediate sobering effect and he noted that Jim did not belabor the point as he turned away to resume his route finding. Lino's regard for the man grew a notch more and he vowed to keep his mind on the task before him.

Minutes crept into hours as they inched their way along the mountain's base. The sun canted over the meridian and flooded their way with light. The terminal snout of a hanging glacier far above them began to gleam as if decorated with spangles. Like the hem of Yolanda's skirt, Lino thought. He did not think in terms of pressure and mass, freezing and thawing, decomposing rock and phase transition, nor of the countless tons of ice stuck to the mountainside and the cataclysmic magnitude of the stress and strain they represented. Jim looked up the precipitous face and took a deep breath. He wondered not if they would succeed, but rather if they would survive the attempt.

As they neared the buttress, obstacles began to present themselves which could not be circumvented. Jim tottered slightly as he eased over a rounded shoulder of clear water ice, his crampons providing only minimal purchase on the glasslike surface. Their oversized packs now required more than casual attention to balance. Jim stopped to provide a quick belay and observe Lino's technique. He was pleased to see the agile Peruvian make the step and reach without hesitation. So far, Lino's performance was exceeding expectations.

It was another hour before the long traverse was over. Lino
was startled to see the buttress suddenly looming above them.
It seemed much, much larger from this vantage and no less
steep than the wall it shouldered up against. When the long
vertical crack in the rock, almost a hand's width, was pointed
out to him, he did not appreciate its significance. Jim gave his
partner a whack on the back and shook him by the shoulder.
"You'll understand tomorrow," he said.

~~~~~

Jim smiled as he watched Lino carefully soak a tightly rolled
cylinder of toilet paper, about the size of a cigarette, in
kerosene and place it on the stove's priming pan. Careful to
use only one match, he ignited it and looked up for Jim's approval. This would conserve their small store of alcohol, normally used to start the Primus. Jim nodded his assent. He was
fast becoming fond of this energetic young man, whose am-
bition sprang from the simple desire to improve his lot and
that of his family.

It was good to be on a mountain again, even this one. Lino
puttered around the small campsite, organizing things and
tending to the stove, leaving Jim time to reflect and ponder
their next move while there was still daylight. He watched ap-
preciatively as Lino expertly cleaned the burner jet with the
stove still running. A memory, long suppressed, was triggered
by the roar of the burner and he thought of Klaus Mettinger.

Klaus was a great alpinist in the classic tradition and an
early climbing partner of Jim's. A white gas stove ruptured
and exploded in his tent on the south rib of Huantsan. Partially blinded, Klaus stumbled out of the tent and fell three

thousand feet to his death. Jim had been with another expedition preparing to climb a neighboring peak when two porters arrived at their camp to bring word. Jim assisted them in reaching the body.

They found Klaus lying on his side, limbs disjointed and askew, limp like a discarded mannequin, his burnt face half turned into the snow. A breeze which blew up the glacier stirred a few white strands of hair as if to imbue him once again with life, but Klaus Mettinger was no more. Perfidious life had deserted his body in the flicker of a moment and all that he had been was consigned to oblivion.

Jim thought of himself. He was only forty. Yet, was this the end? Other men's lives never seemed interesting to him. Merely to live had seemed stimulation enough. He responded to the primal elements: rock, ice and snow. The freedom to move at will from one range to another. But never before had one of his adventures held so much meaning. He had always looked askance at the bondage of others. Now perhaps, it was time to accept the price for his choice. He would exhaust his breath in the great adventure, and when heart and spirit failed, take his leave with dignity and courage. Christ, he thought to himself, I'm getting maudlin.

The sun was nestling down upon a horizon piled with clouds, its evanescent light still bringing a faint glow to the glacier below. Lino pointed to a flock of birds standing silently on the ice beneath them. They faced the sun and except for the random movement of a wing were motionless. What brought them there, Jim could not fathom. "Ravens," Lino remarked. "They search for insects and small birds who fly too high and die in the snow." Jim grimaced and said nothing.

First-Time Visitors

Neither man had actually been to the mountain before and neither was prepared for what they found. Bartolomé and Charlie trailed behind the guides and the film team, who had already dropped over the pass. As they started to descend, Nevado Viracocha, in all its staggering immensity, slowly emerged above a large ridge to their left. "Hold on to your saddle," Bartolomé muttered. Charlie gaped as the gargantuan entity revealed itself. The tents set up in the meadow below looked like colored sequins scattered at its feet. "Tell me this isn't real," Charlie pleaded. "It's real," Bartolomé answered, "every damn bit of it."

No one had to ask where the west face was; the great expanse glimmered before them in the bright light. It possessed an unreal quality, as if it were a vast stage set. Despite the distance, Charlie felt uncomfortably close to the imposing mountain.

As Bartolomé scrutinized the wall, he wondered how anyone could even think of climbing it. Then, with a start, he recognized the shallow buttress, just right of center, that Jim had talked about. It was so narrow and tenuous, it looked like a thread blown against the mountain. His heart began to pound. He fervently wished that Jim were still in camp.

〰〰

When they arrived, the three climbers whom Charlie had drafted in Cuzco were assisting Julian Anderson and Christopher Petty, veteran cameramen flown down by InterAmerican

News Service (IANS). Julian and Chris were excited. Before Charlie could dismount, Chris had taken the reins of the horse and had begun describing the cache of film equipment left from Jim's previous attempt. "These guys," he said, "think we can get a camera up on the lower portion of the face, on the far left-hand side. We could photograph the buttress in profile almost all the way!"

Charlie dismounted and looked up at the glowering expanse of Nevado Viracocha. "Really," he said.

Joining Battle

Jim called the icy sheath over the buttress the silver scabbard. It dangled above Jim and Lino like some pirate's treasure. To their right, the bare rock lower segment of the buttress thrust by them, a giant ribbon of muscle, the bone and sinew of the mountain itself.

The crack was slippery with verglas, a thin black enamel coating. At times the granitic-ice amalgam choked the crack and had to be hacked away. The work was tedious, at times desperate. The crack was a flaw in the black band, a way upward, but it was no gift. Jim was climbing free and protecting his leads with the few pitons they had allotted for this part of the climb. He needed more wide-angle pins than the four he had. This forced him to nest smaller pins together. They were suitable to support his weight, but not to sustain a fall. He climbed with fist jams and careful placement of his feet, toeing into the crack. However, the wide double boots kept slipping out, leaving him hanging by a doubled fist.

The technique was laborious, a constant strain on his shoulders and arms; but if he attempted to straighten his body and stand on his toes parallel to the wall, he invariably came off the rock. The mechanics required the tight couple formed by his hunched body. If a stance felt slightly more secure than the others, he attempted to make a piton placement. Long before the sun had made its way over the mountain, he was bathed in sweat.

Lino did not climb the pitches as did Jim. Instead, as second, he ascended the rope using mechanical ascenders with attached slings for his feet. From the rope, he retrieved the pitons—cleaned the pitch—while Jim rested. Normally, the leader would be bringing up the haul sack with the bulk of their gear, as the pitch was being cleaned, so that the "second" could move directly into the lead upon reaching him. But Lino could not, under any circumstance, lead this rock. Therefore, to further conserve Jim's strength, Lino also pulled the haul sack up upon reaching Jim's position.

Jim continued to study Lino on every pitch, watching for signs of uncertainty or panic. For success or survival, each had to fulfill his responsibilities completely from the very beginning. The spotlight was as much on Lino as it was on Jim.

It took ten tortuous pitches to complete the day and reach their goal. It was a Herculean effort by Jim and he was completely spent at its conclusion. The next to last pitch ended under an overhanging bulge of snow, which drooped from the side of the buttress. From a tenuous position on marginal ice, Jim had to literally chop through the lip over his head and fight his way upward with ice tools and crampons to a stance where he could rest. Another hundred feet of climbing brought him to the backbone of the buttress, where Lino joined him.

This was their first night on the face and a precarious one. In the dimming light, there was no time to take advantage of the surface and search for a better position. Together they hacked out a small platform suitable for a bivouac and arranged themselves for the night. Luckily there was no wind and they ran the stove until their body liquids were replenished and the water bottles filled.

The adventure had begun with a successful day in surmounting the black band. Lino slipped into a blissful sleep and Jim noted the state of his charge with satisfaction. The snow offered some hope of decent climbing and the weather was holding. Tomorrow, he would be strong again and who knew how far they would get. No mistakes, he thought, we just can't make any mistakes. Settling in, he too, quickly fell asleep. Above them, the mindful stars blinked from afar. Nevado Viracocha also slept, his dark face a mystery. For him, there were no summits to conquer, only one to protect. Whatever the mountain god thought, he would make it known in his own good time.

Guidance

"A news team? A camera crew?" Colonel Rohem was not smiling. "How could this happen? What fool in Lima . . ."

From the corner of the room, a fatigued, but alert Major

Zamora lifted his left hand to be acknowledged. "Colonel," he said, "Lima knew nothing about it."

Karl Slesser snorted. "Is the newsman's name Newell by any chance?"

Joaquín nodded. "Yes, that is the name."

"This is a problem." Karl slurred the words, wincing from the pain in his wired jaw. "He is connected. The press is like a giant spiderweb. Just touch one part of it and the signals run around the world. Something will have to be done about this."

Colonel Rohem frowned. "For the moment we will be circumspect. As I understand it, they are here to film Bridgman's climb. Fine—their support will be permitted ingress and egress to the camp. We will let the *norteamericano*'s indigene supporters continue to collect in the basin until we decide it is time to reap the harvest. As for the newspapers, if anyone asks, Señor Bridgman is a wanted man who has committed crimes against the state, including murder. Our presence in the field is to protect the area against Communist-inspired revolutionaries under his leadership. Emphasize the fact that the American ambassador concurs in this."

There was a nodding of heads from the officers standing around the conference table.

"At the appropriate time," the colonel continued, "the troops will be disseminated into the triangle. Those inside can elect to leave or not. It makes no difference to us; the end result will be the same."

Laughter erupted and there was more vigorous nodding of heads. Major Zamora did not share in the levity. It was his job to attempt to arrest Jim Bridgman, a task which he had found extremely difficult. Unlike the colonel he did not see this as a straightforward military exercise in which Jim Bridgman would simply be another casualty of the conflict. His argument that a small force under his command be sent in immediately had been deflected by the sudden presence of the press.

"Remember, gentlemen, patience," Rohem was lecturing. "Haste is destructive and dangerous. Like a fish on a line, let the situation play itself out, then reel the catch in!" Rohem's face was flushed with excitement. It was just like old times.

Emissary

No matter how many times he had experienced it, anticipation fell short of reality. The Andes were not new to Jim, nor Nevado Viracocha; yet, this surface was unprecedented for treacherousness. The top six inches, frozen in the morning, decomposed into a wet slush by eleven o'clock. Beneath it, a three- or four-inch crust was underlaid by either rock, ice or loose snow, depending on position, and was absolutely unpredictable. He felt increasingly concerned over Lino, whose safety was dependent on his not falling. Here and there he had managed a good ice screw placement. However, where the crust broke through onto rock, there had been nothing. It was then Jim was grateful for Lino's naivete.

The heat and glare of the sun reduced his world to a few square feet of snow. He was sweat-blinded and on the verge of desperation, yet still managed to move upward. Using the adze of his ice ax, he scraped the surface above and with high arcing swings planted the picks of both tools. Then, kicking with the front points of his crampons, he moved up and leaned into the slope.

All day long they had been climbing toward a notch in the buttress and still it remained above them. Resting his forehead on the cold ice, Jim sagged against his tools, his breathing loud and prolonged. Off the buttress he noticed a dark speck silhouetted against the reddening face of the sun. It was rapidly growing larger. "That damn condor again," he muttered.

"Jaime!" Lino shouted upward.

"I see it!" Jim answered, trying to mask his exasperation. It had been three nights since they had last put up the tent and he was desperate, almost dangerously so, for sheltered comfort and a day's rest.

The giant bird had swung away from the buttress they were climbing and was now approaching along the face, no more than fifty feet out. As it passed Jim could hear the soft whir of air rustling through feathers and see one leg dangling askew from an old injury. For an instant he could see those red-rimmed eyes looking directly into his own and almost feel the bird's shadow brush over him. Its loud piercing cry made him flinch. "Damn it!" he cursed to himself.

Looking Up

Bartolomé sat with Huaman atop the meadow's crest, looking out across the intervening glacier to where Jim had just begun another pitch on the crest of the buttress. The magnitude of the endeavor confounded him. Not until the Lilliputian figures could be seen juxtaposed against the vast rising expanse of snow and ice could the scale of the enterprise be appreciated. "It begs credulity," the priest muttered. Huaman looked at him and said nothing.

A few minutes later, Rosa joined them. Charlie had provided her with a camp chair, which she unfolded and tamped into place. She remained standing for a moment, her hands on her waist, squinting into the glare.

"I can't see them," she said.

Bartolomé guided her to a tiny blue speck, just beginning to move, midway up the buttress.

"That's Jim?" It was a rhetorical question.

"Yes," he answered, handing her the field glasses.

It was a strange feeling. Rosa found it hard to believe that the distant image was the living, breathing form of her lover; she could not speak to him, hold him or even touch him. It was almost like a dream, vividly real, tantalizing, but without substance. Yet, it was real and more terrifying than any dream. The distance that now separated them was minute on a world scale, but infinite in the reality of Nevado Viracocha.

Bartolomé looked up into her face, "Any second thoughts?"

Rosa looked down, her brown eyes unwavering. "I'm staying," she said.

Bartolomé returned his gaze to the mountain. Good, he thought to himself. Rosa had been anything but a disappointment. He had been worried about her returning to Karoma where she could be easily taken into custody and used for a bargaining chip. Here, she was at risk, as were they all; but he felt better about it. He found something about these mountains reassuring.

Field Inspection

An early morning shower had compacted the sandy soil around the colonel's tent. It felt good to stand there and let the cool, fresh air blow against your face. Mixed clouds surged through the sky in slow motion, raising and lowering over unseen obstacles. Colonel Rohem took a deep breath and nodded to his adjutant. "We'll do the front line first," he said.

His Jeep was waiting a few meters away. The troops had been deployed in the triangle for five days and were understandably disgruntled. It behooved a commanding officer to encourage his men and also enforce discipline. Latin soldiers tended to get morose in the field and he did not want any undue casualties, particularly before the pass was taken.

The colonel was excited, yet at the same time serene. Proceeding into battle was a godlike endeavor; Wagner had understood it well, glorified it. For Rohem, this glory was in no way diminished by the conviction that he could not lose.

The *Presidente*'s chief of staff had pressed him. "Colonel," he said, "the *Presidente* is concerned that you have not moved. When, he wants to know, will the filming be done? Even if the gringo is still on the mountain, he wants you to move in." Civilians were all the same, overanxious and lacking in understanding. It did little good to reason with them.

The man had been reassured and sent packing with the rest of the visitors.

～～～～

Rohem examined the area with narrowed eyes, followed by two nervous lieutenants. The ridges here narrowed sharply toward the pass close above them. He was certain that the approach could be defended only from the pass itself. Four tanks had been brought in and positioned specifically for the assault. They were in ample range to shell the pass and adjacent ridgelines. Everything was in order, trenches dug around the emplacements and two Jeep-mounted machine guns set up behind sandbags. Behind them was line upon line of soldiers, blanketing the triangle and ready to move forward.

Some additional trucks were parked back at the highway, ostensibly for the purpose of transporting captives to the hacienda and thence to the selva. This was purely public relations. It was not intended that anyone other than a token few ever exit the valley alive.

Colonel Rohem continued to survey the terrain. He felt godlike and munificent. It was better that the indigenes had some arms; it would give the appearance of a legitimate battle against true revolutionaries. Numbers within the encampment were growing fast despite their tightening the traffic flow into the triangle. Well, it only meant a greater catch.

～～～～

Bartolomé handed the glasses back to Huaman. "It's him all right," he rumbled, "the Nazi swine."

"We could kill him with some mortars," the Hatun Laika

suggested. Bartolomé grunted. "Tempting, my friend," he answered, "but that would violate the rules of engagement. No,
not yet." Huaman looked at the sky. "Jaime hasn't much time
before the storms return."

Bartolomé rose to his feet. "I'd appreciate it if you had a
word with the *Apu* about the weather."

Huaman smiled. "All right," he said matter-of-factly.

Rest Camp

The strain of continuous leading with little or no protection
was beginning to manifest itself. Jim was becoming more easily frustrated. Midway through this pitch the surface had once
again deviously changed character, acquiring a consistency
akin to an amalgam of frozen pebbles. It disintegrated under
the swing of his ice tools, requiring all of his strength to persevere and win a tenuous purchase. He wanted to scream; it
was just too much. He felt weaker with every minute. No
sooner was one obstacle overcome, than another, even more
insidious, followed.

Somewhere above them was a probable break in the buttress, which promised a tent site. They had been climbing toward this elusive goal most of the day and still it seemed
distant. He had pressed hard, maybe too hard. Lino smiled
less often, but the boy was a man. There was no sign of panic
or a desire to quit. If any such thing were manifest, Jim felt
it himself. He was having to rest more often than Lino. Lino

pretended not to notice, but did observe that he could chop away at the ice in making their platforms virtually without stop, while Jaime took short pauses to regain his breath.

〜〜〜

Lino was very curious about those below. Sometimes he thought that he heard voices, but the wind often sounded like people talking. Jaime said very little, but Lino could tell that the matter weighed heavily on his mind. Jaime was a caring man, *muy compasivo,* and he worried over the others.

There was so much to being on the mountain. Indeed, at times, Lino forgot there was a world below or what his role in it may have been. Now, it was the lowering expanse of the sky, more clear and vivid than he had ever experienced it, the vertical planes of the mountains, the clean, gray granite and shimmering mantles of ice and snow. The tent was his home and now Jaime was his only friend.

Tomorrow, he would ask the condor to speak with Yolanda and tell her that he thought of her and *Mamá,* that this climb was for them and all the people of the village. His chest swelled and he blinked away the tears. Why did he suddenly feel like this? It was unmanly and he was glad for the dimming light that masked his face. Still, try as he might, Lino could not suppress the feeling, the sense of buoyancy and purpose that grew within.

〜〜〜

The blue-black sky had taken on a dull whitish cast, which augured change. Jim, fatigued, noted it with mute and unfeeling surprise. The wind that a moment ago was only a fluttering breeze had changed character. It was now an insistent nagging force, not overwhelming, but constant in the discomfiting pressure that forced him to turn his face away and press against the wall. He hunched his shoulders and stared blankly downward. Below him, Lino had also drawn his hood and was tucked against the wall in his belay seat.

The ledge that Jim had chiseled out of the black ice was barely wide enough to accommodate the half-width of one boot. That morning, he had awakened to a feeling of bone weariness and physical inadequacy. After the first two hours, his meager reserve of energy had already felt expended. The day was supposed to be short and easy, but the elusive break in the ridge still seemed distant. He fought against a growing intolerance for minor frustrations. It was imperative that he keep his poise, no matter how slow the progress. One unthinking move could end it all.

Jim turned his attention to the wall. Placing a twelve-inch ice screw above his head, he retrieved a carabiner from the rack and clipped in. Then, using the ice screw as a handhold, he mantled upward, kicking with his crampons. Swinging his ice hammer, he was suprised to see most of the pick penetrate the surface. To his immense relief, they had reached a section of ice overlaid with hard snow, the best footing to date. Above, an unblemished run of pure white extended all the way to the gendarme marking the gap in the buttress. Twenty-five minutes later he turned the pinnacle on the right and stepped into the saddle. It was more commodious than he had hoped. He could scarcely take the rope in fast enough as Lino flew up the slope to join him, a smile blossoming on the young man's face. It only remained to dig in.

Jim awoke late the next morning with a clear mind and a clamoring hunger. Lino was already sitting up and tending the stove. The pot was near boiling and Jim reached for the food bag. *"Qué malo está el tiempo,"* Lino muttered and pointed through the tent flap. Outside, flecks of snow were being whisked randomly about by the wind. An eerie pale light pervaded the air beneath a black ceiling of shifting clouds. The outer world had been transformed into an immense dimly lit cavern filled with twisting spirals of snow. There was a sense of solemnity about it that reached into the tent and touched them both. Jim spoke in a low voice. "It's all right, my friend. The weather will force us to rest. That will be good."

Lino was puzzled. He didn't feel threatened particularly and Señor Jim was right. Still, he was uneasy, as if in the presence of vast forces that could, unintentionally, harm him. His instinct was to withdraw, to edge away from the abyss outside their tent. It bothered him that his friend the condor might not visit that day.

Camera Crew

After the first three days the camera positions around base camp had been exploited. With Chris filming, Julian interviewed Charlie, who told Jim Bridgman's story and that of the indigene struggle against the coalition of powerful land interests. To better film the buttress, two cameras were then set up on the crest, where Jim had met Lino, and manned by

Chris and Julian. One camera was left at camp to photograph the ever-increasing number of indigenes, which was now approaching two thousand.

Against Charlie's better judgment, the three young climbers, Greg and Travis Peters and Dan Tomkins, had set off for the southwest ridge, hoping to set up a camera position which would offer stunning footage of the climb. They did not know that this was the original ascent route of Jim Bridgman, which had cost him the lives of three dear friends.

~~~~~~~

Charlie and Bartolomé watched as the three figures slowly worked their way along the ridge.

"Do they know what they're doing?" Bartolomé asked.

"I hope so," Charlie answered. "The film would be spectacular from that vantage. But not at the cost of someone's life."

Bartolomé watched for a moment through the glasses. "Looks like they're filming," he said. "One of them is setting up a tent."

"Good," Charlie replied. "Now if they just don't go any farther than that."

Unraveling

Jim Bridgman took a deep breath and prepared to move upward. It was now day eleven on the wall. During the past two days, conditions had been slightly better. Overall, he and Lino had climbed seven thousand feet, no small accomplishment. Still, the summit loomed another three thousand feet above and his nerves were frayed from continuous exposure, improper rest and poor protection. They needed another good bivouac site badly.

Last night's bivy had not been a happy one. All through the preceding day, ice screw placements had been difficult. The ice seemed to possess an uncanny resistance. It took all of Jim's strength to torque them in and the ice easily dulled the cutting edges. Considerable time was consumed wielding a file or searching through the rack for an ice screw with some undefined property. Repeatedly, the tubular screws would stop penetrating after an inch or so. An accumulation of fine white powder would accrue around the base and additional effort would achieve nothing, other than hairline cracks in the ice.

Jim became exasperated at one point and began shouting to no one in particular, "The ice is tight! The ice is tight! Why is the goddamned ice so tight?"

It did seem as if the mountain's cloak was sprung with energy. Ice pitons fared little better and often could not be pounded in at all. Their security depended on a combination of the two, and small ledges chopped into the ice. Repeatedly, they shared the experience of being tugged awake against the strain of a rope after slumping off their narrow perches. This day had begun under a pall of fatigue for both.

They could endure only so many sleepless nights, Jim mused, as he moved up. The farther they climbed, the more remote the summit seemed. A shout from Lino startled him. His

partner was pointing out toward the southwest ridge. At first
he saw nothing, then the bright flash of a reflection caught his
eye. Someone was on the ridge just above his last camp on the
first attempt. For a brief instant he thought Walt, Chuck and
Ralph were somehow alive, that he had to get back them. The
powerful rush of emotion subsided slowly. He waved at Lino
and resumed climbing.

Morning Visit

Bartolomé arose early, and foregoing his morning coffee, set
off for a stroll along the hillsides. He felt compelled to do so.
The morning was fresh and crisp. Agreeable, he thought. Despite the building tension and the threat that hung over them,
he felt calm. His sojourn in Peru had not been long, but it had
matured him. He was sensitive enough to know that something was drawing him out today.

Some indigenes still slept under serapes and blankets. Others tended small fires or nursed a balky Primus stove to life.
Some squatted or sat in the first rays of sunlight. Below them,
their animals grazed in the meadow. Low murmurs greeted
Bartolomé as he passed or stopped to exchange a few words.
They were glad to see the priest, aware of what his presence
among them meant. Long before Bartolomé understood, they
had understood.

A few indigenes clustered ahead, squinting into the light and pointing at the mountain. Jim must be moving up, he thought. Greeting the men, he instructed them in the use of his binoculars and passed them around. It pleased the priest to hear them exclaim as they focused in on the climbers. *"Peruano,"* one man said, his low voice strong with pride. Bartolomé swallowed. "Yes," he whispered to himself, *"Peruano!"*

After an hour or so, Bartolomé began his descent to camp, his stomach rumbling for breakfast. Below him, a man and a woman were coming up the trail. The man shouted up, "Father D'Annunzio?"

Bartolomé stopped. "Yes," he yelled back.

The man looked familiar and as they drew together he recognized Jim's friend from Condoroma, Vicente. "Vicente!" he exclaimed, "it's good to see you . . ."

"Padre!" Vicente interrupted. "There are soldiers everywhere on the puna. My people have sent me to warn you and offer our help."

"Vicente!" the woman called from below and pointed toward the pass. Looking over, they could see two soldiers looking down toward base camp. One appeared to take a photograph and then they abruptly left.

Still staring at where they'd been, Bartolomé's jaw tightened. "How many fighters do you have?"

"Only a third have arms. Old rifles and pistols . . ."

"How many men?"

"If we add the *ayllus* together, maybe three or four thousand. I don't know."

"We will have to know soon, Vicente. When can you leave?"

"Right away, Padre."

"Good," Bartolomé said and sat on the ground. "First, before you leave, I must explain our situation."

Just a Reminder

Jim was struggling with an awkward bulge of ice, which blocked their progress on the buttress. He was anxious to get the job done. Above the bulge, the buttress merged into the west face and there was promise of a chance to cut a platform for the tent. In addition, reaching this position would put the summit clearly in their sights. To his dismay, an ice piton struck rock two inches in and fractured out a square-foot segment of ice, which barely missed Lino.

"Sorry!" he shouted down.

Gathering himself again, he tried to stem a shallow depression in the ice. He managed three or four feet and then, precariously balanced, attempted to place his tools as far above his head as he could reach. The action cost him his balance and he fell out from the wall, turning a somersault, and plummeting downward.

The first piton failed forthwith. The second held and Jim came to a wrenching halt just above Lino, who was jerked tight against the ice by the belay. Other than some abrasion, there was no physical damage. It was the first fall of the climb, a matter of no particular significance on the sunny walls of Yosemite. But here, any fall, however slight, was a potential disaster. If the second pin had failed, he and Lino would have been history.

Lino's eyes were wide open. *"Jefe,"* he said in a concerned voice, "are you all right?" After Jim managed to secure himself, he reassured his partner and decided on another tack. The mountain was going to dictate its own terms. Setting another placement and clipping in, he began an ascending right-hand traverse.

Within a few seconds, he was out of sight. It was with great relief that Lino heard Jim cry "off belay" and felt three long pulls on the rope, signaling that he was tied off. The problem of the ice bulge was solved.

The pitch had ended on a comfortably reclining slope, which steepened toward the summit, but looked relatively unblemished. Jim was ecstatic. They were going to have a shot at it! Wrapping a prusik knot on the haul line, he clipped in and backed down to the top of the bulge where he could observe Lino.

Beneath the bulge was a short section of rippled green and blue ice, almost in the form of columns. Jim watched as Lino struggled with an ice screw that had been forced into the middle. After two or three minutes of exertion he lost his patience and started to chop it out with his ice ax. Jim took a deep breath. He wanted to shout, to stop him, but he didn't know why. Suddenly the thought coalesced in his mind and he started to scream.

The warning died in his throat as the column exploded beneath the last blow, sending heavy fragments of ice into space like a giant mortar. There was a loud, low-frequency "whoosh" as tons of block ice and imbedded rock, which had been partially supported by the column, were disgorged from the face and passed by Lino with only inches to spare. Jim stared numbly at the deep cavity that had appeared beneath his feet. When Lino had cut into the column, he had caused a discontinuity in the distribution of stress within its cross section and the pressure of the combined mass above had been released.

Lino was bleeding from one leg, but appeared to have escaped serious injury. Jim nearly pulled him up the pitch. Within the span of a few minutes they had, by luck, escaped two major disasters and possibly a third. The mountain had reminded them that it surrendered nothing and punished the least mistake severely.

Situation Alert

Bartolomé slowly surveyed the puna north of the pass. From this vantage, the view north was bounded on either side by two ridgelines diverging toward the horizon. Twenty miles removed, the trans-Andean highway, running past the termini of these ridges, formed the base of a triangle.

He could detect nothing. "You try," he said, handing the glasses to the scout. After several minutes, the scout returned them. "Two patrols, Padre, twelve men, and they are going back. Some *campesinos* passed them coming this way, but they did nothing."

Bartolomé sat down on a rock. The military was on maneuvers; that was certain. They had been waiting and would probably continue to do so for a while. However, any attempt at disguising their actions was over. They were now actively probing the terrain and distributing large quantities of matériel. From what he had determined from the stream of *campesinos* filing over the pass, the triangle was completely under military control. Those associated with the news team moved freely back and forth. Others were not hindered going in; but it was unclear whether a problem existed upon leaving.

Bartolomé longed for Jim's counsel. He was not qualified to match strategies with this damn Nazi *comandante*. Still, he had no choice. He must learn to think like a general even if he wasn't one. Surely, his opponent was feeling smug at this moment. The addition of a Peruvian to the climbing team was a real bonus for him; it might double the number of indigenes falling into his trap.

Were buses and trucks being brought in to transport these people or was a mass slaughter being planned under the guise of a battle with revolutionaries? He had to assume the worst. No doubt soon, the triangle would be choked with soldiers and even the scouts would have a difficult time getting through.

The scout looked into his face and saw the anguish there. "What do you want me to tell Padre Raimondi?" he asked. Bartolomé conjured; he had to tell the man something. "Tell him to send the captured mortars and all of the ammunition; we will need them to defend the pass. Tell him that the battle will be fought here and that we will need every man and woman on the *campo*. Tell him to get help wherever he can and weapons. A man named Vicente will contact him. He will have some resources. I can do nothing but wait. We will have to fight these people from all sides, steal their weapons, harass them, slow them up. Tell him to pray; we need a miracle!"

On the Brink

They were between cloud layers for the moment, but Jim knew the respite wouldn't last long. He and Lino were well dug in with no need to worry. However, he could not take his mind off what he had seen earlier in the day. There had been three of them, completing a traverse from above the large step in the southwest ridge to a hanging glacier almost five thousand feet directly below Jim's camp. The wind had been gusting heavily, blowing clouds of snow into the air, and he could see the tiny figures struggling to dig in. Eventually he lost sight of them as a blanket of clouds moved in over the glacier. Conditions permitting, in the morning he would look again.

Until the weather cleared, he and Lino would continue to rest. One more camp, probably a snow cave, would do it. Lino tended the stove, melting snow, as Jim relaxed. Their thirst seemed unslakable and Jim wanted to fill every container they had. Because the tent was crowded with all of their gear, he had been careful to position the stove by the door with the flap partially open at the bottom.

Even so, his precaution could not have prevented the gust of wind which blew under the flap, scattering snow inside the tent. Lino, reacting to close the zipper, jolted the stove onto its side. Hot water instantly spilled across the floor and the burner went out. However, the pressurized tank continued to spew vaporized kerosene into the air through the burner orifice, which was in turn ignited by a residue of burning kerosene spilled onto the floor. Jim's reaction in kicking the stove out the door was almost instantaneous, but not fast enough to prevent the fire ball which singed his hands. Quickly unzipping the door, he lunged through the entry and plunged them into the snow.

Aside from a hole in the floor, the tent was undamaged. Jim's burns were only first-degree and he'd quickly got them into the snow. Still, they would be painful at times to climb with. His thoughts were turning toward the morbid as Lino applied an ointment and bandaged Jim's fingers with gauze and tape. That accomplished, Jim gingerly worked his way into his bivy sack. Lino waited.

"Jaime?"

"Yes."

"I am sorry. I made a bad mistake."

"Anybody can kick a stove over; don't fret about it."

Lino blew the candle out. He had wanted to tell Jaime that the condor had returned, but thought better of it. This time, instead of flying out from the face at the same altitude, the great bird flew close to the wall, directly over their tent. Lino had looked upward into its red-rimmed eyes and felt their energy. He knew that nothing they did escaped him. Every meter of their ascent was a concession by the Supreme *Apu* and his emissary. A door was being opened, but it would not stay open long. Jaime had to understand this.

~~~~~

Outside the tent, the lower cloud layer had briefly pulled back. Had Jim and Lino unzipped the flap and peered out, they would have seen an unusual phenomenon. Far beneath them, in the meadow and on the hillsides surrounding base camp, were thousands of flickering lights, as if the land were sown with tiny stars. Lino would have understood immediately and taken great pride in explaining this action of his people. Nonetheless, as he lay in his sleeping bag, fired with expectation for tomorrow, he somehow felt it, the closeness of his family and friends. They were waiting below with the others, he knew it. Tomorrow night there would be even more stars and he would have his opportunity. *"Jefe,"* he would say, "they have come for us with images of the sun to guide our way and protect us."

Tragedy

The day had been long and melancholy for the Peters brothers and Dan. The avalanches which had cascaded around them throughout the night had dwindled to occasional streamers of snow; but as the sky darkened, they knew the storm was once again turning its attention to them. The windswept traverse back to the ridge now looked impossible and hope for an easy escape from the glacial shelf faded. Travis and Greg sat side by side looking stoically out into the welter of clouds with Dan about fifteen feet above doing the same. Nothing was said. No one wanted to take the initiative. Viracocha had broken the will of the three climbers.

Without warning, they were staggered by a sudden blast of wind, heavy with ice particulates and snow. In the span of a breath the bivouac site was transformed into an incoherent whirl of savage wind and flying fragments of snow-crust and ice. The mood of the mountain had totally changed; there was anger in this display. The three climbers looked about numbly. The high-pitched whine of an even greater blast seemed to be building off the face as they struggled into their bivy bags, their bodies cold and dehydrated. Even the simplest movements were difficult. They hadn't planned to spend more than one night, bringing only one stove whose jet promptly clogged. No one had thought to bring a wire cleaner.

Below them, a chasm dropped nearly three thousand feet to the head of the glacier. To their right, the imposing and impossible shoulder of the buttress loomed like a prison wall. With each precious minute their reservoir of energy diminished. Travis fought against the growing lethargy. We're pretending this isn't happening, he thought; we've got to do something.

~~~~~~

Dan saw Greg reach up and unclip the carabiner to which the haul sack containing their hardware was attached. It was his obvious intent, for greater security, to clip it into the two ice

screws above which anchored their fixed rope. In horror, Dan
saw the open gate snag on Greg's wool glove and, as the
climber tried to free it, he lost his grip on the aluminum oval.
In the tiniest fraction of a second, the heavy blue bag slipped
forever beyond their reach.

It was as if someone had put a gun to their collective heads
and pulled the trigger. Excepting the handful of items in use
about them, all of their climbing hardware, ice screws, pitons,
carabiners, rope, slings, was gone. "Oh, my God," Dan whispered to himself. "We're lost."

He knew they would never survive another night. Retrieving what hardware he could from the site, Dan descended toward Travis and Greg. "I'm going to try climbing up a pitch,"
he shouted. "There might be a crevasse that runs to the right."
Without turning his head, Travis yelled something back which
Dan could not understand. He hesitated for a moment and
then began to climb upward into the mounting storm.

Travis Peters awoke shortly after midnight. A lull in the storm
permitted a few ghostly stars to glimmer through the filmy
overcast. For an instant he thought they were back at camp.
But no, the cold snow told him otherwise. The light breeze
that skipped across the slope to whisk away the vapor of his
breath told him, too. The dim light that cast its low sparkle
on the snow signaled him. Death had them now, firm in his
skeletal embrace. There was no escape and he must, without
flinching, face this demon for the two of them.

Travis knew it instantly, the distant hissing sound that fore-
shadowed doom. The first insidious whisper winnowed its

way through the stupor that passed for sleep and with delicate, but deadly articulation, lay its message on his mind like the gentle and sorrowful placement of a wreath upon a grave. He awoke to his fate with knowing acceptance. There was no thought of escape, no hysteria, no delusions of an impossible miracle. In those last few instants of life, he reached into the deepest recesses of his soul and held fast, with dignity and courage enough for himself and the innocent sleeping form of his brother.

Sickening and visceral, the hissing became louder. A trickle of snow, corn snow like pellets of ice, washed over their shoulders and disappeared into the black chasm beneath. The cold breath of the Mountain God began to blow. The hissing became louder yet, rising and falling. Soon it was a roar, a giant cataract cascading down upon them. Greg stirred and Travis clasped him in his arms, tucking his head against his chest. With all the strength he could muster, he drew him close. Huddled thus, their parkas enclosing them like shrouds, he waited. The indifferent universe would obey its own laws. There were no exceptions. There would be no outcry.

It was several minutes before the avalanche stopped and the river of snow through the couloir reduced to a runnel. At the foot of Nevado Viracocha there was only a swirling white cloud faintly illumined by stars and through it the slow reassertion of silence.

Perils of the Press

Charlie Newell had begun to regret his impulsiveness. Despite Bartolomé's reservations, he had set out from base camp with Diego to reconnoiter troop deployment and garner material for his dispatches. Brandishing a cardboard sign on which the word *Prensa* was scrawled, they had managed to reach the trans-Andean highway without incident. It was there that they had the misfortune to encounter a security patrol consisting of two Jeeps and eight men.

Charlie's Spanish was quite good; the two officers standing by one Jeep were discussing the efficacy of shooting them. One held Charlie's press credentials in one hand and was gesturing wildly with the other. To Charlie's right a foot soldier kept working the action of his rifle and taking aim at an imaginary target. A sharp exhalation of air accompanied each imaginary round as his comrades sniggered in appreciation. To the newsman's immense relief, the more deliberate of the two officers reached into the Jeep and picked up a phone.

"I hope to hell someone's home," Charlie muttered to Diego.

"*Sí, Jefe,*" Diego replied.

The phone conversation was brief and intense. "Get in the Jeep," the officer said. Fifteen minutes later, they pulled up beside several other military vehicles parked to one side of the road. Below the opposite side of the highway, Charlie could see a large rectangular encampment surrounded by a high fence. "Jesus," he muttered to himself, recognizing the internment camp they had heard about. Diego was ordered out of the Jeep and marched across the road. Fearing the worst, Charlie began to yell before he realized Diego was being taken to the camp.

"Do not worry, *Jefe*," his guide shouted back as he disappeared down the slope.

"Mr. Newell, I presume."

Charlie turned around to find himself facing the man whose instrument the imposing array of men and matériel was. "Colonel Rohem," he replied.

"Would you like to accompany me for a brief walk?"

"Certainly," Charlie answered.

Last Camp

" 'For many of our people, life is a thing to be endured and death is a release from that. When the spirit separates from the body, there is no more pain or hunger, labor or cold. In the spirit form, you live on energy from fires beneath the earth. This energy is the life blood of the universe, the living breath of the mountains. It brings the clouds and rain and offers succor to living and dead alike, for they are one and the same.' When last we spoke, my father told me this. Those are his words as I heard them."

Lino spoke in a quiet voice, yet strong with conviction. Jim wondered about these conversations with his dead father that he related with such feeling and certainty. The language was not that of an unworldly boy.

They had established a bivouac in a small but comfortable

cave, laboriously fashioned with ice axes and a snow saw, two thousand feet above the last camp. Instead of one bivouac to reach this point, they had needed two. Jim thought about the three climbers he had seen traversing onto the face. He wondered if they were bivouacked somewhere below, but did not mention it to Lino.

The base of the mountain was black in shadow, their lofty perch still illuminated in the tepid red light of a waning sun. Color bursts of red and orange flared on the horizon like light cast from some vast subterranean forge. As if on command, the sun suddenly began to dim, its seething mass put to bed like a petulant child and the world finally swept into darkness.

"They will light the candles soon," Lino said. "The candles can only be lit when the sun's disk is no longer visible. To do otherwise would offend him, for the tiny flames are also intended as images of his power, to hold the night spirits at bay. The sun would be angered that such acts were thought necessary. It would be a slander against his omnipotence or so our people believe."

Jim managed a wry smile. Today was supposed to have been summit day, but it did not happen. Once again the pitches were unending. The surface was good, a thick crust with decent purchase underneath, really quite easy. The angle was definitely improved and the weather perfect. Still, he could feel fatigue clinging to him with every step and swing of an ice ax. The strain of leading the entire mountain, of performing one gymnastic lead after the other with inadequate or no protection, had finally exhausted his reserves. He was climbing on energy wrung from his body like water twisted from a wet rag. At any instant, he could fail and he knew it.

The pain from his hands was not unbearable, but it was unrelenting. Even now, tied to the mountain and relatively comfortable, he could not totally relax. There was always something to contend with. Despite that, he had to keep a smile ready for Lino.

The power and truth of the *yagé* and its exalted premise were distant now, compromised by human frailty and the malevolent soul of Nevado Viracocha. What was it Bartolomé had quoted to him? "Time discards us, one by one, with casual indifference. Like seeds dribbling from the sower's purse, our spirits are planted in oblivion. Too feeble to protest, we surrender our lives, expunged from our would-be glory by the unyielding will of God."

Was his resolve at last beginning to waver? Or was it simply fatigue? His focus narrowed. I will never be able to duplicate this effort, he told himself and grimaced from the ache in his shoulders. He thought of Lino, already asleep. The dauntless young Peruvian had proved himself. He could not fail him now. Still, tomorrow would have to speak for itself. Whatever he had left, he would give. They would climb through swirling planes of ice and snow and blue-black sky while above them stood the soul of Nevado Viracocha waiting to show its face.

My Turn

Dan was scarcely aware of the dawn, only marginally conscious of being alive. He had survived the night-long bludgeoning of the storm, the avalanches jettisoned over his cringing form, exhaustion, frostbite and the unrelenting will of gravity. His wrists ached from exposure to the cold and his nostrils burned with each breath. The fingers were long since frozen and his feet were stumps devoid of feeling. His limbs were stiff and slow to respond. Balanced on a narrow out-cropping of ice, he fought against an onset of dizziness and tried to bring his mind to focus.

Miraculously, he had climbed through the night, reaching a massive ice accumulation which prevented any access to the upper southwest ridge. Squinting into the glare he looked wonderingly about. He had reached the transition point be-tween life and death. The stage awaited his last gesture.

Time was changing now, the seconds languid and slow. He was aware of the increasingly surreal aspect of the physical world about him. He stared dully at his feet. One crampon was loose but he attached no importance to it. Yet, he mar-veled at the glitter of snow and ice all about. It was as if he were in a cathedral filled with panes of crystal and stained glass. He saw that each glint came from an individual facet. He noted the weave of the fabric on his sleeve, the hickory grain of the shaft of his ice ax and the speck of down that clung to his mitten. He stared in fascination. The world at large did not exist.

It was all related to time, the desperate effort of his mind to turn a few moments into eternity, to preserve life if it could, but at the very least to give its bearer the illusion of longevity. It was a sacred event, the passing of a life, however worthy or unworthy it might be. An odd and compelling stillness sur-rounded the young American, as if Nature paused from her many endeavors in respect. His lower boot began to slip and then held. He was beyond fear and terror now. Let it happen.

House Call

Rosa and Bartolomé sat opposite each other in Rosa's tent. A small table teetered between them with a solitary candle burning in the center. The wavering light did nothing to enhance Rosa's face.

"Hell can't be any worse than this," she muttered.

Bartolomé had been doing his best, but Rosa was inconsolable. "The sky is clear tonight," he said. "Tomorrow, he will reach the summit and raise the spirits of a people. You should be proud of him."

"I am proud of him. I just don't want to be proud of a corpse. He still has to get off that damn thing."

Bartolomé wondered if he was inept with women. Rosa fought to control herself. "I mustn't be short with you, Bartolomé. Without you, I would be utterly lost."

"Jim is going to be all right, Rosa. I know that that is difficult to accept; but, in my heart, I know that soon he will be walking across that glacier to take you in his arms."

Rosa laughed. "*You* are a romantic."

"Even a priest has feelings." Bartolomé lifted his chin in a feigned gesture of umbrage.

"What about the three climbers who were helping Charlie?" She asked. "Chris and Julian are very worried."

"Yes, my dear, so am I. I am afraid that we will never see them again."

Rosa gave a small cry and took her face in her hands.

Bartolomé came around the table and sat beside her; with one arm he pulled her close like a small child.

"It's not going to happen to Jim."

Rosa gathered herself together. In the dim light she could see the concern in the big priest's face.

As she sobbed, Bartolomé held her by the shoulders. "We will survive," he said.

Guests of the Mountain God

Lino watched impassively. He could sense Jim's inner struggling and was concerned. The sky seemed to be descending upon them, an inverted, translucent bowl of cobalt glass, its rim the crenellated horizon of distant mountains. With the exception of a few nearby summits, the surrounding peaks had been reduced to rubble.

Each movement was now a major commitment. Jim had managed a long skein of pitches, taking hours, and a price had been exacted. Clenching his tools for support, he felt a sudden start of fear. He was very vulnerable now and the realization of it struck him with a rush. He swung his ice ax once again and with a sickening sense of despair felt it strike hard ice.

It was urgent that he do something. He could feel the deep pounding of his heart, like the bursts of a steam engine. He began to sweat. Closing his salt-blinded eyes, he fumbled for an ice screw and managed with great effort to get it in. He counted the breaths, fifteen, sixteen . . . twenty. Finally, the lightheadedness subsided and he regained a measure of composure. Careful to make sure he was ready for Lino, he gave three long pulls on the rope and began taking in slack.

Above them, no more than one hundred feet distant, the summit of Nevado Viracocha waited. Jim's breathing was now more regular, but his chest still heaved as he steadied himself to study the remaining problem. Lino, leaning against the slope beside him, was nonplussed, his respiration low and even. This was the last pitch and he was anxious to be done with it. The sudden proximity of the summit had taken them both by surprise.

However, as Jim studied the pitch and listened to the messages emanating from his body, he knew that he lacked the strength to lead it. For a moment he entertained the thought of aid climbing, of placing one ice screw after another and stepping up in slings, but his sense of aesthetics rebelled. Even with that technique, his reservoir of strength would probably not sustain the effort.

The angle had again deteriorated, almost a full pitch of hard ice, convoluted and rumpled, yet smooth like white china. Protruding randomly from the surface were frozen sculptures of feathered ice, glowing as if with internal light. The scene was exotically beautiful, but bespoke a deadly serenity. Nevado Viracocha was no casual host; the table was set with exquisite taste, but there was menace in the welcoming smile. Jim knew that only the most marginal purchase would be possible and that trying to assume a stance for the placement of an ice screw, even to the extent of chipping a small step, could easily precipitate a fall.

He had to try. Nodding to Lino for a belay, he began to

front-point upward. The surface was every bit as hard as he had guessed, his crampons barely scratching the surface. Assuming a rickety stance after ten feet of gain, he tried to place an ice screw, but found the surface totally resistant. It was futile to try another. He had carefully filed all of the ice screws the previous night and a different choice would not improve his chances. The effort had left him slightly lightheaded. His mind raced. They were so close, there had to be a way. He remembered including three Chamonix ice pitons on the rack. Unclipping one, he tried to pound it in, but the ice only shattered. Striking it harder, he watched it deform and bend. Jim cursed in desperation. There was nothing left to do but kick back down to Lino.

A week ago Jim would have challenged this section and made it. Lino knew that. Jaime was very tired; no wonder, he had done things no other man was capable of doing. Lino never ceased to be amazed; it was understandable that he should be tired and time that he, Lino, should assume a share of the risk.

Though the mountain would not let Jim advance, his heart would not let him retreat. His eyes moistened and he felt his throat constrict. Throughout this agonizing, he had been unaware of Lino, patiently observing him and waiting. At last, Lino could restrain himself no longer. He grasped Jim's arm and shook it. His voice was firm and emphatic. *"Jefe,"* he said, "I can do it."

Jim looked at his young companion with uncertainty and pain. He knew what this meant to Lino. Seconds ticked by.

"If you fall, we die."

Lino nodded. There was something waiting for him atop the looming pinnacle of ice and he had to seek it out. That was part of his destiny. Understanding had been slow in coming, but truth was at last emerging. Lino no longer thought of himself as an individual. He was something else, an instrument, a player like one of the masked figures in the festivals. He felt no fear, only the rising tingle of anticipation.

Jim hesitated and then handed the hardware sling to his protégé. "Pick your line, stick to it," he said. "Don't hesitate—keep moving."

Lino took Jim at his word, climbing fast, but with certainty. It was an eerie feeling for the fledgling climber to move out first and feel the rope trail behind him. It was something like being a bird set free, he thought. He found himself much closer to everything, to the elements and the climbing nuances dictated by the varying angles and features of the mountain. The placement of his climbing tools and crampons was indeed marginal, but still positive. Form and strength, that was it—as Jaime had told him.

Jim watched Lino intently; he saw none of the trepidation of a novice climber. Lino was holding form and moving fast. Fast enough that Jim found himself pressed to force the line out over the friction brake.

For an instant Lino stopped and Jim's pulse rate escalated. Then he was moving again and Jim began to feel the first flush of excitement. Lino was nearing the summit skyline. One more placement of his tools and, magically, he was there. Jim saw him pause, the bottoms of his boots projecting into space, the upper part of his body beyond that imaginary line. With one final burst of energy, he mantled over the edge and disappeared from view. Lino had done it!

Lino was surprised by how fast he had ascended. He could hardly assimilate the fact that he was looking across the last three or four meters of gentle rise to the actual summit of the mountain itself. Before him, in that magic few square meters, was the sacred seat of his God, the deific center of his culture. Heeding Jim's admonitions, he paused for only one long breath, and leaning on his tools, kicked up and over the edge. He took two small steps onto the platform and stopped, his eyes fixed on the gleaming summit. It was as if his mind had been plucked from his body and sent spinning in the air, energized by perceptions he never thought possible. He gasped as the mountain seemed to sway beneath his feet. Stupefied, he looked slowly about. He had never known the earth to be so vast, a giant chasm encircling the mountain and extending to a horizon so distant it had to mark the end of the world. The daytime sky, though clear above him, was darker than he had ever seen.

Lino paused to gather himself together before advancing toward the actual top, that tufted fold of snow that had been the object of their pilgrimage for so many long tortuous days. It had been a labor that hardly seemed possible, even now. A compelling fascination lured him up the final curve of sparkling névé until he stood where only the gods had stood before. With each step, he felt the energy rise in his body until at last the pent-up emotion could no longer be contained. As Lino placed his foot on the summit, he experienced a burst of exultation, as if his very being were exploding into light. He began to shout unrestrainedly and dance about, holding his ice ax and hammer above his head. For the first time in many dark, merciless centuries, a native Peruvian had experienced the glory of old, had thrust his arms into the sunlight to receive the embrace of his God. A key had been turned and the door to the sepulcher of a people allowed to swing ever so slightly ajar. Lino closed his eyes and felt the glow upon his face. Only thus could he fully appreciate the moment, only so could he be sure that at last he stood in the golden aura of Viracocha.

〰〰〰

Jim tried to ignore the insistent tugging on the rope. He just didn't have it, but Lino would not relent. He could hear his young companion yelling encouragement from above. Finally he looked up into Lino's anxious face. "Jaime! You can do it! Please try! I will help you!"

With a faint gasp of resignation, Jim unclipped and girded himself for one last effort. Keeping his eyes on the ice before him he began to move, leaning chest-high into his tools. Cupping a hand over the head of each, he kicked and clawed with short movements, letting the rope tension make up the difference. Once again he could feel the onslaught of dizziness, but he fought it off. A few minutes of tedious effort elapsed and then, as if by magic, he found himself staring into Lino's face. With a push and a tug, he struggled over the lip and sprawled on the snow beside his partner. Behind him, he glimpsed the short trail of footsteps. "Is that it?" he managed between breaths. *"¡Sí, Jaime! ¡Sí!"* Lino assured him as he offered Jim a drink from his bottle.

Jim accepted the water and felt himself recover, relieved of the constant strain of climbing. He looked at Lino fondly. "You're a credit to your people," he said. "Let's take some pictures!"

~~~~~

Jim rummaged in his pack for his old Leica. The summit seemed almost anticlimactic to him. There was, of course, a sense of euphoria and well-being, of pride at a great accomplishment. Still, as he fumbled with the camera, there was also a vague sense of loss. He wanted the few moments allotted to him on this summit to be experienced to the fullest. He wanted to feel as he had as a younger man on other first ascents. It *was* great; but it wasn't quite the same. Jim shrugged the thoughts aside. He could reflect on that later. There were pictures to be taken before they began the long descent to high camp.

Concerned Party

Rosa's hands shook, requiring that she brace the binoculars on Bartolomé's shoulder. Adjusting the focus, she slowly scanned upward until Nevado Viracocha's summit filled the field of view. She did not see the climbers at first; then a slight movement signaled her and she stiffened. Jim was just becoming visible, leading and entering the image plane from below. Rosa was awestruck. The exposure through the lens was terrifying, sheer rock and ice falling off below her lover for untold thousands of feet. Jim was moving slowly, seemingly hesitant and less certain than she would expect. She allowed for difficulty and fatigue, but still could not rationalize her fear. Handing the glasses back to Bartolomé, she turned away. "Let me know when he gets to the top," she murmured in a far-off voice.

It was an hour later when Bartolomé announced that Lino was leading the last pitch. All around them the massed indigenes were standing. There were now literally thousands occupying the hillside and the sound of their voices rose in unison as the tiny, minuscule figure of their countryman started toward the summit. They had recognized Lino even as Bartolomé spoke. The priest simply smiled and shook his head. It was now late afternoon and the sun tilted steeply toward the west. In the softening light the emotion exuded by the assemblage seemed to take on a presence of its own, infecting the surrounding air. That this was a momentous occasion for these people, there was no doubt. The basin at the foot of the mountain was filled with human energy.

It did not take long before the cry went up again, echoing out over the glaciers and surging against the rampart of encircling mountains. An immense exhalation of collective joy, the exhilaration of a people with so little to cheer in their daily lives, so long denied any premise for pride.

The sound was a din in Julian's ears, but he stuck to the camera. Dancing figures sprang in and out of focus; the expressions of the celebrants' faces a kaleidoscopic blur in the viewfinder. After several unremitting minutes of raw sound, a chant began to emerge. The indigenes became less physically demonstrative as their voices grew in unison and the sound began to swell in volume. "My God!" he exclaimed out loud. "They're chanting their names!"

Bartolomé watched as clouds began to well upward from behind the mountain. The two climbers had been on top for some time. Not that he would begrudge them their due, but he was concerned. "Come on," he muttered as a giant plume of cloud rose into the sky above the summit. The sun had just begun to settle behind the hillside and as they watched the cloud turned from a delicate pink to a deep crimson red. For almost a minute the climbers could be seen with the naked eye, clearly silhouetted against the subtly shifting background, and then they disappeared.

Rosa was scarcely aware of the placement of her feet on the steep hillside or the jostling of the crowd as they descended to camp. She had seen her man achieve his dream and hoped he would live to enjoy the memory. It had been a long journey for her, too. The gentle pressure of Bartolomé's huge hand on her shoulder made her stop. He saw the downturn of her mouth, the stern set of her chin, and pulled her about.

"He will return in good shape, Rosa," he said, enunciating the words carefully, doing his best to convey a sense of confidence he didn't entirely feel.

Rosa began to sag and leaned into his arms. Bartolomé held her in his best paternal fashion and spoke reassuringly. "Rosa, you have as much to look forward to in your life as anyone here, probably more. I think I know him well enough to pass some judgment. His desire to see you again will see him safely into camp."

Descent

With Lino's help, Jim cut a bollard in the ice for the first rappel off the summit. The effort took nearly half an hour, but they could not afford to leave an ice screw or piton behind. The rappel went smoothly, and despite the waning light, Jim began to chisel another bollard. This time he had to work at an angle and the result was a smaller knob of ice, notched on the up-slope side to prevent slippage of the rope. Lino rappeled first with Jim admonishing him to keep as much weight as possible on his front crampon points. Jim followed and from the end of the second rappel, through the cloud-enhanced darkness, they painstakingly down-climbed each remaining pitch to the tent.

It was nearly dawn before the two climbers reached high camp and the unbelievable luxury of a level platform. Although it was still, snowflakes were beginning to flutter in the glow of their headlamps. For a moment they simply stood there, too weary to speak or coil the rope. Jim waved Lino in first and followed. Even the effort to kneel made his heart race. Scarcely able to bend, he asked Lino to remove his boots. The sky was just beginning to lighten behind the mountain as he covered himself with his half-zipped sleeping bag and succumbed to sleep, too exhausted to remove his clothes, much less reflect on what lay below.

Lino did not immediately fall asleep. On the descent Jim had told him of the three climbers he feared were lost below. It was so sad. Now, he thought, more spirits will be doomed to wander the glaciers until the Supreme *Apu* claimed them.

There were great caverns inside the mountain where the dead were assembled. They could find warmth and companions there if a friendly *aukis* were to guide them. With that hope, Lino also fell asleep. There were no visitations from his father or the old condor, only the fluttering of the tent flap in the wind.

They both slept through the day, awaking only for food and water and a few quiet words before turning in again. On the following morning they awoke to a continuing gray sky and random snowflakes. Visibility was good and following a breakfast of oatmeal they began the final descent.

Parley

The three soldiers approaching the pass were carrying a white flag. A hundred meters or so behind them a dozen more waited. Through the binoculars they looked nervous. The wind was kicking up again and a changing pattern of light and shadow drifted across the landscape.

Bartolomé stepped out to meet them in the company of several armed indigenes. Huaman remained where he sat, watching. The party consisted of one staff officer and two enlisted men. The officer felt awkward saluting a priest, but the occasion seemed to demand it. Bartolomé chuckled and extended his hand. The officer tried not to wince. This priest could crush someone's hand without thinking.

"Colonel Rohem extends his greetings, Padre, and hopes you are faring well."

"Thank the colonel for me and extend my best wishes to him."

"The colonel would like to know if Jim Bridgman has returned from the mountain and if the film work has been completed."

"The answer to both questions is no."

The officer pursed his lips and looked at the priest. Bartolomé wore an expedition down jacket over his habit and long johns underneath. He was a most unusual-looking priest, and to the officer, certainly the biggest man he had ever seen.

"Perhaps you could give us an idea of when these events will take place?"

"I have no idea."

The officer contemplated Bartolomé's answer. "Padre, we have two objectives here. First, at the government's direction, we are to relocate this indigene population to the selva so that they might continue to survive. Second, we are to apprehend the revolutionary leader, Bridgman, and those who bear arms under his leadership. Is it your intention to obstruct these proceedings?"

Bartolomé took a step closer, looking down into the officer's face. "Yes," he said.

The officer took a deep breath. "This is an act of insurrection, of civil war."

"Call it what you will, Captain. But my patience and the patience of these people are becoming strained. You have only to leave and there will be no war." Bartolomé's demeanor was changing, but the captain was slow to perceive it.

"The colonel says to inform you that any resistance will be crushed without mercy."

"Without mercy!" Bartolomé exclaimed. "Even God shows mercy! Who does this fool think he is?" Bartolomé's temper flared. The pressure was telling on him. Suddenly, he lashed out at the nearest soldier, tearing the rifle from his grasp. Holding it by the barrel, he smashed it over a rock, splintering the stock and bending the clip onto a wad of metal. The next blow shattered the trigger guard and scattered bullets on the ground. With a scream, Bartolomé heaved the weapon into the air and watched it fall from sight.

The officer stepped backward. He was not trained for this. The two soldiers with him and those below froze. They knew that to do otherwise would be their death warrant.

Bartolomé gathered his breath. "My apologies to you, Captain, for this untoward display. I am truly sorry. But do tell Colonel Rohem this: every additional second that his criminal associates and leaders live is an act of mercy. God's mercy, not ours. Believe me, these people have already shown their mercy by allowing the *hacendados* to oppress them for this long. Perhaps their final act of mercy will be to give Colonel Rohem and all his supporters a quick and honorable death. Now, get out of my sight!"

The captain was breathing hard as he rushed down the trail. His men had heard the priest's words and they were frightened. This situation, despite their seeming advantage, was not what they had been told to expect. The priest was infinitely believable. Yet, how could the captain convey this to the

colonel. There was no way. He wondered if there was a detail traveling east in the morning.

The Welcoming

Once down, Jim and Lino moved out quickly, anxious to separate themselves from Nevado Viracocha. Jim moved fairly
well at first, but then began to slow. He continued to plod and
stumble for another hour, before crossing over a slight rise in
the glacier and descending into a depression which ran the remaining distance to the exit point. It was there he became
aware of the sound coming from the crest of the embankment,
straight ahead. Removing his goggles, he squinted into the
distance. To his amazement, he realized that the crest was occupied by a mass of people along its entire length.

The sound became louder, rising and falling in cadence.
Shadows criss-crossed the glacier, amplifying the jumbled
confusion of rock and ice. He lurched to one side and cursed.
The glacier was getting under his skin and he was losing what
shred of patience he had left. Lowering his head, he plunged
forward, fighting for breath and balance. His body was re-
belling. Fool, it told him, you no longer have anything to give.

Soon, the din became a roar. There had to be more people
than he could see. Lino returned for him. "Jaime," he shouted
above the clamor. "Lean on me!"

Together they stumbled into the embankment's shadow.
There was nothing left but one hundred feet of dirt to ascend.

A deluge of sound poured from above. Jim could see waving arms and faces exhorting him, chanting his name. Without warning, a swarm of bodies separated from the rest and descended. Jim was engulfed in a melee of delirious indigenes and lifted up the slope.

He staggered against the press of bodies, fighting to remain upright. People reached out to touch or embrace him. Jim tried to reciprocate, shaking hands, patting shoulders and hugging those individuals he recognized, but he was running on fumes.

The jostling intensified and he staggered to one knee. A dozen hands lifted him up above the crowd. Jim gasped for air. For an instant, his mind took in the swelling expanse of bodies and then he collapsed. There was a hush as the climber was gently laid on the ground.

Bartolomé advanced toward the prone figure, throwing people to either side. He knelt beside Jim. "Can you hear me?" he asked. Jim's eyes fluttered but did not open. Cradling the unconscious climber in his arms, he lifted him effortlessly to his chest and set off down-slope with powerful strides. The crowd parted before him. Bartolomé prayed that the doctor they had smuggled in was well equipped.

For Whom the Bell Tolls

Of the large band of men who had ridden in from the mountains, only four continued into Chiquian. They rode directly to the church courtyard and tied up their horses. One of the men, Padre Mariano Raimondi, had to be helped from the saddle. Several of the men could be seen pleading with him, but he waved them off and proceeded to the church steps. It was still early in the day although it seemed much later. A peripheral front was sweeping through the area and the rain was intensifying.

To be precise, the time was 11:17 A.M. when the church bell began to toll. The people were puzzled. Why should the bell be ringing now? Still, the bell continued to toll without stopping: three minutes, five minutes, ten minutes . . . Soon, a few people approached the front steps; then a few more came, curious. A short interval passed and others began to gravitate toward the church. Presently, some could be seen running back into the streets of the town, shouting. Word spread fast. Within the hour, the streets of Chiquian were crowded. People, heedless of the convoys still coming into the township, ran in front of and around the military vehicles. All business came to a halt.

On the church steps, a frail priest stood alone, rain dripping from the sodden hood over his head. They could see he was not well, his poor body racked with coughing. Then a murmur could be heard rising from the throng which filled the plaza area and spilled over into the streets. It was Padre Raimondi! The priest given up for dead! They knew him and revered him, a truly holy man. He was alive!

The wind blew hard, bending the young eucalyptus trees and scattering leaves into the air. The rain seemed to erupt from the sky and then it calmed. Mariano raised his arms as if in supplication. Surveying the crowd, he gathered himself and began to speak.

~~~~~~

Those who remembered in later years would say that, even in the rain, his eyes seemed to burn with fire.

Schedule Concerns

Rosa, who had been waiting with Charlie, moved around the foot of the cot and knelt by Jim's side. Jim's eyes found her and he began to struggle upward. "No, Jaime," she said, gently restraining him. He looked at her, as if in amazement, and moistened his cracked lips. "Rosa . . ." his voice was a hoarse whisper. "Don't talk, my love," she said, "just look at me."

Rosa brushed the hair from his forehead and clasped his right hand tightly. She cringed inwardly as she felt the burnt skin, partially healed cuts and abrasions. She felt his other hand close over hers and squeeze tightly. His eyes grew moist, but would not leave her face; finally they closed.

Rosa studied the sunburned face with its scraggly beard and sunken cheeks. His respiration was so low and he lay there so still. Her shoulders began to shake with silent sobs.

Bartolomé was quietly conversing with the doctor when a low, plaintive cry from Rosa interrupted them. "Doctor!" she called.

Bartolomé felt that tingly rush that precedes knowledge of a calamity. "Oh, God, no," he heard Rosa moan. The doctor stepped quickly to the cot and placed his stethoscope on Jim's chest. "It's all right," he said. "He is just exhausted and his pulse rate is very low."

"Oh, thank God," Rosa moaned and her sobs slowly dwindled away. Silence ensued except for the faint slapping of the tent flap.

Bartolomé motioned the doctor aside. "How soon before this man can mount a horse?"

"What!" Dr. Chavez exclaimed. "This man needs two weeks of rest. Minimal!"

"We don't have two weeks," Bartolomé responded. "We scarcely have two hours."

There was a groan from the cot. Looking over, Charlie was aghast to see Jim struggling to rise, his voice barely audible. "Get the horse . . ."

"No, Jim!" Rosa cried, gently pushing Jim back. "Get your rest and then we will escape. Let the others fight or have Bartolomé call the attack off. We'll tell them that you died from exhaustion."

She started to sob again, violently, and threw her arms around Jim. Bartolomé made as if to console her and then thought better of it.

～～～～

Charlie, who had been writing as fast as he could, trying to chronicle every minute detail of this story, folded the cover over his writing tablet and tossed it into a corner. There was occasionally a time when even a journalist had to put the profession aside.

Hesitation

Rohem looked sharply at his adjutant, who was already rising to his feet. Both men had heard a motorcycle approaching at high speed followed by a loud thud and the roar of an open throttle. Outside, shouting ensued and the repeated cry of "*¡Médico! ¡Médico!*" The colonel jerked his head toward the entrance and the young major dashed out. A moment later he was back. "Colonel Rohem," he said, "perhaps you should hear this directly."

The courier was fully cognizant, despite significant bleeding from bullet wounds to the left thigh and back. He was carefully placed on a stretcher and covered with a blanket. The surgeon waited as Colonel Rohem knelt by the man's side.

"*Comandante,*" he whispered. "The garrison at Chiquian has been overrun. I barely escaped. There were at least two thousand of them; they couldn't be stopped. Many soldiers are dead; but most surrendered. They were . . ." The courier paused, grimacing with pain. "They were taking everything: trucks, weapons, food. The highway to Chiquian is cut off . . ."

"That's enough," Rohem broke in. "You have performed your duty well. Surgeon, see that he receives the best of care."

Rohem reentered the command post in a state of shock. Attacked from behind by a mob? He was incredulous. The adjutant set off to gather the staff officers for an emergency meeting. He sat down to await them, his mind spinning. He had not heard from Zamora in forty-eight hours. He would send someone in to check the situation.

What could have happened? How could the indigenes mobilize like this? Should they still advance in the morning? He knew that he had enough military wherewithal to devastate the entire region but he wanted time to think this over.

Rohem figured that the damn priest was in on this. He respected him for his chutzpah but nobody threatened him or his officers that way and escaped a just reply.

He Will Come

Huaman was waiting outside the tent. He looked inquisitively at Bartolomé as the priest exited. "Have a horse ready for him in two hours," Bartolomé said in a hoarse voice. "Pick three of your best men to ride with him. Jaime is too depleted to even lift a weapon, but he will make the pass."

Huaman nodded. "It is enough. Word of Jaime's success has already flown over the pass and back again. Our men and women rejoice. They will remember us, priest, but only as an afterthought. They will say later that the spirit of Jaime fought . . . beside them."

"Were you always this wise, old man? Or have you simply lived a long life?"

"Oh, I have lived many lives, priest, and each, in some way, has been good to me."

Bartolomé snorted. He remembered the meeting with Jim in Cuzco. Tears streaked the dust upon his face and grew cold. "It will be a big storm. Did you have a hand in it?"

"Perhaps, in a small way," came the studied reply.

Bartolomé shook his head. "Shall we walk or ride to the pass?"

"Walk," Huaman answered. "It will make the day last longer."

Checking Out

Karl Slesser was packing. Colonel Rohem was off on yet another inspection and the moment was opportune for Karl's departure. "Explain it again to me," said the young CIA recruit, voicing his frustration. "Why are we leaving?"

"Basically, because that son of a bitch Bridgman made it," Karl answered, his wired jaw still making speech difficult. "In two or three days, all hell will break loose. In case you haven't been counting, there are twice as many fucking Indians as there are soldiers. Not only that, but there are another four thousand in a makeshift camp behind us."

"But none of them are soldiers; they have shit for weapons."

Karl restrained his laughter. "Did it ever occur to you that they might have us penned up in this fucking 'operational triangle' and not the other way around? Have you noticed the weather? It's changing. What if these bastards come at us in the dark? What good are recoilless rifles and tanks when some crazy fucking Indian is hacking at you with a machete? These people will be motivated now. Bridgman has seen to that."

"Jeep?" the agent asked.

"Jeep," Karl answered.

The Bottom Line

Once on the horse, Jim regained a small measure of confidence. The narrow valley was filled with supporters and all eyes were fixed on him. Despite the numbers, there was little sound; instead, a sense of expectation permeated the air. As the horses began to pick their way slowly through the crowd, individuals called out Jim's name. People crowded close to his horse, but did not impede his progress. The day was dimming fast as a low murmur began to rise from the multitude.

Rosa rode behind Jim with the three indigenes. Above them, Nevado Viracocha looked down through the swirling clouds, his presence somehow magnified in the shadow-strewn twilight. As the party passed, men and women fell in behind, their faces solemn and composed as the ascent of the pass began.

From above, Bartolomé and Huaman watched the mass of fighters move slowly upward in a long serpentine figure. "Heavenly Father," Bartolomé said aloud. Huaman looked at the priest and spat on the ground. "Heavenly Father," he snorted, "all you priests are alike!"

Shadows in the Night

Five miles distant from the pass into base camp, nearly seven thousand indigenes from the environs of Chiquian and neighboring regions waited stoically behind the western ridge of the triangle. They clutched remnants of cardboard, plastic sheeting or anything that would fend off the impending rain. With them, Father Mariano Raimondi waited in the gathering darkness. Above, a hidden notch provided passage over the ridge and down into the army entrenchments. Except for an occasional rush of wind or breath of rainy mist, the storm was still in abeyance; but the tempest gates were about to open. Mariano paid no heed to the increasing cold; his mind was fixed on what was to come.

Only one fighter in three had a firearm. It was therefore directed that they fight in groups of three: one man with a gun supported by two with machetes. The darkness and storm would hide them as they filed through the notch and down into the triangle. Once at the bottom, they would alternate directions, three men to the left, three men to the right, until everyone was distributed along a line at the base of the western ridge. There they would wait until midnight, at which time they would begin to infiltrate the triangle. The fighting would begin when and where it may.

The old man who had led them to the breach in the ridge approached Mariano. A few words were exchanged and Mariano was helped to his feet. With obvious difficulty he walked to the base of the notch, beckoning to the nearest group of indigenes. The men rose, weapons in hand, and began to form a line. Others followed until a long irregular queue stretched off into the darkness.

The line began to move. As the men passed Mariano, they received his blessing. Over and over, the muted words, the sign of the cross. The wind began to rise in earnest. A few solitary raindrops splattered hard against the granite. It had begun.

Engagement

The gale moaned and shrieked over the pass. Spawned on the glacier, it drove heavy and cold into the huddled indigenes awaiting the signal. Despite Rosa's protestations, Jim insisted on mingling with the fighters. Struggling to stay on his feet, he reassured them, offering a handshake here, a pat on the back there. As the storm grew more intense, he realized they could wait no longer. Despite heavy wool mittens, his hands were numb. "This is no good!" he yelled and motioned those nearest him to start over. They needed no encouragement; within minutes the mass of armed men was traversing the pass and taking shelter away from the wind.

The wind now sluiced over their heads, pouring into the black void below. Jim felt Bartolomé's heavy hand on his shoulder. "It's a fit night for demons!" the priest shouted into his ear. They could not see the snow begin to fall, but they could feel it wet and cold upon their clothing. Sleet, rain, hail and snow would be the fighter's lot, but it would not quench the fires burning within. Jim was sure of that.

Their job was the tip of the triangle, including the four tanks and machine gun emplacements. Nothing must be left that the army could use when the sun rose. Victory was in the darkness or not at all. Bartolomé had done a good job, Jim thought. Colonel Rohem was a fool to spread his soldiers all over the puna. Greed and the obsessive need for complete control had vanquished many men.

Carefully concealing the flashlight, as if its beam could be seen in the night's fury, Jim checked his watch. It read 12:01 A.M. Accepting Bartolomé's hand, he was pulled to his feet. Together they signaled the fighters. Exhorting them on, they directed four thousand men and woman down upon the enemy.

A figure appeared out of the darkness and grasped Jim by the arm. He felt a woman's lips against his own and then a soft voice in his ear. "Wait for me. I love you."

Within fifteen minutes, the host of guerrillas had vanished into the night. Jim and Bartolomé were alone with the wind.

~~~~~

Forcing his way against the gale, Vicente led the mass of men from Chiquian through the notch. Only by luck did he stumble upon the small pyramid of stones at the bottom that marked the turning point. Assigning a man to direct the indigenes along the base of the ridge, he turned to the group of one hundred waiting behind him and pointed across the puna. The men immediately began to creep away from the ridge. When the last had disappeared, he followed, his leadership no longer required or even plausible. They knew where to stop and wait. When the battle finally erupted, they would allow the situation to define itself and then infiltrate the area around the command post.

~~~~~

It was impossible to maintain watch in this weather and the sentries knew it. Visibility was essentially zero and anyone exposed to the weather very long would certainly freeze. One could not even hear the approach of intruders in the din. Thus, few made the attempt to patrol their perimeters. Let the officers do it. Most crouched beneath equipment, in foxholes or trenches and tried to survive the night. A few even retrieved their sleeping bags. To hell with it. The indigenes were poorly equipped for such conditions and tough as they were, would not think of venturing out. It would be instinctual with a people who lived so close to the elements.

~~~~~

The first military casualty was a private. He had taken off his parka to put on another sweater. He never noticed the dark shape on the ground. A machete slash across the back of his legs dropped him with a groan; the second stroke nearly severed his head. The sergeant who found him turned around to find two men standing behind him; one held his rifle. The other pointed a revolver at him. A seemingly interminable time passed. The sergeant shook his head. "No," he said. Both men fired.

~~~~~

Colonel Rohem was awakened in his tent by an orderly. "Colonel, please forgive me. You are wanted in the command post. We have infiltrators. Two sectors are under attack." Rohem struggled to rouse himself. Despite the trouble in Chiquian and threats from that unhinged priest, what he was being told was simply not credible. "Tell them I'll be right there," he grumbled.

Rohem sat up and pulled on his boots. As he stood to reach

for his great coat, a flash of light illuminated one wall of the tent, followed almost instantly by a concussive thud. "What the hell was that?" he exclaimed. Pulling his hat down hard, he hurried outdoors, only to stop and stare in disbelief. The night was rife with gunshots and fire flashes from all quadrants. The display seemed to ebb and flow in cadence with the wind.

The communications officer looked up as he entered. "Sir, we are no longer receiving transmissions from the south. Neither have we received anything from our stations along the west. The reports that we do have indicate that our troops are heavily engaged everywhere. All resources are totally committed."

"How long has this been going on?" he demanded.

"About twenty minutes, sir."

Rohem's mind raced. There was nothing further to deploy and he couldn't communicate with the field. It was preposterous, a nightmare. The troops were fighting blindly and he was without the intelligence and communications necessary to redeploy them. "Have any of the field commanders sent runners?" he asked, knowing full well the answer.

"No, sir. At least none have arrived yet."

The colonel sagged. He was completely cut off. He couldn't even see the field his soldiers were dying on.

~~~~~~

The storm had negated all advantage of fixed positions. Throughout the triangle a melee ensued of hand-to-hand combat. Large weapons were useless against an attacker who appeared out of nowhere at your side. If one was reacting to a machete stroke, it was too late for anything. Soldiers who leaped into trenches still could not see to shoot and were victimized with grenades. It was not long before panic set in. Indigenes were silent attackers; almost nothing could be seen or heard except flashes of light and the muted reports of firearms. Screams of human agony came only from soldiers and they were drowned in the wind.

Beneath the pass a fuel drum was ignited, the flames running under one of the tanks. Within seconds it was engulfed and exploded with a loud roar, causing the entire fuel dump to erupt. The remaining three tanks were immersed in flame and exploded almost simultaneously. An immense fireball rent the sky and illuminated the ground. The wind seemed to intensify, shaping the fire into a giant dragon's tongue which licked at the black night and then dove to earth, sweeping back and forth, turning tents, vehicles and men into flame. Exploding 105 mm shells accented the terror.

~~~~~

Sheltered from the wind and warmed by multiple serapes, Jim, Bartolomé and Huaman had the best vantage, such as it was. From the pass, the weapons fire appeared like tiny sparks scattered over the ground. Little sound accompanied the fighting, but they knew the horror that was being inflicted. Several flares were fired into the air, only to be blown onto the ground by the wind. When the tank emplacement went up, Bartolomé let out a roar. Huaman, who sat beside him, pounded his staff into the ground.

The longer this goes on, Jim thought, the greater our chances. Soon, they could make out the progression of the battle. The sparks from muzzle blasts were emanating from a smaller and smaller area. The battle was now concentrated in an irregular shape occupying less than a quarter of the originally contested area. Jim looked at his watch: 3:31 A.M. "We're winning," he said.

Aftermath

Except for the flickering and crackle of a few small, scattered fires, the dawn was unearthly still. A low mist hovered little more than ceiling height above the ground, dispensing a low, pale light. It was morning, but barely so, a damp, leaden gloom persisting as if night were loathe to leave its evil works for day to find. Carnage covered the landscape. The remains of an army, its burnt and ravaged matériel, the bodies of its soldiers, lay scattered for miles.

A visitor, just arrived, would be shocked into silence without fully comprehending what had transpired. It was so still and quiet. Then understanding would slowly begin to manifest itself: the littered corpses beyond counting, the profane mutilation of flesh, the rising stench of annihilation. Then would come denial and fear.

One structure survived, a tent. Inside it, Colonel Rohem sat on his cot and stared without seeing toward the entrance. It was zipped shut. The stub of a candle still burned on the folding table beside him. It offered little light against the shadows. The first nuance of day had yet to be recognized.

Something abruptly stirred within the colonel's mind. It was time to arise and prepare for the morning staff meeting. There really wouldn't be a meeting, but a part of him insisted. He stood and straightened his uniform, brushed the strands of his hair back, and carefully leveled his cap. It wouldn't do to provide a slovenly example for the younger officers. That accomplished, he unzipped the door with a flourish and stepped through.

Outside, reality presented itself in its grisly best. Colonel Rohem blinked; the command post was gone. A wisp of smoke issued from the burnt debris where it had been. "Yes, of course," he said to no one. After a few steps forward, he stopped, suddenly aware that he was not alone.

The area surrounding his tent and the remains of the command post was occupied by indigenes. They were somewhat removed, perhaps a dozen meters, and separated from one another. They stood, sat or squatted, looking at him silently. No one moved. They seemed like specters to him, apparitions from hell, and he could feel terror begin to mount, visceral and immobilizing.

Nonetheless, on some mad impulse, he approached the nearest *campesino*. To his surprise, he realized that it was a woman, as were many of the others. He took another step and made as if to gesture. He stopped. The woman, without rising, slowly lifted her machete and pointed it at him. The blade was smeared with coagulated blood, as were her hands and clothing. His stomach heaved and he began to retreat, backing toward the tent. No one followed.

Once inside, he took the 9 mm Luger from his table and lay down on the cot. Colonel Thomas Rohem would obey the dictates of his tradition: honor, courage, and fidelity unto death. He placed the cold barrel in his mouth. The muffled report was clear through the walls of the tent. Yet, outside, there was neither movement nor spoken word.

Dilemma

On the third day following, Jim was beginning to move around base camp with some agility although his body still rebelled at upward exertion. Rosa trailed at his elbow and Bartolomé, who worried over the two, wondered what would happen now. Despite the probable concession of the government, Jim would remain a wanted man and Rosa, with her responsibilities and heritage, would be a Peruvian forever.

〜〜〜

Jim eased down into the low-slung camp chair and watched Rosa arrange their picnic lunch. They sat facing away from the mountain, looking across the meadow. Sunlight diffused through lofty splotches of snow-white clouds and its warmth mixed with the cool wash of air from the glacier. Rosa returned his gaze, noting the changes, the still haggard, but serene face. His perusal of the neighboring peaks was casual, not intent on route-finding and likely camp placements.

"Bartolomé found us that red to have with the beef," she chuckled and threw Jim a corkscrew. Peeling the foil from the bottle, he laughed. "He didn't find it; he commandeered it from the film guys!"

The levity was strained, artificial; they were play-acting and the strain was tearing at Jim. A moment elapsed before he responded. "We have a terrible problem, Rosa . . ." It was clumsy, brutal and he hated himself for bringing it up.

Rosa reflected, a wistful smile upon her face. This was the conversation she had been dreading. "Yes," she finally answered, reaching over to squeeze his hand. "We must leave here."

A moment elapsed before Jim responded. "There are decisions to make. We live in two different worlds. I can't stay here but I can't ask you to leave Peru; your father and your people need you."

Rosa knew that Jim was right. "Jim," she said, "I will be lost without you."

Jim swallowed as tears began to trickle down Rosa's face. Her mouth quivered and he felt his insides give way. He loved this woman desperately. She was the most incredible person he had ever met. "Goddammit!" he shouted out loud. "We've been through hell! It's not fair! I'll stay here. No one's going to risk coming after me!"

"No, Jim," Rosa said. "It only takes one man, one bullet. If not the government, there are a hundred men around Cuzco who would gladly pay your assassin."

Jim pulled the cork and filled their glasses. He thought of Huaman and Mariano, of the shaman's wise counsel and Mariano's glimpses of the future. Did they know it would end like this? He looked into Rosa's face and saw her beauty blossom in the light, a thing apart. Such happiness could be theirs. He held his glass up.

"To the day then, if this is what we have left."

"I'm sorry, Jim," Rosa said, wiping her tears and lifting her glass. "To us!"

The Shadows Lengthen

On the following morning, before a meadow and hillside full of indigenes, Bartolomé performed a service for all who had died in battle. Afterward, he walked among the families, touching, speaking a quiet word, holding a bereaved woman; their suffering was his suffering. They saw it on his face, in the compassion shown in his eyes.

During the afternoon, a service was given for the fallen climbers. The full rites of the Church were bestowed upon the six young men. His voice wavered ever so slightly as Bartolomé concluded.

". . . and so we all come to that ultimate union, the return of one's soul to nature, the repository and progenitor of all life, the noumenon of the human spirit.

"It is only proper that these young men should rest in Nevado Viracocha's shadow. For it was in the mountains they found their spirits' citadel and there, among the shining granite towers and alpine meadows, that life took meaning.

"We raise no monument to mark their passage. Nature has provided a memorial far beyond human means. Instead, let us take their memories with us, wherever we go, like amulets about our souls, to ward off conceit, indifference and the evils which civilization fosters against us. Let these memories forever remind us of those who, with full conviction of spirit, worshiped life itself."

It was as if everything Jim had suffered in Peru was experienced again, the pent-up grief and rage, the agony, the uncertainty . . . the fear. He began to sob uncontrollably. Rosa put her arm about his waist. "Come on, Jim," she said. "Let's go for a walk."

~~~~~

Afterward, Huaman and Mariano lingered atop the meadow's crest with Bartolomé and watched the indigenes disperse. Heavily laden horses, burros and llamas slowly labored up the pass, accompanied by stoic men and women. The watchers maintained a respectful silence.

They sauntered a short way along the cliff edge, exchanging an occasional remark and looking out over the eerie expanse of glacial ice now being enshrouded in mist. After a short distance they stopped to sit.

Huaman lay on the grass, resting his head against a small mound of earth. As he looked upward a remote speck of black appeared from the clouds encircling the summit of Nevado Viracocha. Huaman made a low sound in his throat and smiled secretly to himself. He knew, before those wide wings could be resolved in sight, who it was. Closer and lower it flew until its dim shadow brushed across the land. One pass and it was gone, vanishing high into the clouds. Ah, my old friend, he thought, what is it the *Apu* feeds you that makes you so strong and lets you live so long? The spirits of old men like me?

Bartolomé tried to convince Mariano to return to Rome for proper treatment. Mariano politely declined. "Do not be impatient with me," he said, his voice distant, yet strong with conviction. "Do not concern yourself over matters beyond our influence. Keep my memory in your heart. Speak for me to the Holy Father and to our Brethren. They will listen to you, Bartolomé, for you have the soul of a saint."

Bartolomé turned his head away. All of his great strength seemed drained. He had not come here for Mariano's last will and testament. He had lost him once, he didn't want to lose him again.

The conversation lapsed and they relinquished their attention to the surrounding nature. Bartolomé noted Huaman watching him. "Father D'Annunzio"—the voice was a near growl—"do you have a prayer for the mountain? It is expected of all priests who come here. The mountain spirits wish to learn whether you are a wise man or a fool!" The growl transmuted into laughter that ended with a fixed, questioning stare.

Bartolomé ignored the jibe. No mendicant friar was poorer than Huaman, his seamed face belying the bone-hard toughness and tenacity that marked his very being. Short of death, nothing could end that unflinching resolve to persevere or continue the struggle of his people. We are like stick figures carved on a talisman, Bartolomé thought, interlocked in a circle: Huaman of culture past, myself a shaman of the so-called enlightened present, and Mariano, a visionary, gazing into realms where time has not even begun.

The two men regarded each other silently. Bartolomé's dark brown eyes confronted Huaman's and did not waver. At last, with a sigh, he responded, "We are, all of us, constantly speaking to God, my friend. Each heartfelt thought is a message heard by our creator. Man speaks to God and the heavenly hierarchy with many voices."

"He must have many ears to hear so many voices," Huaman interrupted with a gravelly chuckle.

Bartolomé winced, acknowledging the display of wit, and continued. "Let me quote a favorite writing: 'The laughter of a child is a prayer more profound than all the litanies and devotions of a thousand religions. The girl who plucks a flower and . . .' "

Bartolomé broke off as if suddenly interrupted, staring with puzzled concern at the vacant space to one side, as if something, privy only to his eyes, were standing there. Huaman pushed himself up with his staff, observing the priest closely with narrowed eyes. Mists were beginning to blow across the glacier and up over the crest where they stood. Mariano, oblivious to what was transpiring, complained of the increasing cold.

The shaman shook Bartolomé's arm vigorously and the Benedictine slowly responded, turning as if in a daze. Huaman, clutching his sleeve, spoke emphatically. "So now, Man of God, you have seen. That is good. Listen to my words. There are no angels in nature, only the spirits of the dead and unborn. Sometimes their voice is sweet like the *quena,* sometimes it is the rumble of boulders falling from the mountain. Every man is a fool to them, because only the living are blind. If we are wise, we learn to listen when they speak and act accordingly. You have been deemed worthy of their counsel. It is an uncommon honor. Accept it as such."

Bartolomé fumbled with the cord at his waist, his breathing deep and prolonged. Mariano by now understood and insisted that his companion sit down. "I shall hold no false god before me," he muttered as if remembering something half read a long time ago. Huaman snorted and spat over the side. "Another pompous priest! Accept what you have seen for what it is, simply a part of nature few see."

"If that is all, why do you worship them as you do? These poor lost souls!" Bartolomé rejoindered, but there was no impetus to his words.

Huaman was patient, but unrelenting. "They belong to the human family as much as you or me. They are the unseen side of our being. The spirits speak for the *Apus* and other gods who watch over the puna. Yet, these gods have no more interest in us than that of a farmer for his crop. Good, bad or indifferent, there will always be another harvest."

With that, Huaman extended his hand and helped Bartolomé to his feet. The wind and mist were blowing harder. Nevado Viracocha was a dim shape looming above them, appearing and disappearing with the shifting clouds. Mariano coughed and made as if to leave. Bartolomé's concern was with his friend, but he could not end the dialogue with Huaman yet. "You chastise me, Hatun Laika. Why? Do you really think that we are so different, that I have no understanding of your world?"

Droplets of moisture were beginning to form on the fringe of Huaman's poncho and along the brim of his hat. He regarded Bartolomé silently for a moment, his face seeming to soften. "There is purpose in my words to you, Bartolomé. I have lived many years, guiding and healing these people as the strength and ability have been given me to do so. Now, the mists are beginning to close about me as they do the mountain. I have few mornings left to see the light spread across the altiplano. But the people will remain, forever, as will their needs. Father Mariano has done well, but he and I, I fear, walk the same path."

Bartolomé listened incredulously. What was this man telling him?

Mariano had started down the meadow a few steps. He paused and motioned them to follow. "Come, Bartolomé," he said, "there is warmth at the camp and hot tea. We can sit in comfort and talk of the future."

Epilogue

And so, like other epics in human history, it came to an end. No cheering crowds or fanfare, no shell bursts in the air, only the rustling grass and wisps of smoke from smoldering fires— the solemn desolation of the battlefield, the wind scurrying over the ground to seek out the fallen, to bestow upon them nature's last benediction.

Later that day, local *campesinos* began to collect the bodies. The corpses of the soldiers were gathered into large piles and doused with gasoline. The fallen indigenes were buried where they fell. A week later, *Presidente* Ruiz announced a great victory over Communist-inspired revolutionaries. Under pressure from political opposition, he also declared the Chiquian district a semiautonomous region, free to elect its own officials and govern its own affairs. History had been made.

Two days afterward, Mariano Raimondi died near camp

and Huaman disappeared into the mountains. May the Gods the shaman served be kind to him. He is worthy of his rest. It was Huaman's request of his people that the mountain never be attempted again. Visits are now limited to base camp and its environs; that is fitting.

Charlie saw to it that Jim had safe passage to the Bolivian border where he would be met by representatives of the Church. To ensure his safety, he and Rosa bid each other farewell at base camp. Their parting was sad, although both a political and practical necessity.

Throughout the following year I corresponded with both parties and read the ill-disguised sadness in their letters. The death of Rosa's father was a devastating blow for her; nonetheless, I was shocked to learn that she had sold her holdings to a combine representing indigene interests and had moved further south to Arequipa. It was thus I took an action which no doubt exceeded the authority of my office. Yet, I hold it is no sin to advance the cause of happiness.

At my persuasion, Rosa de Melgarejo took a needed vacation, boarding a TWA flight from Lima to Los Angeles. While in the city, she attended a charity dinner on behalf of orphaned Latin children given at the archbishop's residence. By sheer coincidence the archbishop had also invited Jim Bridgman to speak on the indigenes of southern Peru.

The archbishop informed me that the two participants were quite surprised to see one another. His Eminence also informed me that one candle mostly serves to make shadows; that it takes two flames to light a room. For the most part I hold with that sentiment, though it did neglect the illuminative properties of brandy. Upon my arrival the following month, I was overcome when asked to perform the ceremony.

Did you foresee that, too, Mariano? Did your ghostly tears mingle with mine? Through all of this, I have been the willing instrument of your spirit; but now, with these last few sentences, I lay my pen to rest. The words are small tribute to what has passed. Still, they represent my heart and all the love that resides there. Be patient, dear friend, it won't be long. I smile at the onset of time and relish the transition to come. Above me, the shadow of the condor grows larger; but there is sunlight on his wings.